ROBIN YORK grew up at a college, went to college, signed on for some more college, then married a university professor. She still isn't sure why it didn't occur to her to write New Adult sooner. She moonlights as a mother, makes killer salted caramels and sorts out thorny plot problems while running, hiking or riding her bike.

Visit Robin York online:

www.robinyork.com
www.twitter.com/RobinYorkNA

Praise for Robin York's Deeper:

'The perfect new adult story . . . West will make you swoon!'
New York Times bestselling author Monica Murphy

'Beautifully written and full of swoony tender moments, toe-curling chemistry, and delicious, twisty angst . . . Stop whatever you're doing and read this book'
Christina Lauren, author of the Beautiful Bastard series

'Gripping, emotional and very sensual . . . with complex and relatable characters, *Deeper* is one part cautionary fable and one part love story – all woven into a gripping plot'
RT Book Reviews

'York wraps a heart-stoppingly beautiful love story around a life-shattering problem and shows the strength of spirit of a young woman who grows up stronger for her broken places . . . will haunt you long after you turn the final page. Highly recommended'
Library Journal

'Strong and effortless . . . West and Caroline are the perfect combination . . . to New Adult'
ChickLit

BY ROBIN YORK

Deeper

Harder

Harder

a novel

ROBIN YORK

PIATKUS

First published in the US in 2014 by Bantam Books,
an imprint of Random House, a division of Random House LLC,
a Penguin Random House Company, New York.
First published in Great Britain in 2014 by Piatkus
Reprinted 2014

A CIP catalogue record for this book
is available from the British Library.

ISBN 978-0-349-40421-9

Printed and bound by CPI Group (UK) Ltd, Croydon, CR0 4YY

Papers used by Piatkus are from well-managed forests
and other responsible sources.

MIX
Paper from
responsible sources
FSC® C104740

Piatkus
An imprint of
Little, Brown Book Group
100 Victoria Embankment
London EC4Y 0DY

An Hachette UK Company
www.hachette.co.uk

www.piatkus.co.uk

For Mary Ann, with love and gratitude

Harder

THE END

THE END.

West

When I had to say goodbye at the airport, I thought, *This is the last time.*

The last time you get to kiss her. The last time you get to touch her.

This is the last time you're ever going to see her face.

And then, after I turned and left, *That was it. It's over.*

I guess I went to the gate. I must have boarded a plane. Someone sat next to me, but I don't remember if it was a man or a woman, what they looked like. What I do remember is thinking everything would have to get easier from that point forward, because nothing could be harder than walking away from Caroline.

It almost makes me laugh now, if you can call it laughter when it comes with the salt-copper taste of blood at the top of your throat. If it's still a smile when you have to swallow and swallow around it, unable to get rid of the bitter flavor of your mistakes.

I went home to Silt thinking I was heading into some kind of

Wild West showdown. I'd call my dad out onto the public street at high noon and we'd draw our pistols. I'd fire straight and true and take him down, and then ... well, that was the part I had to avoid thinking about. That was the part where the screen starts to go dark, the edges drawing in around a black-bordered circle that shrinks until it's the size of a quarter, a nickel, a pinhole, nothing.

Nothing. That was where I would live after I drove my dad out of my life once and for all. Inside that blackness where the pinhole used to be, where the light had disappeared from, I'd pitch a tent, pull a blanket around me, and endure.

I was the sheriff, right? And he was the bad guy. But after I took him down, my reward would be an eternity of nothing I wanted. Maybe a gold star to pin on my shirt.

I was so sure I was the fucking sheriff, it almost makes me laugh, because what happened when I got home was that everything sucked in a completely different way from how I thought it would.

I did the impossible and walked away from Caroline.

After that, everything in my life that was hard got harder.

Caroline

When West's ringtone starts playing in my darkened bedroom, it slips into my subconscious, and I have one of those last-second-before-you-wake-up dreams that's pure sensation—his skin warm against me everywhere, his weight and smell, the muscles in his thighs against the backs of mine, his hand sliding down my stomach. All of that, slow and melting and *West,* until the song finally manages to pierce through the haze of my sleep and pinch me awake.

I fight my way from under the sheet, turned on and pissed off because I know how this goes. The rock in my stomach, the day ahead during which I'll try and fail to shake that flood of sense-memory.

I'm going to have to live through it, and then I'm going to lose it, every good memory I have of West, *again,* when what I want is to drop back into that dream and live there instead.

It sucks. It *sucks,* and I'm so distracted by the suckage that I'm picking up the phone and swiping at the screen with my thumb before I completely register what's going on.

West's ringtone. West is calling me.

West is calling me at one a.m. when I haven't heard from him in two and a half months.

If he's drunk-dialing me, I'm going to fly to Oregon and kick him in the nuts.

That's what I'm thinking when I put the phone to my ear—but it's not how I feel. I wish it were. I wish I could say *Hello?* and hear West say *Hey,* and not feel . . . I don't even know. Plugged in. Lit up. *Juiced.*

I stand in my dark bedroom, aware in every centimeter of my skin that he's breathing on the other end of the phone, somewhere on the far side of the country.

I have too many memories that start this way. Too many conversations where I told myself I wouldn't and then I did.

I have this enormous burden of longing and pain, so heavy I can hear it in my voice when I snap, "What do you want?"

"My dad's dead."

My head clears in an instant, my attention sharpening to a point.

"He got shot," West says, "and it's . . . it's a fucking mess, Caro. I know this is—I shouldn't ask you. I can't ask you, but I just need to tell you because I can't fucking—" A crackling whooshing noise interrupts him, the kind of interference that fills your whole head with white sound. I just stand there, waiting for his voice to come back.

I'm pushing the phone so hard against my ear, my breath shallow and fast, aware with the kind of clarity I've only found in moments of crisis that it doesn't even matter. Whatever he says next. It doesn't matter.

The thing I never understood before West was that there

are some people who, when it comes to them, reason and logic are never going to be in charge.

He left me. He hurt me.

But I stand there in the dark, holding the phone, and I know that in a few hours I'll be on a plane.

SILT

I emerge from baggage claim in Eugene to the sight of West leaning against a dirty black truck. The first thing I think is, *He cut his hair.*

The second thing I think is, *Maybe he did it for her.*

If there is a her. I've never been able to accept that there is, despite what West said.

If she exists, she's not here. I am.

West looks scary. Stubble covers his scalp, a dark shadow that throws the shapes of his face into relief: jawline, cheekbones, eye sockets, protruding brow, jutting chin, scowling mouth.

The muscles in his crossed arms belong to a brawler.

The West who left me in Des Moines more than four months ago was a guy, sometimes a boy, but this person who's waiting for me is a big, hard, mean-looking man, and when he glances in my direction, I freeze. Mid-step. I'm wearing a white cardigan over a new green top that cost too much. Designer jeans. Impractical flats. Ridiculous clothes for August, because it's always cold when you're flying.

I wanted to look nice, but I got it wrong. I got everything wrong, and yet I think nothing I've done is as wrong as whatever is wrong with him.

He straightens and steps forward. I start moving again. I have to.

"Hey," I say when we meet a few feet from his truck. I try on a smile. "You made it."

He doesn't smile in return. "So did you."

"Sorry you had to pick me up."

I'd texted right before I boarded the first flight to tell him I was coming. I didn't want to give him a chance to say no, so I just gave him my flight number and announced when I'd get in.

When the plane landed in Minneapolis, I had three texts and a voice mail from him, all of them variations on the theme of Turn your ass around and go home.

I waited until I was boarding for Portland to text him again. I'll get a rental car.

Walking off the jet bridge, I got his reply. I'll pick you up.

Since that was the outcome I'd been angling for, I said, Okay.

It doesn't feel okay, though. Not even close.

West wears cargo shorts and a red polo with a landscaping company's logo. He's tan—a deep, even, golden brown—and he smells strongly of something I don't recognize, fresh and resinous as the inside of our cedar closet after my dad sanded it down. "Did you come from work?" I ask.

"Yeah. I had to take off early."

"Sorry. You should've let me rent a car."

West reaches out his hand. For an instant I think he's going to pull me into his body, and something like a collision happens inside my torso—half of me slamming on the brakes, the other half flying forward to crash into my restraint.

His fingers knock mine off the handle of my suitcase, and the next thing I know he's heading for the truck with it.

I stand frozen, gawping at him.

Get your act together, Caroline. You can't freak out every time he moves in your direction.

He opens the passenger-side door to stow my bag in the back of the cab. The truck is huge, the front right side violently crumpled. I hope he wasn't driving when that happened.

By the time he emerges, I'm comparing the musculature of his back to what his shoulders felt like under my hands the last time I saw him. The shape of his calves is the same. He's West, and he's not-West.

He steps aside to let me in. I have to climb up to the seat. The sweltering cab smells of stale tobacco. I leave my sweater on. Even though I'm too hot, I feel weird about any form of disrobing.

I turn to grab the door handle and discover him still there, blocking me with his body.

That's when I figure it out. It's not his hair or his tan or his muscles that make him seem different: it's his eyes. His expression is civil, but his eyes look like he wants to rip the world open and tear out its entrails.

"You need to eat?" he asks.

I don't think the simmering cynical hatred I hear in his voice is directed at me. I'm pretty sure it's directed at *everything*. But it sends a shiver of apprehension through me, because I've never heard West sound like that before.

"No, I'm good. I had dinner in Portland."

"It's almost three hours back to Silt."

"I'm good," I repeat.

He's staring at me. I press my lips together to keep from apologizing. *Sorry I came when you called me. Sorry I needed a ride from the airport. Sorry I'm here, sorry you don't love me anymore, sorry your abusive asshole dad is dead.*

My own father didn't want me to come. At all. I had to quit my job a few weeks early and hand over almost everything I'd earned as a dental receptionist this summer to pay for the plane ticket—a move Dad called "boneheaded."

He doesn't trust West, and worse, he doesn't trust *me* when it comes to West. Which means we argue whenever the subject comes up. We fought like cats and dogs at breakfast this morning when Dad realized he wasn't going to be able to talk me out of this.

To make matters worse, we're close to being ready to file the petition in my civil suit against Nate, my ex-boyfriend, for infringing my privacy and inflicting emotional distress. Dad wants me close at hand so we can read through the complaint together four thousand more times.

He's a judge by profession, a single parent of three daughters, and a fretful micromanager by nature. Which makes him, in this situation, kind of unbearable.

I reminded him that poring endlessly over documents is what he paid our lawyer a zillion-dollar retainer for, but Dad says this is a learning experience for me. If I want to be a lawyer myself, I ought to pay attention.

I *am* paying attention.

I'm trying, at least. It got hard to pay attention right around the time West told me he was seeing someone else.

When he called me last night, all other thoughts flew out of my head.

The upcoming trial is important. Keeping my employment commitments is important. But West is *more* important. I'm not going to abandon him when he needs me.

"You don't have to make a big fuss," I say. "I'm just here to help."

Without another word, he slams the door and gets behind the wheel, and we're on our way.

I thought Eugene was a city, but after we leave the airport we're instantly in the middle of nowhere, and that's where we stay. It's so green, it makes me thirsty.

West turns right, heading toward the mountains.

It's nearly seven, so we won't get to Silt until ten. I don't know where I'm staying tonight.

I'm going to be sitting in this truck with West in the dark.

I take off my sweater. West fiddles with the air conditioner, reaches across me to redirect a vent, and suddenly it's blasting in my face. My sweat-clammy skin goes cold, goose bumps and instantaneous hard nipples.

He turns the fan down.

"You're doing landscaping?" I ask.

"Yeah."

"Do you like it?"

The look he gives me reminds me of my sister Janelle's cat. Janelle used to squirt it between the eyes with a water gun to keep it from jumping on her countertops, and it would glare back at her with exactly that expression of incredulous disdain.

"Sorry," I say.

Then I try to count up how many times I've apologized since I walked out of the airport.

Too many. I'm letting him get to me when I promised myself on the plane I wouldn't let *anything* get to me. This is a convoluted situation. Someone's dead, guns are involved,

West was torn up enough to call me—my job is to be unflappable. I'm not going to get mad at him or act heartbroken. I'm not going to moon around or cry or throw myself on him in a fit of lust. I'll just be here, on his side.

I'll do that because I promised him I would when he left Iowa. I made him swear to call me, and I told him he could count on me to be his friend.

He called. Here I am.

After marinating in tobacco-scented silence for a while, I find myself scanning West all over again, looking for similarities instead of differences. His ears are still too small. The scar hasn't vanished from his eyebrow, and the other one tilts up same as always. His mouth is the same.

Always, for me, it was his mouth.

The scent coming off him is like a hot day in the deep woods—like a fresh-cut Christmas tree—but it's not quite either of those. On the seat between us, there's a pair of work gloves he must have tossed there. I want to pick them up, put them on, wiggle my fingers around. Instead, I look at his thigh. His faded shorts, speckled with minuscule pieces of clinging bark. His kneecap.

I look at his arm from the curve of his shoulder to the banded edge of his sleeve where the polo shirt cuts across his biceps. He doesn't have a tan line. He must work with his shirt off, and the thought is more than I know what to do with.

The last time I saw him, we were kissing at the airport, holding each other, saying goodbye. Even though I know everything's different now, it doesn't entirely *feel* different. It's cruel that it's possible for him to have told me what he did and for me to still be sitting here, soaking him up.

I'm not over him. I've tried to reason myself into it, but I'm learning reason doesn't have anything to do with love, and West has always made me softer than I wanted to be, weaker than was good for me.

Before we crashed and burned, though, I liked the person I was with him. He made me vulnerable, but he helped me be stronger, too.

"You want to fill me in on what's going on?" I ask.

A muscle ticks in his jaw. "I've been at work. I don't know what's going on."

"What was happening when you went to work?"

"My dad was dead."

"Where's Frankie?"

Last I heard, his sister and his mom were living with his dad at the trailer park where West grew up. West had dropped out of college and moved home to Oregon so he could protect them, but there's only so much you can do to save someone who doesn't want to be saved.

His mom wouldn't leave his dad, and West wouldn't go near the trailer with his dad living in it. That meant West wasn't seeing Frankie as often as he would have liked. It bothered him not being able to get close enough to protect her the way he wanted to.

"She's out at my grandma's," he says. "I have to pick her up."

"Does she seem okay?"

"I can't tell."

"She wasn't there, was she? When he got . . ."

"Mom says she was at a sleepover."

His knuckles are white on the steering wheel. I watch the color drain from his skin all the way to the base of each finger as he squeezes tighter.

"You don't believe her?"

"I'm not sure."

Then we're quiet. He's got a cut on his right hand in the

space between his thumb and his index finger. The skin is half scabbed over, pink and puffy around the edges with curls of dry skin. I can see two places where it's cracked.

A burn. Or a bad scrape.

Back in Putnam, I'd have known where he got a cut like that. I'd have nagged him to put a Band-Aid on it or at least spread some lotion around so it would heal better. I probably would have made a disgusted face and told him to cover it up.

I wouldn't have wanted to touch it, the way I do now—to reach out and stroke that newborn pink skin with my fingertip.

I'm dying to know how he would react. If he'd jump or draw away. If he'd pull over and turn off the truck and talk to me. Touch me back.

"What do you smell like?" I ask.

He lifts his shirt to his nose to sniff it. I glimpse his belt buckle, and the sight slices clean through the twine I'd used to tie up a tightly packed bundle of conditioned sexual response. My cheeks warm. Pretty much everything below my waist ignites.

I have to turn away.

When I glance back his eyes are on me, which only makes it worse, because for a few heavy seconds counted off by my thumping heart, West doesn't look angry. He looks like he used to when I was prone in his bed and he was crawling up my body after stripping off my panties—like he wants to own me, eat me, pin down my wrists, fill me up, ruin me for any other man.

I let out a deep, shuddering breath.

West concentrates his intensity on the road, frowning at it as though it might at any moment sprout a field of dangerous obstacles he has to navigate the truck around.

The charged silence lengthens. He exhales, slow. "Juniper."

It takes me an eternity to remember I'd asked him what he smells like.

"Is that a tree or a bush?"

"Both," he says. "Kind of."

He taps the steering wheel with flattened fingers. His left knee jumps, jiggling up and down, and then he adds, "It's a tree, but most of them are short like a bush. Oregon's got too many of them. They're a pest now, crowding other stuff out. The landscaper I work for uses the lumber for decking and edging, but I've seen it in cabinets and stuff, too. They make—"

He stops short. When he glances at me, I catch a strained sort of helplessness in his expression, as though he's dismayed by how difficult it is to keep himself from talking about juniper trees.

He swallows. "I was chipping up scrap wood for mulch. That's why I stink."

I wait. His knee is still jittering.

Come on, I think. *Talk to me.*

"They make gin from juniper berries," he says finally. "Not the Western juniper we have here. The common juniper over in Europe."

"Is that sloe gin?"

"No. Sloe gin is made with blackthorn berries and sugar. You start with gin and pour it over the other stuff and let it sit forever."

For the first time since I landed, I feel like smiling. Whatever's wrong with him, however twisted and broken he is, this guy beside me is West. *My* West. When it comes to trivia like gin berries and juniper bushes, he can't help himself.

West is a crow about useless information, zooming down to pluck shiny gum wrappers off the ground and carry them back to his nest.

The girl who took my place—does she listen when he does this? Does it make her like him more?

If there even is a girl.

That same intrusive thought I've had a hundred times. A thousand.

Whoever she is, she's not the one he called last night.

"I like the smell," I tell him.

"When I'm here, I don't smell it. But when I fly from Putnam to Portland, it's the first thing I notice getting off the plane." This time when he glances at me, his eyes don't give anything away. "It was, I mean. When I used to do that."

"I bet when I get back to Iowa, I'll smell manure."

"Only if you time it right."

The silence is more comfortable this time, for me at least. West remains edgy, tapping his fingers against the steering wheel.

"Is this your truck?" I ask.

"It's Bo's. He lets me use it."

Bo is West's mom's ex. She and Frankie lived with Bo until she left him for West's dad.

Bo was at the trailer when West's dad got shot.

Sticky subject.

"Is he still in jail?"

"No. They questioned him and let him go."

"Was he . . ." I take a deep breath. "Did he really kill your dad?"

"He won't say. He was there, shots were fired. There were two guns. I don't know which one discharged, or if it was both or what. For all I know, it could've been suicide." The anger is back, flattening out his voice so he sounds almost bored.

"Not likely, though, if they took Bo in for questioning."

"What the fuck do you know about what's likely?"

"Nothing. Sorry."

That's where the line is, then. Junipers are an acceptable topic of conversation. His dead father is pushing it. Speculation about what's going to happen next? Out of bounds.

West leans forward and flips on the radio. The music is loud, hammering hair-band rock.

I turn it off. "When's the funeral?"

"Whenever they get the body back from the coroner."

"Oh."

"I'm not going."

"Okay."

More silence. Dark green forest closes in on both sides of the road. We're climbing now, heading into the foothills.

"How long are you staying?" West asks.

"As long as you need me to."

He stares at me so long, I start to get nervous we're going to drive off the road. "What?"

"When's school start?"

"The twenty-eighth."

"Two weeks."

"Two and a half."

"You're not gonna be here two and a half weeks."

"Whatever you need."

West looks out the driver's-side window. "You shouldn't have come."

I've already thought the same thing, but it hurts to hear him say it. "It's nice to see you, too, baby."

"I didn't invite you."

"How sweet of you to notice, I *have* lost a little weight."

His eyes narrow. "You look scrawny."

Stung, I drop the act. "I'll be sure to put on a few pounds for your visual enjoyment."

"If you want to say *Fuck you, West*, go ahead and say it."

"Fuck you, West."

His jawline tightens. When he reaches for the radio, I knock his hand away.

"I don't know what I'm supposed to do with you," he says.

"You're supposed to let me help."

"I don't want you anywhere near this shit."

"That's sweet, but too bad."

That earns me a criminal's glare. "You don't belong in Silt."

"I guess I'm about to find that out for myself."

"I guess you are."

He reaches for the stereo again. This time, I let him turn it on.

I think about how we're driving toward the Pacific Ocean, which I've never seen.

I think about West and what I want from him. Why I'm here.

I don't have any answers. I'm not kidding myself, though. Inside a makeup pouch at the bottom of my suitcase, there's a leather bracelet with his name on it.

I shouldn't be here, but I am.

I'm not leaving until I know there's no chance I'll ever wear that bracelet again.

The road drops away from the pavement on West's side of the truck.

The guardrail doesn't look like it would be much help if he yanked the wheel to the left and sent us sailing out over the edge.

Not that he'd do that.

I don't think.

We climb up and up through a corridor of trees, winding around broad curves to the sound of rushing water. The light fades.

I can't get over the green. It's green in Iowa in August, too, but there the color hugs the ground in long rows and flat lawns. Here, it's all trees. More trees than I've ever seen in one place, crowding the road and pulling my gaze up to the sky.

After a while, we descend, sweeping in slow, easy curves downhill as though we're skiing on an extravagant scale. This heaved-up world is our field of moguls, the tires rocking us back and forth like freshly waxed skis on perfect powder.

I've been to the mountains, skiing in Telluride and Aspen with my family, but Oregon is different. The road's so narrow, the forest so dense. It feels primeval, unfinished.

We swoop and curve. The silence stretches out and grows stale.

This drive is interminable.

West reaches past my knees to open the glove box. Careful not to touch me, he extracts a pack of cigarettes.

"You're smoking now?"

"Hand me the lighter, would you?"

I can see it—cheap bright pink plastic—but it's too deep for him to reach. I leave it where it is.

"Smoking is disgusting."

We hit a straight section. He leans over me as far as he has to in order to retrieve the lighter, which is far enough to press his shoulder into my knee.

The lighter snicks and sparks when he sits up, the smell of the catching tobacco acrid, then sugary. The ripples from our brief moment of contact move through my body, lapping against my skin for a long time.

West blows smoke in a stream out the window to dissipate in the dark.

I feel like smoke, my edges dissolving with every mile that passes, every flick of his hand over the wand that makes the high beams come on, a flood of light, then another flick, dimming to yellow. The darkness concentrates his potency, makes him more solid and me less substantial, immaterial, unreal.

When he leans forward to turn down the radio—an obvious prelude to conversation—I have to pull myself back from somewhere far away.

"What's going on with Nate?" he asks.

"Nothing."

"He stopped posting the pictures?"

"As far as I can tell. They pop up sometimes, but that's going to happen. I don't think it's him doing it anymore."

Nate spent most of last school year posting and reposting our sex pictures online while I wasted dozens of hours contacting site owners to get them removed. It was the world's least fun game of whack-a-mole.

He finally stopped after I took the problem to the dean's office. When the college began to investigate, I hoped he would end up expelled for violating the campus technology policy, but it didn't happen. He'd been too sneaky, and he's a convincing liar. How else would he have convinced me he was a nice person for all the time we were going out?

The college let him off the hook with a suspension of his Internet privileges—a slap on the wrist—but the disciplinary investigation must have shaken him up, because he's backed off the attack.

"You get a trial date yet?" West asks.

"No, we're not done working on the complaint."

"What about the Jane Doe thing?"

Filing as Jane Doe rather than Caroline Piasecki means my highly recognizable name won't come out in connection with the case, and the public records of the suit won't identify me.

Which means, in turn, there's a chance that my entire economic and political future won't be tainted by what Nate did and what I'm doing to get back at him.

"My dad knows someone who knows someone who says with the judge I'm going to be assigned, it shouldn't be a problem."

"So when do they set your trial date?"

"After we file the complaint, which is any day now," I say. "Dad says it will probably be at least twelve months until the trial."

"It'll be nice to see that fucker raked over the coals for what he did."

"I guess so."

"You *guess* so?"

"It's going to cost a fortune."

"How much?"

"Maybe a hundred thousand dollars, according to the lawyer. Could be more."

West whistles.

"And he says it could get ugly, like a rape case. They'll attack my credibility. So I'm trying to get ready for all that."

"Doesn't sound easy to get ready for. Douchebag lawyers grilling you about your sex life."

"Don't forget my mental stability."

"Your mental stability's just fine."

"I meant that they'll grill me about my mental stability."

There's a smile flirting with the corners of his mouth. "Fucking great. Have 'em call me, I'll tell 'em what a basket case you were at the bakery last year."

"That'd be great, thanks."

"My pleasure."

I press my hands against my thighs so I won't press them into the ache in my chest.

It's too easy. Talking to him. Remembering.

If I close my eyes and pretend, it's almost possible to forget all the bad stuff between us and drop into my memories of those nights at the bakery when I was falling in love with West.

Maybe he feels it, too, because he leans forward to turn up the music.

I look out at the dark green shapes of the trees, the blurred branches. The trial drops away as I let myself think about why I'm here. What I want. My purpose.

West.

But after a while, even West slips away, and then it's just dark.

Cold air coming in from the driver's side of the truck snaps me awake.

We're parked on the street in a neighborhood of nearly identical houses—all of them small, crowded on tiny lots.

West stands outside the open driver's-side door. His face through the window is stark, shadowed.

"Is this where Frankie is?" I ask.

"Yeah, my grandma's."

He shifts so he's holding the top of the car door with both hands, leaning into it, studying me through the glass. It's as though he's using the door as a shield so he can look at me, *really* look at me, the way he hasn't yet.

He rakes his eyes upward from my shoes. Right turn at my knees. Left turn at my thighs. Lingering over the parts that used to be his favorites.

It's like in my dreams—my mind too fuzzy and slow to defend me against the heat of West's lava-dipped icicle gaze. I just want to crawl across the front seat of the truck on all fours until I crash into his body and he's on me, over me, hot hands and wet mouths and every single thing I've missed that I need.

A few hours in the truck, and my lofty thoughts of friendship and loyalty are nothing but a sticky layer on top of weeks' worth of longing.

West's expression has gone dark. "You're staying here tonight," he says.

"What, to sleep?"

"Yeah."

"Where are you staying?"

"Out at Bo's."

"How far is that?"

"Twenty miles."

"I want to stay wherever you are."

He comes from behind the door and jacks his seat forward, pushing himself all the way through the space behind it so he can get hold of my bag.

When he starts rolling it up the walk to the front door, I get the idea that this decision he's made isn't negotiable.

I hurry after him. "Who's inside?"

"Based on the cars, I'm guessing Grandma, Mom, Frankie, a couple of my aunts."

I wasn't aware he had aunts. Or, until he mentioned her earlier, a living grandmother. "Anything I should know about them?"

"Except for my mom and Frankie, I haven't seen them in six years."

"Seriously?"

He frowns. "You think I'm fucking around?"

I don't. My stomach hurts. "Sorry. How should—who should I say I am?"

"Tell them whatever you want." He rings the doorbell.

I have time to take a breath and think, *This is going to be weird,* before the door is pulled open directly into the kitchen.

The first thing I notice is that there's a woman sobbing at the table.

Like, *sobbing*.

Two other women and three kids are crowded into the room with her, but I don't pay much attention to them, because the second thing I notice is that the woman who opened the door has West's eyes *exactly*.

Nobody has eyes like West's. Even West doesn't, since his eyes look one way one day and another way the next, depending on the light and his mood and all kinds of factors I can't pin down. I've wondered what it says on his driver's license, because there is no word for the color his eyes are.

It's trippy, seeing West's eyes in the wrinkled face of a woman.

Other than the eyes, the resemblance is scanty. She has to tip her head way back to talk to him, because this woman is *short*. She's round in every direction—boobs, hips, butt— with salt-and-pepper hair cut close to her head. She's takes a drag off a cigarette held in her left hand, and I notice when she puts it to her lips that her fingers seem to take off in a new direction at each swollen knuckle joint.

"Will wonders never cease?" she says.

Far from a welcome. I kind of expect her to exhale right in West's face and then slam the door, but she turns her head to the side instead and says, "Michelle, look who's here."

I know that Michelle is West's mom. She looks up.

Her eyes are like dark holes punched into dough.

"Who's that?" Her voice is hoarse, terrible to hear. I want to cover my face with my hands.

"This is Caroline," West says.

She blinks. Rubs at her eyes. Blinks again. "Caroline who?"

Behind a closed door between the kitchen and the other room, a toilet flushes. West asks his grandma, "What's she on?"

"She's been like this all day."

"Fuck." He inhales deeply. "Can we come in?"

"Introduce us," his grandmother says.

"Caroline, this is my grandma, Joan. Grandma, Caroline." He points across the kitchen. "Aunt Stephanie, Aunt Heather, and my cousins Tyler, Taylor, and . . . I don't know that one."

"Hailey," the woman named Heather says.

"Hailey," West repeats. "Good to meet you, Hailey. I'm West."

I shake West's grandmother's hand and offer a weak, "Hi."

"I brought her to stay with Frankie," West says.

"I'm with Frankie," Joan replies.

"You've got other stuff on your plate."

"I can take care of one kid."

The bathroom door opens, and I recognize West's sister at the same time her face lights up to see him. "West!"

Relief washes through me—more than I'm prepared for.

I've never met Frankie in person, but when West and I were together, she and I started texting. I don't know if he's aware that we never stopped.

Not that we swap the secrets of our hearts. Frankie's ten. She sends me pictures of cute boys and really bad jokes. I send her links to stories I think she'd like, or I just ask her how she's doing.

How's school? How's life?

I never ask her, *How's West?*

I guess I figured that was over the line, but standing here now, it's utterly hilarious that I thought I had lines. I mean, I'm in Silt, Oregon. *Obviously* I have no lines.

West's got his arms around Frankie, his face in her hair, his eyes closed, and I can't look away.

He wants me to stay here, so I'll stay here.

He wants me to watch over his sister, so I'll watch over her.

There's nothing I wouldn't do for West Leavitt.

Frankie and I bunk down that night in the attic. It's one big low-ceilinged room full of boxes and swollen garbage bags, a broken chair, the ironing board and mop bucket. Clashing squares carpet the floor—deep brown shag next to a red Turkish print next to a pink nubbly one.

Samples from a carpet store is my guess. Not of recent vintage.

The attic makes my nose run. It started as soon as I lay down, and now my eyes are watering. I keep sneezing.

Even if I weren't wired, it would be a joke to think I could sleep.

Frankie's beside me, each of us with a sleeping bag on a

pallet made of blankets and a thick egg-crate mattress pad. Every time I'm sure she's finally nodded off, she moves.

Before he left, West took his sister out on the porch and talked to her for a while. Then he went into the living room with his mom and spoke to her in a low rumble while his grandma draped an afghan over Michelle's shoulders.

I stayed in the kitchen talking to Frankie while West's aunts talked to each other and his cousins argued loudly about who got to sleep in which bed when they got back to Stephanie's that night.

After Michelle fell asleep, Joan drew a pocket door closed between the living room and the kitchen, and the whole crew of aunts and cousins cleared out. Frankie was only too happy for the opportunity to ask me a dozen more questions. What was my trip like? How many airplanes? Were they big or small? Where did I get my sweater? How much did my shoes cost? How long was I going to be staying, and why hadn't she known I was coming?

I did my best to answer, but I was tense waiting for West's reappearance. When he finally came back through the pocket door, he went straight to Frankie.

When will you be back? she asked.

Tomorrow after work. Caroline's gonna keep an eye on you.

Anything in particular I'm supposed to do? I asked.

Stay with her. Call me if anything gets strange.

I wanted to say, *Define strange,* but he looked so tired, I decided to let it go.

Things are already strange. I assume they can only get stranger.

I sneeze loudly and then sniff, wishing I'd packed tissues. Stupid allergies. Dust and mites, mold and dander—all it means is that I never know when someplace is going to set me off. I keep Claritin in my purse, but all I found when I fished around was an empty plastic pill bubble, half-squashed.

I'm going to have to go down the narrow wooden staircase that brought me up here and try to find Joan. Ask if she's got something I can take.

I hope she's not asleep already.

When I shift to my side, preparing to move, Frankie says, "Caroline?"

I freeze. In front of me, there are bare two-by-fours with wiring stapled to them. A water stain, dark at the edges, bowed plywood in the middle. A small square window and the moon outside, nearly full.

Behind me, there's a little girl whose father is dead.

West wanted me here, with her. But what did he want me to say?

"Yeah?"

"Do you think he'll leave again?"

"Who, West?"

"Yeah."

I turn toward her and prop myself up on one elbow.

Her sleeping bag is close enough to mine that I can see it rise and fall with her breath.

Hers is My Little Pony. Mine's Spider-Man.

Her eyes are so big in the dim lighting. She's got her mother's brown eyes and sharp chin, but the rest of her is West— cheekbones like wings, eyebrows that come to a peak, a wide mouth, and thick, dark hair. She's beautiful and so *young*, her front teeth a little too big for her face.

"I don't know," I say honestly.

"But what do you think?"

"I think . . . I guess he'll do whatever he decides is best."

She's quiet. Then, "Did he ask you to come?"

"No."

"Why did you, then?"

"I thought . . . I could help."

She rises to her elbow, mirroring my position. "What can you do?"

"Not much," I admit. "Keep you company, if you want me to."

"Can I tell you something?" she asks.

No. Don't tell me anything. I don't know what I'm doing. But that's just cowardice. I've learned to ignore it. "Sure."

"Mom told them I wasn't there. But I was. I saw what happened." Her eyes gleam, wet. "I saw."

"Do you want to . . . talk about it?"

She shakes her head. Her tears brim over.

I disentangle my arms from the sleeping bag and put them around her, pulling her close and rubbing her thin small shoulders. "Shh," I say to this shaking girl. "Shh, shh, it'll be all right."

I have no idea if it will.

After a while, her breathing settles and slows. I can tell when she falls asleep—she gets heavier against me.

I've been holding back a sneeze for a while now, inhaling deeply and squeezing my eyes shut. As soon as I can, I ease out from beside her and slip down the stairs.

West's grandma sits with a mug at the table, knitting. A wall-mounted TV flashes a muted newscast. A radio plays oldies, while a crackling noise pours out of what I think might be a police scanner.

Bright pink letters across the front of her long white sleep shirt say "San Francisco."

Her arms are pale, the flesh loose and veined with red fireworks.

"She asleep?"

"Yeah."

"Tough kid."

I guess she is. She kind of has to be.

"You want some coffee?" Joan asks.

"Is it decaf, or . . . ?"

"I don't drink decaf."

"No, I'm good. I was just going to duck into the bathroom for a second."

The toilet seat is freezing. There's a hole in the plaster above the head end of the tub, positioned so I imagine someone creating it with the back of their skull. Tapping until they dented the sheetrock, pounding until the plaster crumbled.

I sneeze three times on the toilet.

"You have a cold?" she asks when I come out.

"Allergies."

"You need Sudafed or something?"

"Any kind of antihistamine would be great."

She gets up carefully, the movements of a woman who's no longer comfortable in her body. A minute later, she's back with a bottle of generic allergy medicine and a glass of water.

"Thanks." I take the pills, then sneeze again.

She pours herself more coffee and sits.

"You and West are close," she says.

My head is full of snot. It's too late for me to feel clever, too dark outside for bullshit. "We were."

"He left Frankie with you."

"He doesn't want me here."

She gives me a pitying look. "Doesn't *want* to want you here, more like it."

We're quiet. The kitchen fills with the crackling murmuring gibberish of the scanner and the love-complaint of some long-ago vocalist on the radio.

"He tell you how long it's been since he let me get a look at his face?" Joan asks.

"He said six years, but he didn't say why."

"His daddy—my son. Last time he took up with Michelle before this, it ended bad, and West was in the middle of it. West come over here, told me I had to choose sides. Everybody had to choose. Either him and his mom and Frankie, or my Wyatt. Nobody was gonna be neutral anymore."

She pulls the sugar bowl close and spoons more into her mug.

"I guess you chose your son."

"I thought West would come around."

I smile at my fingernails. "West doesn't really come around."

"Not for six years, he didn't."

I wish I'd taken her up on the coffee. Sleep is an impossibility here, and I'm envious of her steaming mug.

The idea of swallowing that bittersweet heat.

"My son was no good." She addresses this remark to her clinking coffee spoon, slowly revolving. "I don't know why. It wasn't anything I did, I don't think. The other three came out okay. But Wyatt was always full of himself. A bully."

She drinks deeply from her coffee, then frowns at it. "Too much sugar now."

I feel like I'm supposed to say something, so I say, "I'm sorry."

"Michelle's no better. You saw what she's like. She'll be sniveling for weeks—months, maybe—and never give a single thought to what it does to her daughter or what she leaves her son to deal with."

It's eerie when Joan finally looks at me. West's eyes. A stranger's face. Familiar strength that I know how to count on. "Did you come to take him back with you?" she asks.

"I don't know."

She drains the mug and stands to set it by the sink. Looks through the window at the moon.

"Take him out of here," she says quietly. "He's not going to get another chance."

I spend the next morning washing dishes and shelling peas with Frankie at Joan Leavitt's kitchen table.

Afterward, Joan tries to teach us both how to knit. Frankie catches on faster than I do. I keep wrapping the yarn around the needle, which makes holes.

Joan says I'm good at making holes.

For lunch, she warms up canned tomato soup and fixes grilled cheese sandwiches with Kraft singles and margarine. There's a constant stream of traffic in and out of her kitchen— friends, neighbors, extended family, a woman with four children who I eventually figure out from the conversation is from Joan's AA chapter. Joan is her sponsor.

I'm not introduced. The company ebbs and flows. Joan pops outside for a cigarette and pops back in, running water in the sink, talking on the phone, turning up the radio. Always, if her hands aren't otherwise occupied, she's knitting. She has a red bag that snaps to the belt loop of her pants, and she carries the needles in her hands and knits without looking, twelve-inch squares in brown and blue, green and red.

Her living room is draped in her knitting—two afghans on the couch, one on the La-Z-Boy, an overflowing basket of yarn in the corner. There's a set of stitch pattern reference books tucked beneath the coffee table.

I sit with one thigh touching the afghan wrapped around West's mom and the other leg pressed up against Frankie, who seems to need that.

All day long, she pushes herself against me.

She's an alarming blend of kid and woman. Knobby knees and boobs, careful eye makeup and huddled posture. I understand why West loves her. Frankie is everything soft in him, every impulse right at the surface. Loud and funny, hot-tempered, quick to forgive.

Your hair's so pretty, she tells me.

Show me how you do your makeup.

Teach me how you make your scarf look like that.

She doesn't say anything more about what she witnessed. She doesn't cry.

I wonder if I should tell someone that she saw the shooting, but who would I tell? Her mom knows the truth, whatever it is. Her grandmother, her aunts and uncles—either they know or they don't. I can't imagine breaking Frankie's trust, turning over what she told me to somebody whose allegiances aren't clear.

The only person I can see myself telling is West, and West isn't here.

In the afternoon, we hear that Bo has been taken in for questioning again. West's mom bursts into tears. She cries about Wyatt being dead. She cries about Bo being in jail. I can't figure out which thing she's more upset about.

Frankie stares at the TV, her eyes wide and wet.

I put my arm around her, and we watch soap operas.

West doesn't text. He doesn't call. He doesn't come, even though he said he would.

That night, I comb through the online version of the Coos Bay paper on my phone after Frankie's gone to sleep, trying to fill in the blanks.

Shots reported at the trailer park. A gunshot wound to the chest. Ambulance to the hospital. Dead on arrival.

The neighbors say an argument got out of hand.

The paper says there were only two witnesses: Michelle and Bo.

Bo's been questioned, released, questioned again.

I want to make a narrative out of these plain, blank facts. I want a story I can tell myself, but there's only Michelle's tear-streaked face. Frankie curled into a ball on the couch, her head on my lap as she watches TV. People coming in and out the door into the kitchen, talking to Joan, leaving food, running errands.

I text West.

What are you doing?

When are you coming over here?

Should I get a car?

He ignores me.

Even when we were dating, West never wanted me to know about Silt.

Here I am, though, and before he forces me back out of his life, I'm going to learn as much about this place and these people as I can.

My second day in Silt is the same as the first, except I listen harder, pay closer attention, and send West four hundred texts.

How's it going?

What's up?

Need anything?

He doesn't respond, so I try random declarations.

Watching Days of Our Lives w/ Frankie.

Having split pea soup.

SP soup looks like snot, but tastes good. Discuss.

Then I give up and just start typing whatever comes to mind.

When do you get off work?

Am I going to see you tonight?

Think I'll go out for a beer.

Shoot pool in a short skirt.

Check out the local nightlife.

Do you like Raisinets or Sno-Caps better?

Milk Duds or Junior Mints?

Ocean or mountains?

I want to see you.

Come for dinner.

To my surprise, he does. His aunts and his grandma crowd around the table in the kitchen with his mom, and there are cousins big and small with paper plates, fruit salad with whipped cream and marshmallows, stringed chicken cooked all day in a Crock-Pot.

When he takes his plate to the couch, I follow. I sit beside him and ask, "How was your day?"

"Got a lot of texts."

"Anything interesting?"

He stares at the TV with his plate balanced on his lap and bites into a pull-apart roll slathered in butter. "Nope."

But he slants me a look, and the smart-ass tilt to his mouth makes me flush with heat.

I've seen that smile in bed, over dinner, in his car, in the bakery, in every corner of our lives together.

I miss that smile.

"You can't ignore me into disappearing," I say.

He just chews and swallows, staring, straight ahead.

I lean close and whisper so only he can hear me. "I'm not leaving until I know you're okay."

Everything about him gets still. He doesn't even breathe, and I'm holding my own breath in sympathy, so caught up in him that I don't even realize it until he draws air deep into his lungs and turns toward me. His face bare inches away.

His thigh hot alongside mine.

His eyes, his nose, his mouth, his face.

God.

There can't be another woman. Not between me and West—there *can't* be, because if there were, I wouldn't feel like this. I *couldn't* feel like this. This alive. This real.

Not if he didn't feel it, too.

"So if I tell you I'm okay, you'll go?" he asks.

"I have to believe it."

My white shirt is reflected in his eyes, a glare against the darkness of his pupils.

His nostrils flare. I know he feels something. I know he's got things he wants to say to me. So why won't he open his mouth and say them?

After he left Putnam, West shut down any conversation that included the words *move* or *transfer,* any talk of seeing each other again. Everything is black or white for West. His mom went back to his dad, so he had to go back to Frankie.

All he got of her was one afternoon a week at the McDonald's near her school. An hour for West to look his sister and his mom over for bruises, interpret their answers to his questions, wait for the day he found out something was wrong.

The rest of the time, he worked. He slept. He went to the bars with Bo, and every now and then got drunk enough to call and tell me the truth as he saw it.

We were over. I shouldn't keep trying to be his friend. I shouldn't text him.

We were over, so we shouldn't be talking on the phone at two in the morning, except we *were*. Because he'd called me. And once we were talking, we found ourselves joking, meandering around until he said something or I did and we slid down into the dark together, hands where they shouldn't be, saying everything we'd been holding back.

Miss you.

Want you.

Need you.

Still love you.

Baby, I can't. I can't.

He'd tell me I deserved better, but I could never make myself believe there was anyone for me but West.

I watch the color rise in his cheeks. I look at his throat, where his pulse beats. I feel the heat coming off him, the want.

He can lie to me in a text. He can lie over the phone. But he can't sit here and lie to me with his body.

"Make me believe you're fine," I say. "Tell me you don't miss me. You don't want me. You're not thinking about me all the time, as much as I'm thinking about you." I reach out for his thigh and find a grip above the knee. *"Tell me."*

The muscles in his leg twitch beneath my fingers. West wraps a hand around the back of my neck.

He leans in close.

I think he means to say something harsh, to convey the hard truth of our hopeless situation. I should brace myself for it, except I can't. That hand on the back of my neck makes me soften instantly, everywhere.

This is how he used to kiss me. Just like this. And when

he lets me this close, looks at me this way, I can see right into him and catalog every feeling chasing its way across his face.

His longing. His lust.

His need for me, his craving for my softness, his desire to claim something tender in this blighted life of his.

I can see anguish, too. Agony.

I watch agony overpower his tenderness, wrestle its way to the forefront, and shut down his expression until all the feeling left is in his lawless, angry eyes.

"Stay with Frankie," he says. "That's all I want from you."

He stands and walks out of the room, like that's a normal thing to do. Get up in the middle of everything, step over the crawling baby, stuff his plate in the garbage can and go.

Go wherever.

Go somewhere I can't follow him.

I think about borrowing a car, asking for directions out to Bo's place. I could park and knock on the door, find West, corner him. I could flatten my hands on his chest and shove him.

Say what you're thinking. Admit what I mean to you.

Talk to me about what you're going to do now that he's dead.

Promise you're coming back to me, convince me you love me, tell me you're sorry.

What stops me is how badly I want him.

I want to follow him around the way Frankie follows me. Push myself up against him, seeking comfort.

What stops me, too, is what I saw. What West let me see: that he's hurting badly, and his hardness is the only defense he's got.

I'm here for him. Not for myself. *Stay with Frankie,* he said.

That's what I do.

My third day in Silt is like the first two.

West makes himself scarce and refuses to answer my texts.

My dad calls and I ignore him. Four times. I can't be here and still be thinking about what's going on back home, not if I want to stay sane. It's too much.

And I'm weary of talking to my dad. He's obsessed with the trial. Talking to my dad about trial stuff ate my entire summer—the trial and West, West and the trial. Lying awake nights in my bedroom at the house where I grew up, I felt sometimes like I was disappearing. Like I was nothing but the aftermath of last year: what happened with Nate, what happened with West.

Instead of taking Dad's calls, I do my detective thing in the morning, insinuating myself into conversations, learning the names of all West's cousins, the personalities of his aunts and uncles, the simmering feuds and complicated webs of animosity that fuel this family's daily dramas.

There are a lot of dramas. I can see why West opted out for six years.

Michelle has to go in to the police station for an interview. Joan teaches Frankie and me to play backgammon, and we have a tournament at the kitchen table while she makes chili, knits, and talks on the phone with her daughters, one after the other, each of them pissed about something.

Michelle comes home with a headache, cries when Joan asks her what the police wanted to know, and falls asleep on the couch.

Frankie gets bored and wants to play Skip-Bo. When Joan tells her she doesn't have it, Frankie says she's got it at the trailer. Also at the trailer are her clothes, her toiletries, her cell phone, the blanket off her bed, and everything else in the world a ten-year-old girl could possibly want.

"Can we go get it?" she asks. "Please, Caroline?"

"I don't have a car, remember? I can ask West."

"He'll say no. They *all* say no." She folds her arms and collapses on top of her cards in despair.

"It's a crime scene, hon."

But late in the afternoon, Joan takes a phone call out to the porch. When she comes back inside, she tells us the police have classified Wyatt Leavitt's death accidental.

They're releasing the body. The funeral will be tomorrow.

That night, after Frankie falls asleep, Joan walks up the attic steps.

"You decent?"

"Yeah." I'm wearing a long-sleeved T-shirt and yoga pants. Decent enough.

"Come with me."

A short drive later, we're parked in front of a dark trailer with crime-scene tape across the door.

The knob turns easily under her hand. She shows me how to duck under the tape.

Breaking and entering, I think. *Contaminating a crime scene.*

Technically, it's not a crime scene anymore. But even if it were, I think I'd be here. I need to see this place. I need to know it, because this is where West came from.

This is his past.

I take it in—the musty smell, the cheap paneling over thin walls. The scratched tabletop, its wood grain a sticker half peeled away, revealing the white of the backing.

Joan comes out of the bedroom with her arms full of clothes and says, "Get me a trash bag from under the kitchen sink."

I do as I'm told, thinking about where West would have kept his things. What he might have called his own and how he would have protected it.

He never wanted me to see this.

My cell rings. I fumble getting it out of my pocket, inadvertently accepting the call. My father's voice says, "Caroline?"

"Hey, Dad."

"I've been calling you all day."

Joan comes out with another load of clothes. I squeeze the phone to my shoulder and hold open the trash bag. She stuffs the clothes inside.

"Sorry, I'm keeping busy."

"Doing what?"

Trespassing.

Invading the privacy of the man I love.

Banging my head against a brick wall.

Only I don't think West is a brick wall, as much as he looks like one. The bricks he surrounds himself with are no more real than the wood-grain surface of the tabletop.

"I can't talk right now," I tell my dad.

"When can you talk?"

"I don't know," I say. "I'll call you."

"You'll have to do better than that. I set up a meeting for Tuesday, because I have some questions about the complaint. I need you to weigh in on a few things before then. Will you be back? Or . . ."

I can't listen. Outside, the heavy thump of bass draws closer. Lights cut across the window and pan over the wall, illuminating a dark decoration against the wallpaper.

A spatter pattern.

Blood.

I disconnect the phone.

Joan comes out with a handful of jewelry and Frankie's Skip-Bo cards. "Let's get out of here," she says.

I want to move. Escape. But I stand another minute in the beating heart of West's nightmares, because for so many years, escape was impossible for him.

We ride back to Joan's house with the windows down. I turn my phone over and over in my hand, thinking about my dad.

West's dad is dead. I saw his blood.

Joan must have seen it, too. Her son's life, spilled across the walls. Wasted.

I came here to help, but there's so little that's in my power to do. All I can do is stay. Love him. Hope.

I carry the bags up the stairs so Frankie will see them when she wakes up.

My fourth day in Silt is the funeral.

West stands by the coffin with his mother.

I try not to stare, but I can't stop. His thighs strain the trousers of his suit. The jacket is so tight across the shoulders, he looks like a thug in a gangster movie. When he bends down to hug one of his little cousins, I notice how shiny the pants are across the backside, and I worry he's going to split them.

Maybe he borrowed it, but the ache in my body says no. This is his best suit. This is his suit from *before*, maybe the suit he graduated high school in, wore to prom, I don't know.

It doesn't fit him, and I want to cry.

He looks so angry.

He didn't want to come. His mom couldn't talk him into it. His grandma knew better than to try.

Frankie wanted him here.

She's all the way on the other side of the room with her aunt Heather, who has three kids with different fathers and lives on disability in western Idaho. Heather is rubbing her lower back like it hurts. All this standing around talking to people makes *my* back hurt, and I didn't get hit by a falling pallet at a warehouse ten years ago.

We've been here for six hours. It's hot and too dry, we're tired, and there's nothing to drink or eat.

Every few minutes, Frankie looks around until she finds West. Her shoulders ease.

He's trying so hard to make this work out for her. As though, if he does that, he won't have to deal with it himself.

I suspect he thinks that he *is* dealing with it, but when he drops his guard his face tells me the truth. When he looks off in the distance and lets that angry mask fall for a second, half a second, an instant, I see.

I saw him watching Frankie talk to an older teenage cousin, everything raw in West exposed in his face—protectiveness, aggression, fear, love.

God, I miss his face.

I miss the mornings when I'd wake up before him and look and look until I could close my eyes and see him there, the tangle of his eyelashes, the shape of his mouth, the scar in his eyebrow.

I miss the nights when I'd sit on the couch and he'd be on the floor below me, book open on his lap, one arm thrown over the cushion behind him, and his fingers heavy on my thigh. How he'd read something interesting and turn to tell me, his smile cockeyed and bright, my world full of him all the way out to the edges.

When he looks in my direction, I catch his gaze and hold it, and it's my yearning that propels me across the floor toward him. It's the click of our connection, as powerful as ever, magnetic even from across a room. It's my hope that maybe I can say something, maybe—

But a couple gets there ahead of me, the woman touching West's elbow and sharing condolences. A beautiful woman with black hair, older than me by a decade, perfectly made up. I envy her poise and her boobs and her fuchsia wrap dress, but mostly I envy that she's touching West and I'm not.

I look away.

Right into the open coffin.

I don't know whose idea that was. I'd assumed it would be closed, because hello, gunshot wound? But I guess they just pack the holes full of whatever and slap a suit on the body, because there's West's dad, laid out like . . .

He looks so much like West.

It's creepy how much he looks like West.

Like West, dead.

I'm not tricked, I'm not stupid, but my heart is, apparently, and my body's in a galloping panic, sweating and hot, tears in my eyes.

Look away.

The woman is hugging West. Up on her toes, pressing her breasts into his chest. It's a little too much hug, you know? With hips in it, and hips aren't supposed to touch when you hug at a funeral.

Look away.

Separated from them by a few feet, there's a man talking to West's mom. Older, distinguished gray hair, great suit. Michelle is crying again, although it's dignified funeral crying. He's offering her a hankie, and the hug is still going on to his right. His mouth looks like mine must—tugged down at the corners, as if he's wishing the hug would die a painful death.

As though he'd like to tear the hug off them, throw it on the ground, step on it.

Look away.

Coffin again. I burp, taste vomit, wobble a little on my heels, and stagger, prompting me to reach out to steady myself.

White satin lining, cool against my skin.

I remember reading that funeral homes charge the grieving a fortune for stuff like satin linings and urns to put the ashes in, and you don't get any choice because it's not like they'll let you turn up with a reusable Ziploc tote and say *Fill 'er up.*

Everything costs money. West's grandma is living on Social Security and her dead husband's medical benefits from a union job he had with the railroad. If she didn't own her house outright, she wouldn't be able to get by. As it is, Michelle's been giving her money for groceries.

Michelle "borrows" about five hundred bucks a month from West, sometimes more. She's not working since Wyatt got killed. This dusty pink carpet, the tasteful hush, the rows of side tables full of flowers—West is paying for it. Paying to embalm the man whose fists crashed into his face.

I look at the corpse again, because that's all he is now, a corpse. I stare at his face until I can see the makeup—mascara on his lashes, creamy foundation, blush.

Not West. Just some asshole who donated the sperm.

I'm glad he's dead.

The man who's been talking to West's mom touches his wife's elbow and leans down to say something in her ear. She lets go of West finally, smiling, nodding.

They say their goodbyes and move away.

West glances at me. Cuts to the coffin. Mumbles, "Stay with my mom."

He walks away.

Damn him.

Damn him for lying to me, damn him for not talking to me, and damn him for pretending there was ever someone else.

There was just West, here, convincing himself he could never come back to me. That there wouldn't ever be a way for us to be together again.

West deciding I'd be better off if he let me go.

What's she look like? I'd asked him. *Does she make you laugh? Do you love her?*

No reply.

I spent a day fuming, analyzing, talking, drinking, and came back at him with *Do her knees go weak when you kiss her? Does she smile when you fuck her? Does she say your name?*

I was drunk and bold that night. Righteous, shouting.

West hung up on me.

My best friend, Bridget, had to pry the phone from my hand, because I was shaking with anger. I didn't feel the tears until she wiped them away.

I study his retreating back, his stifled shoulders moving through the room. Moving away from me.

I understand him better than anyone alive. I just don't know what the fuck to *do* about him.

West's grandma liberates me.

She whispers, "Go on," and takes Michelle's arm.

I weave between the rows of chairs set up for the service

in half an hour, out of the room and down the broad main hallway of the funeral home, with its fussy old-fashioned couches and its wall art no one could ever possibly object to—mostly shepherdesses and cows, with a seascape thrown in for good measure.

West is nowhere in sight. He must have gone outside to smoke.

Near the exit doors, I see the man who'd been talking to West's mom by the coffin. I start to pass him, and he says, "You're Caroline, aren't you?"

"Yes."

He extends a hand. "Evan Tomlinson. May I speak with you for a moment?"

Tomlinson. *Dr.* Tomlinson. West calls him Dr. T.

This is the man who paid for West to go to Putnam. "Of course."

From the viewing room where West's dad is, I hear a door slam. Someone going outside? They'd have to use the big set of double doors by the coffin. The door scrapes open and slams shut again.

"I was surprised to find you here," Dr. Tomlinson says. "I understood West had cut all his ties to Putnam."

"He's tried."

He sinks his hands into his trouser pockets. His eyes flick across my face, seeking. I guess he finds whatever he's after, because he says, "I'm going to cut right to the chase. West Leavitt making wood chips is a waste of a life. It's a waste of intelligence, and we don't have so much intelligence to spare in this world that I like seeing it thrown away. I've been trying to get him back to Putnam, and I'm hoping you can help."

Yes.

Yes, I can help.

Yes, yes, yes.

"What did you have in mind?"

"As an alumnus and a major donor, I've been offered the opportunity to recommend a student to the college for a legacy scholarship. It's an attractive deal—tuition and board are covered, and all West would have to demonstrate is an ability to benefit."

So far, so good. I can't think of anyone with greater ability to benefit from a Putnam education than West.

"If you control a legacy scholarship, why didn't you recommend West for that before?" I ask. "Instead of paying his tuition and everything yourself?"

"This is a new thing I've been developing with the financial aid office since I sent West to Putnam. I think it was my sponsoring him as a student there that got their attention."

"I see. And have you mentioned this to West?"

"I have. He turned me down. He wouldn't say why."

"When did you ask him?"

"Just the other week. Before his father . . ." He loops his hand in the air, encompassing everything surrounding us.

. . . got shot.

. . . ended up here.

"Did you mention his sister when you made this offer?"

"No."

"He won't leave her behind."

"He's too young to be responsible for that girl."

I shake my head, unwilling to agree or disagree. Sure, West is too young, but what does that mean anyway? He's the age he is. He's the person he is. He's been responsible for his sister a long time, and he's going to take care of her regardless of what Dr. T or I think. Regardless of what *anyone* thinks.

"Dr. Tomlinson—"

Just then, the funeral director comes through the front door. He's red-faced, and he reeks of panic. "Where's Mrs. Leavitt?"

"She was in the viewing room."

"She isn't now. Could you do me a favor and look in the bathroom? It's important that I find her."

"Why? What's going on?"

"There's a . . . some unpleasantness in the parking lot, and if anyone can put a stop to it . . ."

I'm already on my way out. I'm familiar with West and unpleasantness. He has a bad habit of swinging instead of thinking. I have a bad habit of walking into his punches.

Outside, I find a crowd bunched tight between two parallel rows of cars. I duck and weave like an eel to get a view of the action, and then I'm not sure what I'm looking at.

West has both arms out, holding his uncle Jack apart from a man I don't know. "No respect!" his uncle is shouting. "No excuse for this fucker!"

The guy being yelled at has a shaved head. He's built like a brick wall in a suit. I clue in to his identity when he flinches at the word *killer*.

Bo.

There are others shouting, too, adding to the chorus of voices. Frankie's in the crowd behind him, white-faced, silent.

"Calm down," West says to his uncle.

Jack is Joan's son—West's dad's brother. He doesn't work. I overheard his wife, Stephanie, telling West's aunt Laura that she put the kids to bed last night and then spent two hours driving around looking for him so she could drag him home and dry him out for the funeral.

He sounds like he's plenty wet now, though. "I'll fucking calm *down* when that fucktard is gone from my brother's fucking funeral!"

"He came to pay his respects."

"He should be in jail!"

"That's for the police to decide."

"He shot Wyatt, West! Cold fucking blood! I can't believe you're taking his side. Fucking *staying* with him, driving his truck around—it disgusts me."

I'm close enough now to smell the liquor fumes coming off Jack. I search for West's mom, knowing she and Bo are the two poles of all this conflict. Two points in a triangle whose third point has been removed.

When I find her, that's when I know this situation is going to get a lot worse before it gets better.

I once went out after a storm with my dad and saw a downed telephone pole in the road, the severed end of a power line showering electricity into the dark night. That's what West's mom's eyes are like. That much energy, loose and sparking. Lacking only a glancing touch to cause damage beyond measure.

"You got some nerve, coming here," Michelle says. She jerks her chin up. For one frozen instant, I see a strong resemblance to West. It's in her jaw. In the fire in her eyes. "After what you did?"

Her voice is rising.

"After what you said to me, what you promised, and now you're disrupting his funeral? His *fucking* funeral, Bo! You take him from me and you can't leave me that much?"

She's stalking toward him now, warming up. Bo's protests are too quiet to affect her gathering momentum. Her curses fall on him like rain. Dark and cold.

They pelt him, and he squares his shoulders. Looks into the distance, past her. It's not until she tries to slap him that he lays a hand on her, but one hand is all it takes.

She tries to wrench her arm away, shouts in pain when she fails, and bloodlust ripples through the crowd, a tangible wave of ugly impulse.

I want to keep it from getting any worse, but no one I see has a stake in stopping this. Laura is so nonconfrontational, it's a shock her spine hasn't dissolved. I'd hoped Stephanie could be counted on to prevent her husband from behaving like a jackass, but the excitement in her eyes says she loves this. Heather's not someone to be counted on. The cousins are strangers to me. The funeral home director is missing.

My gaze collides with West's. He mouths the word *Frankie*. The least I can do.

I look for the fastest way to get to her. It's a straight line, so I cut through the empty space between Bo and West, ducking under West's outstretched arms.

"Come with me," I say. "We have to find your grandma."

Her eyes are on Bo. "He shouldn't be here."

"I know. Come on."

I pull at her arm, and she falls against my side. We zip indoors, casing the joint for Joan. Family room, bathroom, hallway, coffin room. We find her alone in an empty visitation room. When I tell her what's going on, she just sits there, gazing at a lit cross in a niche.

"Please," I beg.

She meets my eyes, and her gaze tells me she's no stranger to this kind of thing. The people out there are her family. She made them with her body, watched them make others, weathered years' worth of this behavior.

Drinking problems, health problems, abuse, alienation, violence, death.

I wish she'd at least had a chance to bury her no-good son with some dignity, but I want her to step in and help West even more.

"He's on his own out there," I say.

She closes her eyes. Sighs.

Gets to her feet.

When she walks across the threshold, I want to go with her, but I'm worried about Frankie. I can't protect her and be with West both.

It's killing me not to know what's happening to him.

"Will you stay here?" I ask.

She bites her lip. Shakes her head.

"I'm supposed to keep you out of trouble, but your brother . . ."

Is out there.

Is the only thing I care about anymore.

"You really love him, huh?" she says.

I feel the tears coming up, but I take a deep breath and swallow them back down. "Yeah."

"I won't come all the way out," she says. "I'll stay in the doorway, so I can see what's going on."

"Good enough."

We hustle toward the front of the funeral parlor. I'm half-way down the hall when she takes my elbow. "Caroline?"

"Yeah?"

"I'm sorry."

Her apology rings in my ears as I hurry away.

Sorry. As if this is her fault.

I hear sirens in the distance. Did the funeral director call the police? I think he must have, and it feels like overkill until I step through the door and into a disaster.

I see a man in a suit jacket throwing a punch. A woman teetering on high-heels, bent double. I hear a high-pitched whistle, the smack of bone against bone.

I watch a stranger head butt another stranger, the spray of blood the single most repulsive sight I've ever witnessed.

This is a brawl, I think. *This is what a brawl looks like.*

The chaos is random, not coordinated like in a movie, and I can't locate West, can't even penetrate the first layer of heaving bodies, which is hard for me to understand because there aren't a hundred people in this parking lot. There are . . . twenty? Twenty-five? I should be able to get to the middle of them.

I try, but my instinct for self-preservation is too healthy. Every time a hip or fist or elbow comes at me, I jerk back.

Then suddenly the melee breaks open and I see West's mom and Bo. He's got his arms around her from behind. She's completely wild in his grip, shouting obscenities, trying to break loose. She looks like the madwoman in the attic, her hair wild, voice rough, mascara streaking down her cheeks.

I glance toward the entrance and locate Frankie where she said she would be. Seeing this.

I'm sorry, too, Franks.

Bo's trying to get Michelle out of the middle of the tumult. West's grandma is helping, I realize—she's the one who cleared the path, the one whose shrill whistle keeps cutting through the noise—and West is holding the crowd off Bo's back.

He shoves someone. Throws a punch.

He takes a hit to his cheek, his head snapping back, and then I'm running right for him. Sprinting toward West as the air starts to flash and bleed red.

The screams of the sirens split the sky.

A policeman has West facedown over the back of a patrol car with his legs spread. His forehead is mashed against metal, the seam between the shoulders of his suit jacket split open, the white of his shirt showing through.

"Excuse me." I grab a passing officer's arm. "Excuse me!"

She shakes me off, talks into her radio. I step closer to the car and try to get the attention of the guy with West. "Is he being arrested? What about his rights? He didn't do anything, it wasn't his fault, he's not a criminal—damn it, you're not *listening* to me—"

West barks, "Caro!"

How mean he looks with that bruise blooming on his cheek. How much like the man they think he is. A roughneck brawling at a funeral.

"Knock it off," he says. "Let them do their jobs."

"But it wasn't your fault!"

"They'll fucking figure that out if you give them a few seconds' peace."

When a third cop takes my upper arm in a tight grip and leads me away from West, I bite my tongue. I end up against the building, beside Joan.

"I can't believe this," I say. "He was trying to *stop* it."

"If he keeps ahold of his temper, he'll be fine," she says.

"Nothing about this situation is fine."

I press the back of my head into the building's vinyl siding and try to breathe.

West's mom is bundled into the back of a patrol car, where she abruptly flips from blank catatonia to screaming again in her hoarse, ravaged voice.

"His funeral!" she's yelling. "His fucking funeral!"

Bo gets taken to the station in another car. West's uncle

Jack goes to the hospital with a broken nose, and the rest of the aunts and uncles and cousins disperse. I don't know if they're heading to the hospital, the police station, or if they're just done with the whole scene.

West is allowed to stand, and he gives his statement in the parking lot out of my earshot.

An officer comes over to talk to me. I tell him what I know. It takes longer than I thought it would, and by the time I'm finished West is nowhere in sight.

The lot is nearly empty.

The funeral director appears at my elbow. "If you'll come inside, miss."

I can't think of any reason not to follow him. My feet operate on their own set of instructions. My face feels stiff. I think I might be a little shocky.

He shows me into the viewing room, where a small group stands in front of the coffin—West, Joan, Frankie, the Tomlinsons. All that's left of the mourners, I guess, because as soon as he deposits me next to West, he takes a place at a lectern beside the coffin.

"What's going on?" I ask West.

"Funeral."

"Now?"

He finds my hand, squeezes it once hard, and lets go.

It soon becomes clear that whatever program was planned has been tossed out the window. We're treated to a short, generic speech, and then we're all asked to step out into the other side of the room behind a fabric-covered panel while they close the coffin.

The Tomlinsons hold an angry-whisper conference in the corner. If I had to guess, I'd say Dr. T wants to leave and his wife is refusing.

I can't imagine why she would want to stay.

Frankie is folded in a chair, her arms wrapped around her knees. West sits beside her. He's missing from his face, all the anger wiped away and replaced with the impassive blank nothingness I remember from when he was at Putnam and we were both denying how we felt about each other.

I don't want anything from anyone that expression says.

It makes me want to give him the world on a plate. Give him absolutely everything he could ever desire.

It makes me want to apologize for his lot in life and for the differences between his world and mine, because West is amazing, and his life sucks.

His life is always going to suck if he stays here, in his mother's orbit, and assigns himself the job of keeping order.

There isn't anything I can do about it.

After a while, the panels roll open. The coffin is wheeled outside on a sort of pallet. We watch them load it into the hearse to drive it uphill to the cemetery, which is just behind the funeral home.

At the graveside, West remains impassive until we're invited to throw flowers or earth on the coffin. Then he steps out of the circle of mourners to where a shovel leans against a nearby utility truck, grabs it, and digs into the pile of dirt at the head of the grave. Tossing in one shovelful after another until the earth stops sliding off the domed lid and starts to accumulate.

This is not, obviously, what the funeral director had in mind, but no one seems inclined to put a stop to it. Joan leads Frankie back inside. Mrs. Tomlinson follows. Dr. Tomlinson didn't show up at the grave at all.

West and I remain, along with the funeral director, who's giving me a pleading look.

I shrug.

West shovels. His eyes are fevered, his cheeks pink.

The funeral director returns to the building.

I start to wonder how long it takes to fill a grave. I can't imagine leaving him here alone.

Spotting a second shovel in the back of the truck, I retrieve it and carry it to the dirt pile. West's gaze locks with mine.

We stare at each other.

There's no tenderness in it. It's a clash of wills.

It's him saying, *Stay the fuck out of this,* and me saying, *Make me.*

It's him snapping, *I don't want you here. You don't belong in Silt. I don't need you.*

It's me shouting, *You don't fucking know what you need. Stop being so stubborn. Take what I'm trying to give you. Take it.*

What I want to do is drop the shovel and walk over to where he is. To slip my arms around him, press myself against him, flatten my breasts into his chest, kiss him until he has no choice but to kiss me back—to kiss me the way he used to, sparks striking into a burn so fast and hot that sometimes we couldn't get our clothes off quick enough, couldn't manage to do more than unzip jeans and shove underwear out of the way just far enough to join our bodies together.

It's unbelievable how badly I want that back. How urgently I wish we could get lost in each other, find joy again.

I understand, though, that it's not what he wants from me.

I take off my heels, sink the blade into the soil, move it through the air until it hovers over the gleaming black surface of the box West's father will rot in.

The thump of earth landing on steel gives me a cheap satisfaction.

I'm awkward with the shovel, losing more dirt than I get

in, dropping some of it on my feet, where it gets between my toes, moist and muddy. Within a few minutes, my back starts to hurt. Then my hands.

West moves fluidly, his body graceful in action. The blade of his shovel sings.

Still, it takes a long time. I get blisters.

I don't stop.

The sun drops toward the horizon.

When we finish, he takes my shovel and returns them both to the truck. He stands beside the grave, hands loose and empty.

He looks like a boy—so much like a boy that I understand viscerally that he was as young as Frankie once. He was a kid who wanted a father and got nothing but disappointment. A boy who got punched, kicked, abandoned, and then told to stop holding on to the past. To let it go.

His mother, his grandmother, this whole family—they all asked him, again and again, to give his father one more chance. Maybe this time Wyatt would be different. Maybe this time life would be fair and kind, and happiness would be possible.

It never was, though. Not for West.

I don't know how he can survive here.

I don't know how he's not crushed, because it crushes me just to watch him. This whole place—it's beautiful, that winding road from the airport, the trees in the mountains, the buttes and the ocean. It's not fair that it's beautiful, be-cause it's so outrageously cruel to the man I love.

If West stays here, this place will kill him.

I step closer, skirt around the grave until I can feel the heat coming off his arm.

I touch him, my hand on the curve of his shoulder. "West."

It's not fair to ask him for anything right now, but I don't want to take from him. I only want him to lean on me. I want to give him rest, oblivion, escape. *Something.*

I've been trying to give him space, trying not to dig up feelings he can't handle when he's already got so much to deal with, but I can't take it anymore. I can't believe that this is *better*—that somehow it's *better* for West not to have whatever comfort I can give him, it's *better* for me to be three feet away from him and telling myself I can't get closer, not now, not tomorrow, maybe not ever.

How the fuck is this better? For who? Not for me. Not for West.

Surely not for West.

I move around to his front and insinuate my hands into the space between his arms and his sides. I rest my cheek against his heaving chest.

"If you want me," I say. "No strings. No anything—just, if you want to forget for an hour. Whatever you want."

I tighten my arms around him. He's so much harder than he used to be. All this armor between him and the world. I want him to know that I see it there. I know what it is, and if he wants to take it off with me, he can.

I love him.

I love him so fucking much, and this is all I've got to offer that he can possibly take. So I squeeze him as tight as I can until he yields.

His weight bows into me. Not all, but a fraction of it. A crack in the blank concrete wall of his self-denial.

His hand comes to the back of my head, the nape of my neck, pressing my face into the ragged sound of his breathing.

"Caro," he says into my hair.

It's the first time he's said my name like he used to. Like it's precious.

Like I'm precious.

"I can come out to Bo's," I whisper. "Or we could find a motel. Whatever you need."

When I lift my chin, his eyes are closed, so I kiss him.

I kiss his mouth. The margin of it. The swell of the bruise on his cheekbone.

His soft lips, his lowered eyelashes. This boy I love.

I kiss beneath his jaw, my tongue flicking out to taste his sweat, his skin, and then his hands are on me, lifting my chin, and he's kissing me back.

It's no tender reunion—it's a swan dive right into the middle of where we used to be, a plunge into blind lust and tension and sex. His tongue, his frustration, his taste, his heat, his lips on mine, his hands guiding me, giving me all of that, *all of it,* and I get carried away.

Stoned on the taste of him, high on possibility, I tell him, "It's going to be okay." Not because I believe it, but because I want to. "We'll get through this."

And that's all it takes for me to wreck it.

All it takes for him to take his hands off me and draw away.

When he opens his eyes, I can see my error written there. Because what sounds like hope to me isn't hope to West. It's just a reminder that he can't have anything he wants.

"There's no *we.*" He steps back. Brushes his hands over his thighs. "I don't need anything from you."

I know what he's doing. Of course I do.

He does, too—he has to, because his words are so patently ridiculous. My chest is still heaving. My lips are wet and full. My whole body aches, and West is saying, "You should think about going home."

It hurts.

God. It hurts so much.

But even as it hurts, I don't *believe* him. I've had West inside my body. I've locked my gaze with his for that first deep thrust, and I know what he looks like when he wants me. I know how he kisses when he's hurting, how he craves the oblivion our bodies can make together, the comfort afterward, the tired quiet space to talk in, to tell me what's weighing him down.

I know better than anyone how to read the language of West denying himself what he wants.

So I let him walk down the hill alone. I watch his broad back get smaller, watch him pull off his suit jacket and ball it up and throw it in the Dumpster outside the funeral home. I watch him disappear around the corner of the building, and I count off the time in my head.

Ten minutes.

Then I'm going after him.

The funeral home is hushed. Quiet as a doctor's office or a chapel, places people aren't supposed to enjoy themselves.

Suspended places.

The door into the viewing room stands open, but there's no one in there. No one in the hall, no one in the family lounge area.

I walk out into the parking lot. The sun has dropped beyond the horizon line, and although there's still enough light to see, dusk is gathering.

I'm tired. I want a hot shower and a warm bed, and I'm going to make West take me to Bo's tonight. Even if he won't touch me, I'm sick of sleeping on carpet squares in an attic that makes me sneeze. I don't want to wake up tomorrow morning with crusty, red-rimmed eyes.

Joan's Chevy sedan is gone. She must have taken Frankie back to her place.

I walk to the truck and check the door. Unlocked. Once I'm settled into the passenger seat, I text him—Where are you?—then glance at my email.

Tired and lonely, I text my dad.

Just wanted to check in. I'm fine.

I think how lucky I am, how extraordinarily lucky. Being with West's family, seeing the way they are, helps me remember that my life has basically been amazing in every way that matters. Sure, I lost my mom, but I wasn't old enough when she died to remember having her. Who I remember is my dad, and he's always been there for me and my sisters. Crabby and controlling, yes, but I've never doubted that he wants the best for me. Not for a second. And whatever minor differences I have with him, they're always going to be just that: minor.

I send another text. I'm glad you're my dad. I love you.

I wait a minute, but he doesn't write back. Neither does West.

I lay my head down on the seat and close my eyes, hoping West will turn up before it gets too chilly. Even in the summer, it's cold here at night. Something to do with the mountains.

West would know why, if I asked him.

I fish my earbuds out of my purse and put a song I like on repeat at low volume.

Sleep comes down on me slowly, stealing into the song, rocking me to safety.

The next thing I know, I come awake to a *thump*. My hand clutches closed around my phone; when I sit up and look out the windows, I don't see anything. It's completely dark now, the parking lot just a gravel patch with no streetlights to illuminate it.

I hear a woman's laugh, low and intimate.

There's another thump—a body making contact with the side panel of the truck.

A quiet squeak against glass, and now I crane my head farther around to see something moving against the narrow window of the back part of the cab. A shadow, fuzzed at the edges. I realize it's a woman's hair when she says, "No one can see us out here."

A cloud of black hair, and the back of a dress that would be purple if it were light enough to tell color from shadow. The woman who hugged him too long beside the coffin. Mrs. Tomlinson.

West's voice replies, "You'll have to be quiet."

"You know I can't."

"You need something to shove in your mouth?"

She laughs.

"Turn around," he says.

A clack against the window. Her wedding ring.

It's the ring that makes it real. The white streak of her teeth. I'm dizzy. So disoriented, I close my eyes.

That makes it worse.

For a long moment, I'm falling, stuck inside a pocket of time, drenched in violent revulsion as though it's been dropped on me from above. A bucketload of antipathy, a full-body *no*.

No, this can't be happening.

Her ring taps against the glass again. "Yeah. Yeah, I missed that mouth."

I don't hear what West says. I can't see him.

I can't see him because he's down on his knees with his face between her legs.

I turn away from them, blinking into darkness.

When I was three, I fell into a lake in the winter. We went to a dock where you could throw bread crusts to ducks and geese—me and my two older sisters with my dad—and I think Dad must have taken his eyes off me for a second too long.

I remember fear when I backed away from something that scared me.

I remember surprise when I fell.

I don't remember being afraid in the water. Only sinking into a cold so absolute, a descent so inevitable, that I accepted it.

That's what this is like. I know it's happening. I know I'm angry. I know my hands are shaking, and I'm nauseated. But all of that is as unimportant as the frantic shouting of my sisters muffled by the water.

I'm cold.

Encased.

Sinking.

I drift without moving as the sounds she makes become more frantic.

We could compare notes.

Is he doing that thing with his tongue, Mrs. Tomlinson?

Oh, he must have just scissored his fingers. That gets me, too.

How many times have you done this? Did it start when he was your caddy?

How old was he then? How many different ways did you use him?

He's using you now.

They aren't my thoughts.

It's not my own ironic detachment, it's just a random defense. A mouthy guard at the door. The real me is awash in rage and shame and sorrow so deep I'm not even allowed access to it.

I have to sink away. Let the water take me.

I'm annoyed when my phone vibrates in my hand. I glance at the screen and see that I have new texts from my dad and West.

In funeral home office, West's first text says.

I'm going to be a few minutes still.

Wrapping things up w/ director.

If we were inside the funeral home, I'd have to feel something right now. That's what they're for, these places we create to receive grief, to allow it and mute it at the same time.

But in the cab of this truck, drifting down into the cold with the scent of tobacco in my veins, I'm protected from having to feel. Suspended, for now.

I read the texts from my dad while West brings Mrs. Tomlinson to orgasm.

I love you too, C.

What's the word there—any idea when you'll be home?

A third one arrives.

Let me know when, I'll pick you up.

She's noisy when she comes. I didn't know people were that noisy outside of movies.

This scene is a parody, a terrible movie I can't turn off.

Gravel clatters. West getting to his feet. He must see the interior of the truck illuminated by the screen of my phone. Her, too, now that her eyes are open.

The sounds they're making probably mean something.

I'm supposed to care.

I'm supposed to say something when West opens the truck door and looks at me with nothing in his expression like surprise.

Looks at me with a blazing sort of pride, an arrogant tilt to his eyebrows that tells me he knew.

He knew exactly what he was doing.

I don't say anything. Not even when he calls me by name.

"Caroline," he says—my whole name, which he hardly ever uses.

I refuse to speak even when he takes me by the shoulder and shakes me, "Fucking say something," and Mrs. Tomlinson's making soothing noises, "West, West."

I'm sinking, and I don't have to talk to him.

I don't have to do anything.

He drives me to the airport in the morning.

Up the mountain. Down the mountain. Wordless.

It's not until I see a sign that says we're twenty miles from Eugene that I start thinking how this is it.

I mean, this is really *it*.

When West left Putnam last year, I took him to the airport, and I didn't know if I'd ever see him again. It was horrible, but not as horrible as this silent car ride, because what I didn't understand last year is that everything about that departure was outlined in hope.

I didn't know if I'd see West again, but I hoped I would.

He didn't know if he'd ever get back to Putnam, but I know he hoped, too.

We hoped we could be friends. We hoped we could be more.

And the slow death of hope—the suffocation of a future—that's hard to live through. It's no wonder he couldn't take it.

It's no wonder he told me he'd met someone, just to give himself a reason to stop calling. To give me a reason to stop waiting for the phone to ring.

All of that was hard.

It's not as hard as this.

This is the wasteland after a volcanic eruption—everything

hot and black, covered in sulfur, the sky the color of ash. There's nothing for hope to feed on in this car. He took it all.

He killed it on purpose.

"I know what you did," I say into the silence.

His hands tighten on the wheel. "Say what you need to say, Caro."

"You're hoping I'll yell. I bet it would be easier if you could remember me that way. You could think about how it ended, and then you wouldn't have to remember the rest of it."

He's quiet.

I'm not.

I've never been a quiet person, and everything that's happened to me in the last year has driven whatever quietness remained right out of me.

I wish I had a microphone for this. A sound system and a crowd of a thousand.

I wish everyone in the world could hear.

"I love you."

That's the first thing I have to say to West Leavitt, and I hear his surprise in the sharp sound of his inhale.

"I came here because I love you, and I helped you the best I could because I love you. I need you to know that there isn't anything I wouldn't have done to make this work between us. I didn't know it when I got here, but I sure as fuck know it now. If you'd asked me to take time off school, move out here, help you get your sister on the right path, I would've done it. For *you*. If you'd said to me you wanted to raise her, you and me together, take her from your mom and set up a house somewhere, I'd have said sure, yeah, let's do it, even though it's scary. For *you* I'd do it. All I've ever said to you is yes, and I was going to keep saying yes, because you were worth it. The way you made me feel. Your mind and your heart and you. Everything about being with you was worth it."

His eyes are on the road, so I look at it, too, but there's nothing there.

"Look at me," I say.

He won't.

"You look at me," I repeat. "I deserve that much from you."

The truck slows. He signals, then pulls onto the side. Cuts the engine.

He turns toward me, and it's harder.

But it's already so hard, there's no point in flinching away from it now.

"You have to leave Silt," I tell him. "Take your sister, because God knows you won't leave her, but you *cannot* stay. You'll never be happy here. You don't know how."

His eyes cut away from me. Out the window, toward the mountains.

"You told me once when I needed to hear it that I hadn't done anything wrong, so now I'm going to tell you. You *did* do something wrong. That performance last night? It *was* a performance. I'm not going to pretend it was anything you wanted, that you got carried away with lust or some bullshit, because that was fucking calculated. It was mean, and it was wrong. But I know what you did, West. I know why you did it. And the same way I needed to hear that I hadn't done anything wrong with Nate, that *I* wasn't wrong even when a hundred strange assholes on the Internet were talking in my head at me day in and day out—"

His eyes cut to me.

"I never told you that?" I ask. "Yeah. Voices in my head,

insomnia, misery. The whole thing. And you were the one who pulled me out of that. *You* were."

"You did it yourself."

"*Everyone does everything themselves,* West. By themselves, to themselves. *Everyone.* But sometimes they do it because they have a reason, and you were my reason. You told me I was fine, I wasn't broken, I wasn't wrong, and I believed you. *You made a difference.*"

I knot my hands in my lap. Not sure now that I should be saying any of this.

Never sure, actually, that I could make any kind of difference for him the way he did for me.

"I'm not the person you need to hear it from, I guess."

There's a plane low in the sky. Landing at the airport. I look at his face again. "But I might be the only person who's going to tell you. Your dad sucked. Your family . . . well, nobody wants to hear anything bad about their family, but West, they're never going to stop taking things from you. Not ever. There's never going to be a day when you look around at your mom and your sister and your grandma and say, *Okay, they're fine. I can go live my life the way I want now.* It's not going to happen, any more than I'm ever going to get my sex pictures off the Internet. You can't wait for it to happen. What you have to do is find a way to get out from under it, knowing it's never going away. You have to make your own life, because if you don't, you just won't get to have one at all, and that's the worst fucking thing I can imagine."

He makes a sound in his throat. I don't know what it means. I don't know how he feels, but this is the only chance I'll get. I'm going to lay it all down in front of him, because *he* taught me how to cut through the bullshit, and it's one of the most important lessons I've ever learned.

"You know, that's the thing that made me cry the hardest last night, even after what you did to me? Even with how mad I am, how fucking gross I feel every time I even look at your mouth or think about hearing what I heard—thinking about how *you made me hear it*—it's even worse to think I'm going to leave and you're going to drive back to Silt and die there. Die there every day."

I swipe at my face. Mascara all over my hand. What a disaster.

"It's sick, you know that?" I say. "This heart of mine, limping along?"

"I don't get it," he says. "I don't get why you're being . . ."

"Because I love you. I don't want to, okay? I think there are some things that are so hard, you shouldn't have to do them, only no one can take them from you. There are feelings so sick, so obviously unhealthy, you shouldn't have to feel them. But there they are. I still love you, and I'm not ever going to see you again, not *ever*. You did that to us. Not your dad or your family, just *you*. So I could hit you. I could rage at you right now, and call you every ugly name I know, and I know a lot. I could tell you how much I'm hurting, or I could get out of the car, slam the door, hitchhike to the airport because fuck you, fuck you, *fuck you, West, how could you do this to me? How?*"

He wipes his palms up the back of his head. Drops his forehead onto the steering wheel and covers his face with his forearms.

"What I can't do is pretend I don't know what you did," I say. "Or pretend I don't still care about you."

I look one more time at him. All of him. His lowered head and his shoulders, his torso wrapped in a blue T-shirt, those long legs sticking out of his shorts.

We're so far from where we were when we met.

Lost in the wilderness, and there isn't any way back.

"Don't waste your whole life," I tell him. "You're not going to get another one."

Collapsed over the wheel, he turns the ignition.

I can hear him breathing. Thick, deep breaths.

It's five full minutes before he's got it under control.

I'm calm now. Emptied out.

When he lifts his head, he flips open the glove compartment, careful not to touch my knee, and extracts his cigarettes. The lighter is out of reach.

I pluck it out and give it to him.

I find his bracelet in my purse and leave it in the glove box while he watches. It looks like a child's token.

"Give up the fucking cancer sticks, too," I say.

When he exhales smoke out the window, I watch it disappear into the sky.

I remind myself that this place we're in now—every green thing I see—all of this came after the fire and ash.

There's hope in the world.

I just have to find it.

BLACK BORDERS

Fade to black.

That was my plan.

Some fucking plan.

Caroline left the morning after my dad's funeral. I spent the next four weeks in Silt, and the screen of my personal Wild West movie was supposed to darken from the edges to the middle until there was nothing left but a quarter-size hole, a nickel, a dime, nothing.

Show's over. Welcome to the rest of your life. Enjoy your time in this paradise of emotional numbness.

Drink some beers. Fuck some chicks. Rock on.

I was delusional. I can only guess, now, that my delusions were supposed to protect me, because it's not like any part of my life had given me reason to believe awful shit gets less awful through repetition. Worrying you're not going to be able to buy groceries—worrying your baby sister's going to cough her lungs out from the croup—worrying you're going to die alone and never again make love to the only woman you want—it always fucking sucks.

It sucks and sucks and sucks and sucks, and it never stops sucking. There's no end to it. No bottom. No black curtain that falls down and makes it so you don't have to feel it.

It's like Caroline said. There are some things so terrible you shouldn't have to go through them, but you do have to. They're yours to feel, yours to put up with.

Your life to live, whether you like it or not.

I drove back to Silt and went to work.

I fed juniper into a chipper and thought about the future for the first time in months. I thought about Caroline. What she'd said. What I'd done to her. I thought about how hard I'd tried to keep her from seeing me here, seeing me struggle to keep it together.

I knew she would, if she came to Silt.

I figured I couldn't stand it if she did, and I was right. I couldn't stand it.

Couldn't stand what she told me.

Couldn't stand that she saw right through what I did to her—the shame I felt when she didn't cry or shout and I figured out I'd been trying to trick her into changing her mind about me because I couldn't just tell her the truth.

I loved her. Every day, every hour, every single fucking awful minute, I loved her.

And even loving her, I hurt her, because I thought I had to. What else would have made her leave? A smart woman like Caroline, loyal, caring—she would've done anything for me, including stay. I guessed it, and then she told me, so, you know, gold star for me. Three cheers for West, figuring out what he has to do to drive the love of his life away. Eat Rita Tomlinson out against the side of Bo's truck—that's gonna get the job done. That'll get it done every damn time.

I disgusted myself.

I hated myself.

But Jesus, I loved Caroline. She was always braver than me. Better than me, smarter, able to see her way to the heart of things. She looked at me and saw a man worth rescuing, but I'd already made up my mind not to be rescued.

I put her as far away from me as possible, because I was going to have to stay in Silt, and I couldn't stand it but I *had* to stand it.

I had to.

This was my life. The script I got handed when I walked onto the set.

Only, I looked at the script again after Caroline left, with my dad's corpse cooling in the ground in a box I bought with weed money, and I figured out I was never the fucking sheriff.

Nobody with any goodness in them—any sense of justice or rightness—could have done that to her.

I'd done it.

So who did that make me?

I've got a list in my head: Shit That Has to Get Sorted.

At the top of the list is "living situation," so on Monday of the week after the funeral, I drive by my grandma's house after work to talk to my mom.

She's on the couch wrapped in the afghan she's adopted. The TV's on, but she doesn't look like she's watching it.

She looks like shit, actually. Her hair is limp like she hasn't washed it, and I notice chipped polish on her toenails.

I sit down next to her. "What's on?"

She hands me the remote. "Garbage. You can pick if you want."

I accept it. Flip through a few channels.

I'd asked my grandma to take Frankie out for a burger so I could hash some things out with my mom, but now that I'm sitting here I sense disaster on the way. I can read Mom's moods like the weather, and she's not at her most stable.

It's not her mood that worries me, though. It's mine. There's a dark cloud over my head. If I thought I could put this off another week or two, I would.

"Did your girlfriend move out to Bo's?" she asks.

"No. She went home."

"Thought she might be sticking around, the way she looks at you."

The way Caroline looks at me—

I throw a wall up there.

The way she touched me, the way she tried to comfort me, the way she took off her shoes and dug that grave with me—

I build the wall taller.

My voice is dry when I ask, "What's there to stick around for?"

The pillow next to me on the couch has a deer on it. A naturalistic forest scene I remember thinking was real cool when I was a kid.

Tacky. That's how this place looks to me now. My whole life here, shabby and low-class and tacky.

That's one part of going to a rich-kid school in Middle America that I never knew to expect. You spend two years in classrooms with six-inch-wide heartwood pine molding stained deep, academic brown, and when you go back to where you came from it all looks a hundred times worse than you remembered.

Your default settings have shifted. Hondas and Toyotas instead of American cars. Handcrafted instead of machine made. Local and organic and artisanal whatever-the-fuck, and you can mock it when you're there, but that doesn't keep Hamburger Helper from tasting like warm piss and chemicals the next time you try to eat it.

"I don't like you staying out there with him," my mom says.

"Bo's all right."

"You don't know. You weren't at the trailer that night."

"How could I have been?"

"You're never here. Even when you're home, you're thinking about how much you'd rather be somewhere else. With Caroline."

Mom trills Caroline's name as though only snobs are named Caroline, and I'm instantly pissed.

I breathe deep, try to shake it off. She's right that I shouldn't have left. I lost track of my place in the world, went to Putnam, let myself believe there might be more for me, and look what happened. If I'd stayed here, Mom would probably still be with Bo. My dad never would've come around, couldn't have moved into the trailer because that's where *I'd* have been living.

None of this mess would've happened if I'd stayed.

"I'm here now," I say.

But Caroline's whispering in my head.

She's saying, *They're never going to stop taking things from you, not ever.*

I should've told her I don't expect them to.

That's the part Caroline doesn't get, because she was born with a silver spoon in her mouth, and she grew up thinking she could be anybody she wants to, do anything she sets her mind to. The world belongs to Caroline, but it doesn't belong to *me*.

I'm from Silt. I was born to take care of my sister and

watch out for my mom. I belong to this place and this family, and that means they take from me, and what I'm here to do is give them what they need.

I can't leave.

I can't dream big dreams.

I can't have college, or Caroline, or anything outside the borders of this place, because if I leave here I leave Frankie vulnerable to Mom's careless mistakes and whatever narrow vision of the future she can form when she can't see past the mountains to guess at what might be possible for her.

If I work hard, keep my head down, and take care of business, I can give Frankie the world. That's the best I can hope for.

"I want to get a place in Coos," I tell my mom. "Someplace big enough for the three of us."

"Coos?"

"Franks can go to middle school there if we have an address in the district. They've got better teachers."

"Frankie's not smart enough for it to matter."

"Yeah, she is."

My mom sighs. We've had this argument before. "You have enough money for rent and a security deposit?"

"Yeah, but if we want someplace nice you're going to have to be working, too."

"I quit the prison," she says. "I can't work at the same place Bo's at."

This isn't true. She was fired.

Bo told me he argued with the human resources people for an hour, trying to get them to keep her on. He's been there fifteen years and thought he might have enough pull. In the end, though, Mom wasn't worth their waiting on her to come back.

One more lie. One more disappointment.

Shrug it off.

"You still have Dad's car?" I ask.

"Yeah, but I told Jack he could have it."

"Why the fuck would you do that?"

"He always liked that car, and he wanted to have something of Wyatt's."

"I can't keep driving Bo's truck if I'm not paying him rent money and you're treating him like you are. Where's that leave us? One job and no fucking car—how are we supposed to get by?"

"I don't know, West! I can't cope with all this with your dad gone!"

"When could you cope with it?" I snap. "*When?* When could you *ever cope?*"

"Don't take that tone with me!"

"I'll take it if you deserve it! All you've done since he got shot is cry and feel sorry for yourself and then cause a fight you could've stopped at the funeral. It's *over*, Mom. We've got to move on, because there's shit to figure out—where we're going to live, how we'll get new school clothes for Frankie, a physical. Is she still on the state health plan?"

"Your dad took her off it."

"Jesus *fuck*. So we've got to get her back on and sign up for the Oregon Trail card again. The funeral about cleaned me out, but I've got enough money left for a cheap car. If you can get a job nights, I'll stay on days at the landscaper, and I'll find an apartment on the bus route so Franks can get to school. I think—"

"West."

"*What?*"

She's rubbing her hands over her face. She looks pale, smells ripe. "I can't do any of that."

"*Why not?*"

"I can't . . . I can't think. I can't sleep. I want Wyatt. It's hard for me to even see you, you look so much like him, and—"

"Just don't look. Don't think. I'm not asking you to think. All I'm asking you to do is help me get Frankie sorted, get this paperwork rolling. I'll put you on my accounts at the bank. We'll do the lease in both our names, and that way—"

"West," she interrupts again, her voice a whisper.

"Fucking *what*?"

She's crying again. Always crying.

I remember how my dad used to complain. *You're always fucking crying, Michelle, and when you're not crying you're nagging me. Useless cunt.*

It should make me feel poisoned, that echo, but instead it makes me hate her.

I've spent half my life trying to be her helper, her partner, her boss. It's not a job I'd wish on my worst enemy.

"I can't," she pleads, wiping her eyes on her sleeve. "I just *can't*."

"What do you want me to do? Everything? While you sit here on Joan's couch and cry?"

"Joan will let me stay."

"Joan's *his* mom, not yours. He didn't marry you. He didn't stand by you, he didn't treat you good, he didn't respect you or love you or even *stop himself from kicking your ass whenever he felt like it*. Why are you doing this? Why cling to this sick fucking memory when Frankie needs you?"

She blows her nose and lowers the tissue. Her mouth is hanging open a bit. She looks wrecked.

My hands mash the pillow. I want to do violence to something, but it's not her. Her body is the first soft thing I remember, her smile the one I'd work for when I was a kid. Her radiance was the treat I'd earn if I made the right jokes and read her mood correctly.

I'm a dick to keep pushing at her when I know she's not exaggerating—she really can't do this.

"Frankie doesn't need me," she says. "She's got you."

She says it so matter-of-fact, it sounds like the clang of a cell-block gate swinging shut.

Frankie's got me.

I had Caroline.

Not anymore.

I stand up. Pace back and forth in front of her. Jam my hands into my pockets, take them out, cross my arms, rake my fingers through the stubble of my hair.

I know where this conversation is headed, and I'm not ready for it.

"You want me to take care of her," I say. "Until when?"

"Until I'm feeling up to it."

"When's that gonna be?"

She shrugs and looks at her lap. "Until I can work. Get a car, save some money up for a place."

I bite back a laugh.

Never. That's when she means. She's never going to feel up to it.

I turn and look at her, wishing I could feel more tenderness—some of the friendship we used to have, if not actually love.

I do love her.

I just don't like her or respect her or trust her anymore.

And I can't carry her. If she's giving me my sister to carry, I'll take that weight on, but I can't handle my mother, too. Not if she won't help me.

"Fine," I say. "But if we're gonna do that, we'll make it

official. You give me power of attorney for Frankie. I need to be able to make decisions."

Her eyes are huge. "I'm still her mother."

"I'm not trying to steal her from you. Power of attorney isn't the same as custody. It just means you're giving me permission to do shit like enroll her in school, sign her up for health insurance, that kind of thing."

"How do you know?"

"I've looked it up." *A dozen times since I was twelve.*

"Will we need a lawyer?"

"No, it's pretty simple if both adults are willing."

"Both?"

"You and me."

"Oh." A shadow crosses her face. "You're only twenty."

"I turned twenty-one a couple weeks ago."

"I missed your birthday."

"Yeah."

And for whatever reason, that's the thing that crumples up her face, sets her off crying for real.

I sit down again, letting out a slow exhale and holding my arms open so she's got something to fall against. She sobs and tells me how much I look like him.

Just like him, just like him.

It's breaking her heart.

Three weeks later, Dr. T shows up at my work right when I'm climbing into the truck to get Frankie from school.

Bo told me to keep it. Said he doesn't need it and implied he knows I do.

Nothing quite like charity to make you feel like a worthless sack of shit.

I pull the door closed and throw Dr. T a wave. The idea is

to pretend he's here to check out the water features in the showroom or buy a new garden gnome.

Hands on the wheel. Eyes on the rearview. Put the truck in gear.

It doesn't work. His arms are waving in my peripheral vision. He's jogging over, and then he's right beside my door making that gesture that means *Roll down the window,* so I have to.

The window sinks away, and shame crawls over me. It leaves slimy trails up and down my arms, hollows my stomach, snatches at my breath.

It's always like this with him.

When I first met Dr. Tomlinson, back before I graduated high school, we were friends. Maybe I'm fooling myself to remember it that way, but that was how it felt. Like we had things in common, stuff to talk about, ideas we would kick back and forth as we worked our way through eighteen holes in sync. Fucking simpatico.

Then he introduced me to Rita.

I can't look at him anymore. It takes a monumental effort just to meet his eyes. Every time, I'm waiting for him to say it.

You fucked my wife.

"I wasn't sure where else to catch you," he says. "Your phone's disconnected?"

"I changed to a different carrier."

"You're supposed to be able to keep your same number these days, even when you switch."

"Yeah, there was a mix-up."

He's not dumb enough to believe this, but he's too polite to say. "Do you have twenty minutes?"

"I've got to pick up my sister."

My paycheck deposit showed up yesterday, and I promised

I'd take her to buy a few things for school. She grew out of all her leggings and stuff from last year.

"I was hoping to talk to you about that scholarship."

This isn't the day, then. The you-fucked-my-wife day.

As the realization hits me, so does my disappointment.

I've been waiting for the other shoe to drop with Dr. T for six fucking years, and it's getting so I want it to. I *want* to be accused by him, attacked by him, fucking blamed by this man for every wrong thing I've done.

I'm a villain. I deserve venom. A kick in the ribs. Disgust.

He claps a hand on my shoulder, and I flinch.

"I know you've had a hard year. I understand why you felt you had to leave Putnam, but it seems to me you've got an opportunity here to turn things around."

The shame. Jesus, the *shame,* crawling all over me. I'd do almost anything to get out of my body right now, get away. Part of why I left Silt in the first place was so I'd never have to sit across a table from Dr. T, listening to him ramble on about my best interests while Rita slid her bare toes up my leg.

"I've really got to go," I say.

"I'll ride along."

He walks over to the passenger side and lets himself into the truck, just like that—a reminder of how easy it used to be with him. Walking the course together, shooting the shit on his back deck with the view out over the green and the sun sinking down into the ocean.

I liked him.

I thought if I worked hard enough, put Silt far enough behind me, I could be Dr. T—trousers and four-hundred-dollar shoes and a white shirt he doesn't have to worry about staining because his Mexican housemaid drops off his dry cleaning and picks it back up wrapped in plastic every Tuesday.

I wonder if everybody else's dreams begin to look like dumb fucking nonsense after a dose of reality, or if it's just mine.

He buckles his seat belt. I back onto the highway.

"I talked to someone in the financial aid office about your case last week," he says.

"You shouldn't be doing that."

"I know you turned me down, but I keep hoping you'll change your mind. You have so much potential. You remind me of the way I was at your age, and I can't stand to see you throw it away. I keep thinking there's got to be a way I can do this for you."

"You've done more than enough already. And I'm sorry about that tuition that got wasted spring semester. I'm gonna see about paying that back to you."

"You don't have to pay it back."

"I want to."

He turns in the seat, fixes me with that sharp gaze of his. "West, I've been trying to see this whole situation from your perspective. I know taking money was always hard for you. I've said more than once that the way I see it, money's a neutral thing, not good or bad. But if I can use what I have to help someone like you, that's not neutral, it's overwhelmingly positive. I understand it's hard for you to see it that way, okay? That's the reason I've hoped that this scholarship might be something you could accept. Because it's not me, not *my* money. This is a Putnam scholarship. They're only going to give it to you because you deserve it."

I don't deserve anything.

"All you have to do is fill out some paperwork, and the

scholarship is yours. The college tells me they already have records showing you're a student of exceptional merit."

Exceptional merit. I'd laugh if the phrase didn't make my throat tighten.

I licked your wife's cunt. Up against this truck. While Caroline watched.

"It could be good for your sister, too," he says. "I heard she's living with you now. You could take her along. Give her a fresh start."

I watch the white line on the highway, willing my mind to go blank.

I can't think about what he said, because when I start thinking about shit like whether I could take Frankie and leave, just *go*, I pore over every angle of it. I work through every possible way it could go down, and then I shut them off, one after another.

I don't have to reach for impossibilities because they're all right there in front of me—the impossibility of tearing Frankie away from everything she knows.

The impossibility of juggling work and child care and classes all at the same time.

The impossibility of taking one more favor from a man I've screwed over in every conceivable way.

I can't tell myself I deserve to, not when I can conjure up the smell of Rita Tomlinson's perfume and the blank white horror in Caroline's expression.

Wanting things makes me miserable.

Wanting things makes me look at trees and guardrails when I'm driving, makes me ponder whether I should buy a bottle of whiskey and take it out to Bo's, drink it in the driveway until I'm ready to unlock his gun cabinet, load up his .48, and put an end to this.

"I can't," I say.

"You can," Dr. T insists.

"No. I can't. I just fucking *can't*."

After that, he's quiet. Too quiet.

His hands are folded in his lap, his gaze on the middle distance. It takes him another mile to speak. "I had another question I wanted to ask you."

"Shoot."

"It's about Rita."

My arms are made of lead. My foot's a block on the gas pedal.

"I noticed at the funeral," he says, "and after the funeral when I tried to speak with her . . . but I'm not being honest if I say it's the first time I wondered." He pauses. Flashes me a quick, uncomfortable smile. "I'm concerned she might be somewhat obsessed, I guess. With you."

Obsessed with me.

Is that what you call it?

"She talks about you a lot. *We* talk about you, of course, in the usual way, but since you've been back in town, her interest seems like . . . too much."

He wipes his hand over his mouth.

"I know this is an awkward question, but has she behaved in any way that's inappropriate? That might cause concern?"

He wants me to reassure him.

He's scared, because he's figured something out, but he won't let himself see the real shape of it. He doesn't want to add one and one and get two, so he's looking at me to tell him, *Hey, no worries, it's three. Look. I'll show you the math.*

I flip the signal and turn the wheel. The truck bounces into the middle school parking lot.

"No," I say. "Nothing to be concerned about." And then I manage a smile. It takes everything I've got to make it look real, but I give it everything, because I don't want Dr. Tomlinson to know what his wife is like.

It's bad enough that I do.

"Nothing at all."

Scrutinizing my expression, he brightens. "Oh. Okay. Good. Well, look, if you'll do me a favor and let me know if there's anything I should be concerned about, I'd appreciate it."

"Will do."

I slow. Brake. Put the truck in Park.

School kids are streaming from the building, running, laughing. I see my sister come out the door alone with her head down, hair hanging in her face.

She doesn't look like a kid. Not when I see these other ones. She's different from them, marked, like there's a line around her.

New clothes will help.

Maybe we can see about getting her hair cut.

"And just to go back to the scholarship for a minute," he says. "Promise me you'll at least think about it. The semester's already rolling, but the person I talked to said it won't be too late if you hustle out there."

I open the door. Hop out of the truck.

"West."

"Sure. I'll think about it."

I say it just to shut him up.

When Frankie arrives, I make the introductions, load her into the back, drop him off at the lot, and keep going, toward the strip where Ross's is.

"Who was that guy?" she asks.

"I used to caddy for him."

"What's he want?"

"He wants me to go back to Putnam."

She's quiet for a while, looking out the window. "Caroline's at Putnam."

"Mmm-hmm."

"Where would I go if you did that?"

"I told him no, Franks."

"But if you did."

"You'd go with me."

"Without Mom?"

"Without Mom."

"Isn't that against the law? Like, since she's my mom?"

"I could take you if she says it's okay."

"Oh."

That's all she's got to say on the subject. *Oh*.

She tries on jeans. I get angry and then angrier until I'm incapable of producing any response to her fashion show that satisfies her. She gets pissed at me for not being excited, and I guess that's fair, because I'm pissed at her for saying *Oh*.

I'm pissed at myself for wanting her to say something different.

Want is a bottomless black hole, sucking at me. Tentacles of faith and hope and trust, wisdom, good judgment, principles, pride—everything I don't have—pulling me down.

I can't. I fucking *can't*.

I pick up a bottle of whiskey on the way home.

Ten minutes after Frankie goes to bed, I pour myself a glass.

"Hey, Joan." I grab the bag with my lunch out of the fridge. "What's up?"

"Are you at work?"

"No, I'm on my way in."

I pull the apartment door closed most of the way with my

foot, dangle lunch from a few fingers so I can use the rest to snag the knob and operate the key in the lock.

"You're going to be late."

"I'm never late."

I hear her exhale. Blowing smoke out on the porch. "No, I don't guess you are."

Stepping up into the truck, I glance at the glove box, but I leave the pack where it is. I'm trying to cut back. Caroline wants me to quit.

Again and again, I come back to Caroline.

Come back to her accusations. Come back to the sight of her in her funeral dress and muddy feet, shoveling dirt.

I come back to Caroline's laugh, Caroline's mouth, Caroline's body naked against mine.

I come in my hand in the shower, inside her, inside my own memories.

It's almost a month since she left Silt, and I need to quit Caroline worse than I need to quit smoking.

"So listen," Joan says. "Your uncle Jack is talking to a lawyer."

He put my name down on the paperwork at the hospital, told them I'd pay for breaking his nose. Some fucking nerve. "I'm gonna pay the bill."

"This isn't about what you did to his face—it's about your dad. The ambulance-chaser Jack's hooked up with thinks he can make a case against Bo. Emotional distress or whatever— like what what's-her-name's family got against OJ."

A civil trial, she means. Since the authorities aren't pursuing a criminal case, my uncle's going to take justice into his own hands. "What kind of case has Jack got? He's a dead-beat alcoholic dickbag. What's he going to say, Dad's death made him *more* of one?"

"Watch your mouth. That's my son you're talking about."

"Sorry."

She sighs. "These guys only make their money if they win," she says. "The lawyer must think it's worth his time. I'm telling you because of Frankie."

"What about her?"

But I have a sinking feeling I know exactly what.

Frankie wakes up thrashing in the sheets, shouting. Sometimes "Daddy." Sometimes "Bo."

Always, "Don't!"

I stand in the doorway of her room and say her name, *Franks, Franks, Franks,* until she stills because she's heard me, and that's usually when she starts to cry.

I wish I knew if I was fucking her up.

I sit in the living room after she's asleep and think about how if Frankie ends up depressed, ends up cutting herself, ends up dead, ends up pregnant at fourteen—it'll be because of me.

Something I did or didn't do, some sign I missed that it was my job to see.

"They could make her testify if there's a trial," Joan says.

"No fucking way. Even Jack isn't that big of an asshole. He's got to know I'd kill him for even trying it."

"I think that's the idea. He's got it in for you since the funeral."

"I can take care of myself."

"But if he gets at her—"

"She was at a fucking sleepover!"

Joan sucks at her cigarette so hard I can hear it. Exhales. "Day before the funeral, Frankie talked to Stephanie."

Jack's wife. Shit.

Shit.

"Stephanie's telling everybody Frankie was there at the trailer when Wyatt got shot. Frankie will get dragged into this thing if it happens—it's not going to do any good to pretend she won't."

She's right. Fucking Leavitts—there's a reason I stayed away from them so long, and the reason's that it's always like this. Drama after drama, fighting and feuding, arguing over money and sex and drugs and whatever the hell else they can think of. They feed on it. They *love* it.

Jack's going to put Frankie right in the goddamn middle of it.

"Can't you talk him out of this suit? Bo hasn't got much money. Whatever went down in that trailer, I guarantee you Wyatt deserved it."

"When have I ever been able to talk a Leavitt man out of anything?"

I laugh. Don't mean to.

I don't have any control over myself.

I don't have control over anything.

Six years ago, Frankie was too young to be hurt by this kind of Leavitt bullshit, but I wasn't. I cut ties to the Leavitts because they wouldn't take my side, wouldn't protect me and my sister from my father.

They won't protect us from this, either. *I* have to.

"Thanks for the warning," I say.

"Let me know when you decide what to do."

I disconnect and drop the phone on the seat next to me.

The morning is cool, the sun bright over the mountains. The wind's blowing through the cab of the truck, rattling the paper bag with my lunch in it.

I'm young and healthy, alive. Free of my father. I should feel good.

I should be able to find a way to feel good about the giant fucking palm smacking into my back, shoving me toward Iowa.

Take your sister and go. That's what Dr. T is trying to get me to do.

That's what Caroline said to me, in no uncertain terms.

But all I can think, looking at the green on the hills, at the black ribbon of asphalt, at the blue sky, is this is one more fucking thing in my life I don't get to decide about.

I see Iowa in my mind's eye. Summertime in Putnam. Green lawns and brick buildings, marigolds and window boxes, students everywhere.

The hope spikes right into me, spikes my pulse, makes me breathe too shallow so I start to get dizzy and I have to pull over by the side of the road and slam my hand into the steering wheel and tell myself, *No way, no way, no* fucking *way.*

I think, *Take Frankie somewhere else.*

Mexico. Oklahoma.

Anywhere would do—anywhere that's far enough away from Jack and lawyers and courtrooms to keep her safe from all the traumatic assholery heading our way.

We could live by a river in an adobe hut. I could learn to train horses. We could eat frijoles and tortillas and I'd be inside that fucking Cormac McCarthy novel I read in my first-year seminar, but it would be better than letting the hope back in.

Before she left, Caroline told me, *You have to find a way to get out from under it, knowing it's never going away. You have to make your own life, because if you don't, you just won't get to have one at all, and that's the worst fucking thing I can imagine.*

She says that to me over and over.

She says it in my head every day, and every day I say the same thing back to her.

The way I've lived—the life I've had—I can imagine worse things than you can.

It's not so bad to waste your life. It's not so hard. What's harder—what's fucking impossible—is thinking you've got a future and then losing it.

I don't think I can survive it a second time.

In the glove box, I locate my last pack of cigarettes and light one up. I smoke it fast, sucking in deep carcinogenic lungfuls, trying to get used to the fact that it doesn't matter if I can stand to live in Putnam or not.

I don't have a decision to make.

We're going to Putnam, because there's a two-hundred-thousand-dollar education waiting for me there. A bachelor's degree that means something. I'd be an idiot to turn it down when I can grab it and use it for Frankie.

I burned my life in Putnam to the ground. I don't want to wade among the ashes and pitch a tent over top of what's left of it, but I will. I haven't got a choice.

Later, I'll call Dr. Tomlinson.

WILDERNESS

Caroline

Every year, winter takes me by surprise.

Fall comes and shears the edge off summer, mellows out the temperatures for a few golden days of gorgeous perfection, and then when I'm ready to live the rest of my life in those stolen moments, *snap*.

It turns cold one night. Just like that.

Growing up, I'd deny what it meant. *No, not yet. It's not time yet.*

I'd ignore the signs. I'd leave my jack-o'-lantern on the front porch long after Halloween, celebrating a season that had passed until black spots showed on the flesh around the pumpkin's mouth and it started to look ancient and wizened.

Once the first frost did it in, my dad would make me take it out back and chuck it into the woods. *So long, fall.*

But the autumn of my junior year at Putnam, I was ready for the days to get shorter and the temperatures to drop. I braced myself for the cold, preparing to carry on in a Putnam without West, a life without West.

It would be cold for a while. Lonely. But I'm an Iowa girl. I was used to the cold. I knew how to bundle up against it, muffle my breath behind a scarf, muffle my needs so I could endure the early nights and the long winter.

My dad finished annoying the lawyer, and my complaint against Nate got filed in mid-September. Sixty days to respond. Plaintiff identified as Jane Doe.

The trial date was set for the end of next year. I braced myself for four seasons of waiting and strategizing, subpoenas and scrutiny, depositions and petitions to compel.

I thought I had it under control.

Then I got a text from a number I didn't know. It was West, telling me he was coming back to school.

Another to say he was bringing Frankie.

A third to let me know I shouldn't worry, because he'd keep his distance.

I think what I was supposed to do when I got those texts was freeze. *Snap.* Go cold, just like that.

It would have been easier if I could have locked myself off. Safer to tend my rose garden of ice crystals, pretending to love the cold.

But I was through with pretending.

I got those texts, and I felt joy—pure and deep, as real as anything I'd ever had with him. I felt vindicated, because this would be another chance. The future he'd killed off, now brought back to life.

And maybe our future was an ugly, shambling thing. Maybe it was half-dead, scarred and foul—but it was ours, and I couldn't pretend I didn't want it. I couldn't even pretend not to be elated, burbling through the days after I got the news, wondering when and where I'd see him again, how it would be, how it would feel.

That sounds stupid. Naive.

I know how it sounds.

And I know, too, that a jack-o'-lantern on the front porch is only a jack-o'-lantern until midnight on October 31. One minute after midnight, it becomes a rotting pumpkin. My father used to explain it to me every November.

But it's the same pumpkin, right? It's the pumpkin you bought, carried home, planned over, cut carefully into. It's the pumpkin you gutted and scraped at, lit up, placed proudly on display.

It's the same fucking pumpkin the day after Halloween that it was the day before, and the fall when West came back to Putnam, I was through with people trying to tell me how to feel and what to love.

When there are pictures of your cunt on the Internet and strangers emailing to tell you they want to jizz in your face—when that's happened to you and there is a way in which it will never stop happening—you have to get really comfortable with the notion that the only person who's allowed to define how you feel about anything is *you*.

I shared an off-campus house with seven friends and friends of friends, including my best friend, Bridget, and West's former roommate, Krishna. Bridget and Krishna nagged at me. *What happened, what happened? You can talk to us. You should tell us. We need to know.*

Everyone wanted to talk to me about West that September. What happened in Silt. How I felt about it. What I was going to do when he came back to Iowa. Even my friend Quinn, who was studying in Florence that semester, pestered me over email. *I heard you went out to see West. I need details.*

Everyone wanted to talk about it, but really they wanted to tell me how to feel.

It ticked me off that there was so obviously a right and a

wrong way to respond to what West had done, and that everyone seemed to think I was doing it wrong—in denial, confused, lost, deflecting.

Fuck that. I felt how I felt. I wanted what I wanted.

Outside, the weather turned cold, then colder.

I saw West everywhere, and I burned.

I'm driving back to campus when I spot him getting out of his truck at the Kum and Go.

I check that the oncoming lane is clear, jerk the wheel to the left in a U-turn, and pull up to the curb across the street.

My hands tremble in my lap as I watch him walk into the store. He's wearing short sleeves over long sleeves. His shoulders stretch the fabric. I drink him in—that back, that ass, those long legs in boots.

I get wet just from looking. Greedy. Full of an anxious, amped-up craving for contact.

I want to talk to him, push into him, hit him, fuck him. Crash into him and find out what happens next. Something. Anything.

The plate-glass front of the shop is crowded with brightly colored posters and signs, but I can see the top of West's head at the counter. I lean closer to the windshield. My throat is hot, my breasts full.

I left Silt six weeks ago. West's been back in Putnam fifteen days.

Every time I see him, it gets a little stronger.

The first time I saw West after he came back, he was outside the art building, and I was walking with Bridget to my seminar. A clutch of smokers gathered by the door, West off to the side by himself, blowing a white cloud into the air.

He didn't greet me.

I knew to expect it. He'd done it to Krishna already. He's doing it to everyone.

West works and goes to class and stands off by himself, because that's how he wants it.

I spot him out windows, passing by the giant phallic sculpture at the center of our campus.

I see him in the library at the circulation desk, waiting to be helped.

I go out for groceries and discover the shape of his head, the curve of his shoulder, as he holds a package of cold ground beef in his hands by the butcher's counter and studies the label instead of turning around to say hi to me.

When I close my eyes, there's his defiant, arrogant face as he opens the door of the truck after he finished eating Mrs. Tomlinson's pussy. He wipes his mouth, even though he never did that. He tilts up his chin and says, *How about that, Caroline? Am I good enough for you now? Still want to rescue me? Still think you can love me? Huh?*

When I sit on the bed in my rented room and look out at the alley behind the house, an apple core three feet from the garbage can, I see West resting his forehead against the steering wheel of Bo's truck, shuddering by the side of the road.

None of what I feel is as simple as anger or betrayal or disgust, because there's always this other thing.

The thing that makes me do a U-turn when I spot his truck.

The thing that pulls me out of my car when he emerges from the store with a carton of cigarettes, free arm swinging, keys glinting in the bright light of this sunny September day.

I can see how angry he is from twenty feet away.

He can be as angry as he needs to be, and I'll still feel like this whenever he comes near. I can't help it.

He stops when he spots me. I don't wave or speak or beckon to him. All I do is watch. Witness him.

You exist. I exist. Here we are.

He gets in his car and drives off toward campus, and I track his progress until he turns the corner.

I'm smiling for no reason.

I just feel so alive.

Some things can't be unseen once you've seen them.

This is what I'm thinking the next morning, standing stock-still on the threshold of our kitchen, clutching a water bottle in my hand and transfixed by the unexpected sight of Bridget and Krishna making out.

It's seven-thirty in the morning. I was, prior to this moment, barely awake.

Now I am *so* awake.

Awake enough to notice a lot of things other than the obvious thing, which is my teeny little freckled redhead best friend tongue-wrestling with the resident campus manwhore.

Like, I notice that they're both in their running clothes, and they smell ripe. After two years of rooming with Bridget, who runs track, I'm more than used to the odor of warm armpits and high-tech fabric, but this time it's coming off both of them together.

Their mouths are making this wet smacking sort of noise. Krishna is *owning* Bridget. One-hand-on-the-back-of-her-head, one-right-above-her-ass, bending-her-backward-over-the-counter *owning* her.

His hair and shoulders are wet. Her thighs. Their arms.

Rain. It's raining out there. The rain is drumming against the house, and Bridget is kind of . . . squeaking? She's making a noise that's so obviously compliant that it makes me think of animals, *mating* animals—like, hamsters, maybe, which I wish it didn't because I once actually saw hamsters mating and it isn't something I want to see again, or think about, and Jesus, neither is this.

And yet I can't move.

I can't move, because this isn't a first kiss or a fourth kiss or an eighth kiss. They have done this many, many times. This has been *happening.*

When?

When did this start happening?

Krishna's hand is sliding beneath Bridget's back, rucking up her shirt, his skin so dark against hers, and my brain is just hammering at me, *when, when, when?* Last school year? Over the summer, when Bridget took more than one long weekend to visit Krishna in Chicago for reasons that now seem flimsy as tissue paper?

As flimsy as her sports bra, which presents no obvious barrier to Krishna's hand. It's working its way around to the front. It's going to get there, and no. No.

This is wrong. It's wrong in the way things are wrong when you don't expect them, but it's wrong in other ways, too, that I can't even get a handle on because they hit me in one big mass, a cumulous cloud of emotions, foggy and cold, impossible to sift through, especially because *it keeps happening.* His hands are over her breasts now. They're moving, they're *tweaking,* and she likes it. So much.

I have to clear my throat against the possibility that Bridget's hamster noises will actually kill me.

Bridget *leaps* away from Krishna. Her hand flies to her throat. "You scared me!"

I lift my water-bottle hand, now frozen into a claw. "I just wanted a drink."

This is the worst thing to say, it turns out, because it makes them step farther apart, clearing a corridor to the sink that I have to walk through.

I have to not-look at Krishna so hard. And not-hear the way they're breathing. And not-consider how wrong it is that none of us seems to have anything to say at this awkward moment to end all awkward moments.

Bridget. Krishna. The two talkiest people in a whole universe of talkers, now totally silent.

The water running into the bottle is louder than any running water has ever been.

I can feel them looking at each other behind my back. I can feel the conversation they're not having, the frantic exchange of messages through hands and eyes.

I turn off the tap. Set my bottle in the sink. Pivot to face them and say, like it's no big thing, "So this is a surprise."

Bridget is the color of beet juice. "It's not what it looks like," she says. "Because, you know, it looks like we were going to—"

"It's exactly what it looks like," Krishna interrupts.

"It's *not*," she insists. "Caroline's going to think we were sneaking around and we didn't want her to know, but that's—"

"We were sneaking around," Krishna says. "We didn't want you to know."

Bridget punches him in the arm. "Stop it!"

"Stop what? Telling the truth?"

"No! You're making it sound like we're—like I'm—and it's just not . . ."

"Not what?"

"Not like *that*. Dirty. And sneaky. And . . . I don't know. Convenient housemate hookup."

Bridget's expression is searching, earnest in a way that's painful for me to take in.

Krishna aims his can't-give-a-shit grin at her. "Nothing wrong with a dirty, sneaky, convenient housemate hookup."

It's ghastly. She stiffens. The flush drains out of her face.

She gets smaller.

Krishna claps her on the shoulder like they're old army buddies. "I'll leave you girls to it. I need to grab a shower."

We listen to the stairs creak underneath his climbing feet.

"Oh my God," I say when he's traversing the hallway over our heads. "Bridge."

She shakes her head. "Don't make me talk about it."

"I kind of think we should talk about it."

"Yeah, I know. I just . . ."

She covers her face with her hands, and I wrap my arms around her, hoping that's the right thing. It feels like the right thing, even though I'm having trouble switching gears from my own reactions to caring about hers.

It gets easier when I realize she's shivering.

"How long has this been going on?" I ask.

"I don't know if it's going on."

"It looked like it was going on."

"It's complicated. I would have told you, but it's so complicated, and I could never tell if we were on or off or neither, so I didn't know what to say. I still don't know what to say. At all."

"Can I say what it looks like?"

"Ugh. No."

"You sure? Sometimes it's good to hear what it looks like."

"It looks like I'm in love with Krishna and he's just fucking me because I'm around all the time, and he's going to break my heart and then pretend he doesn't care because he's a guy and that's what guys do, and meanwhile I'll be moaning about how he has hidden depths and you just don't understand, but you'll know better because you think Krishna's only good to be friends with but not someone you can count on, and you've never really been able to like him as much since he let West get arrested, because you're hopelessly in love with West and you're always going to take his side in everything forever."

Her hair drips on my neck.

I give her a squeeze.

"Okay," I say. "So at least you know what it looks like."

"I am fully aware, on every level you can possibly imagine, exactly what it looks like."

"And you're saying it's not like that?"

"Unfortunately, no. It is like that. Sometimes."

"What's it like when it's different?"

She inhales deeply. Bites her lip and casts her eyes at the ceiling, searching for words. "It's like falling into . . ."

She shakes her head. "It's like . . ."

A chill runs up my spine. I've known Bridget for over two years. I've never seen her at a loss for words. "Bridge—"

"I can't describe it," she says with a shrug. "But it's good enough to be worth all this other crap, apparently, which I can't even tell you the epic amounts of crap I've been dealing with. What he just did, walking out of the room like that? That's *nothing* compared to what he's been dishing out every time he gets spooked, which is fucking constantly, and if we weren't—"

"Constantly fucking?" I interrupt.

She hides her face behind her hands. "Yes. God."

"Go on."

"If we weren't constantly fucking, I would have *so many bad things* to say about him."

"You can say the bad things and also fuck him constantly."

"I know, but it feels so disloyal. I *like* him."

"You maybe love him?"

She hides her face against my shoulder. "Don't say it. It's too stupid."

"I have the market cornered on stupid."

When she looks at me again, her eyes are bright with tears, but she's smiling. "You know what I used to think? It's awful. You're going to think I'm awful."

"Probably not."

"I used to think only stupid people made mistakes. Like, people who were too stupid to know what the right thing to do was, so they did the wrong thing, and I was smart enough to see all that stupidity coming, so I would never be like them. I thought my mom was stupid for not knowing my dad was having an affair, and my dad was stupid for having one. And, God, I'm sorry that I'm saying this, but I thought, after what Nate did—"

"You thought *I* was stupid?" I blurt out.

"Kind of? I mean, not across the board, but about that one thing, yeah. Like, I thought I'd never let a guy do that to me, and I couldn't see why *you* had unless you'd just sort of stumbled into a pit of stupidity temporarily, and then stumbled back out."

"I can't believe you thought that."

"I know. But what I'm starting to figure out with Krishna . . ."

". . . is that it's possible to be smart and still do really stupid things?"

"And know you're doing them the whole time," she says. "That's the worst part."

"It is," I say, nodding. "I've had this exact same thought. *Oh my God, I am being so fucking stupid. I should be ar-*

rested for containing this much stupidity in one person. And then, like, *God, he's hot, I love him, I am totally going to do this anyway.*"

"It *sucks*," she says.

"Donkey balls."

"Ginormous donkey balls."

"It sucks ginormous *hairy* donkey *scrotums*," I confirm.

"Hoovers them up."

"Deep-throats them."

"While they take pictures and post them on the Internet," Bridget says.

"And go down on other women to drive you away."

"And *tell you about all the women they've fucked while they're taking off your pants.*"

"He did not."

"He did too."

"What a vile excuse for a human being," I say. "You should totally ditch him."

And then we're laughing, leaning into each other, holding on tight, and I'm glad I saw her with Krish, even if it was kind of gross.

I'm glad I see West all over Putnam, even if he's living in his little bubble of isolation.

It would be great if I had godlike powers to make the world less cruel. I could change everything. I could bend West's life toward mine instead of away from it, make everything different so he never would have chosen to do what he did, never *could* have chosen it.

I bet Bridget feels the same way—like she'd change whatever went wrong in Krishna's life to fuck him up, and then he'll stop jerking her around and admit they have something. But who would Krishna be if he weren't . . . well, *Krishna*?

And who would West be if I changed his whole life to make it so he never disappointed me? Not West.

I don't want anyone but West.

I'd rather fuck up and have something—some messy undefinable not-quite-relationship that feels awful but also transcendent, electric, *important*—than keep away from him and have nothing at all.

I'm going to figure out a way to get him back. Everyone can think I'm stupid if they want to, and tell me I shouldn't, and say I'll regret it. Everyone can believe it's a bad idea—even me.

Maybe it is a bad idea.

I don't care. I'm doing it anyway.

My phone rings at the library that same afternoon, drawing nasty looks. It's four o'clock, a quiet time for serious study, and I forgot to set it on vibrate.

I fumble in my bag until I find it way down in the pocket where I don't usually put it, and by then it's been ringing so long I'm hot with embarrassment. I decline the call, a local number I don't recognize, and go back to my response paper.

A minute later, the phone starts to vibrate in my pocket, and I feel . . . I don't know. Weird.

Weird like the hair is standing up on the back of my neck.

Weird like when people say they *just have a feeling*. That déjà vu thing.

I accept the call, shutting my laptop and shoving it in my bag.

"Ms. Pia . . . Pia . . ."

"Piasecki," I say.

"This is Jeff Gorham. I'm the counselor at Putnam Elementary, and I have Frankie Leavitt here needing a ride home. I haven't been able to reach her brother. I've got you listed as an emergency contact on the ride form, is that right?"

I have no idea. But as I push out the library door and into the overcast fall afternoon, I say, "Uh, yeah. Did you try his cell?"

"Frankie did."

I hear a garbled voice on the other end of the line, and then the counselor again. "Would you be able to swing by and pick her up?"

I glance at my watch. I have a meeting in an hour, but the elementary school isn't far. "Sure. I'll be there in ten minutes."

My car is parked on the east side of campus. I find myself rushing to get to it. Jogging, impatient, freaked out. Those words—*emergency contact*—set off some kind of alarm in the back of my brain.

Plus, you know, the obvious thing. West.

He must have put my name down on that form, but I bet he hated doing it.

I bet he's going to hate this even more.

When I pull up outside the school, Frankie's sitting on the steps with a guy who looks young enough to be a Putnam student. I step out of the car, wave in her direction, and wait to see if they're going to beckon me over. I don't know what kind of rules govern who gets to pick up a ten-year-old from a public school.

I guess all Frankie has to do is tell him I'm the one she's been waiting on, because in a second she's free. She walks to my car with her head down. When she gets in, her backpack hits the wheel well with a heavy thump.

"Sorry," she says, before we've even pulled away from the curb. "I missed the bus. I didn't know Mr. Gorham would call you."

"That's all right," I say. "Where should I take you?"

"Home, I guess."

"Which is . . . ?"

She points straight ahead. "That way."

The whole drive feels unauthorized, like I'm breaking some law. Guilty, too, because she's texted me a bunch of times since they got to town, but I've been trying to disengage. I'll wait a day or two to reply, then respond in short, generic phrases. Afraid she'll cling and I'll have to explain that her brother and I are . . . whatever we are.

"So you tried to call West?" I ask.

"I told Mr. Gorham I did, but I didn't want to bug him at work. I thought I could just walk. Mr. Gorham said no."

"How far is the walk?"

"I don't know, a few miles, I guess. You go left up here."

After the turn, I study her surreptitiously. Her eyes are puffy as if she's been crying.

"*Did* you miss the bus?"

She shrugs, turning her face toward the window. I guess that means no, but she doesn't want to talk about it.

"You need anything to eat? A snack or something?"

"Nah. There's plenty at home."

"When will West get back?"

"Around twelve-thirty."

"At night?"

"He works swing shift."

"What are his hours?"

"Three-thirty to twelve, mostly. Sometimes they run ten-hour shifts and he works four-thirty to two."

"And you're just by yourself at home every night?"

"No. He's got four days on, three days off."

"You're too young to be alone that much."

Frankie's expression turns mulish. "Go right here."

We end up at a small white farmhouse in the country. Where most people would have grass, huge metal sculptures litter the dirt. Gravel has been laid down between them in a kind of path.

I've heard of this place. Laurie Collins, the guy with the woman's name who makes all these sculptures, is a permanent visiting artist. He's famous at Putnam because he's the one who made the giant metal phallus sculpture, but I think he's famous more generally, too. The college tour guides make a big deal out of him.

"You're staying with Professor Collins?"

"No, over the garage." She points to the side of it, where a wooden staircase leads up to a door.

I pull to a stop. The farm seems like a nice enough place. Pleasant, perfectly safe. The farmhouse has cheerful yellow curtains and a bright blue door.

But there's no traffic, nobody in sight.

It must be so quiet in that apartment when she's alone.

"Thanks for the ride." She opens her door.

"Hold up."

Frankie stops.

"I've got a meeting soon, but maybe you want some company? You could come with me. We're just making posters for this march. The Student Government office has huge rolls of paper and giant markers, and we can decorate them however we want. And then after maybe we could grab dinner? Unless you've got homework."

"I do," she says, "but if I get home early enough I can do it before bed."

"What time is bed?"

"Nine o'clock."

"So if I get you back by seven, that should be enough time?"

"Yeah."

"Unless you don't want to hang out with a bunch of college students . . ."

A muscle twitches in her jaw. She looks so much like her brother, it wrenches my heart. "I'll come."

"Good."

She drops back into the car.

I make a three-point turn in the driveway, and we're off.

The farther we get from the apartment, the better I feel about the decision I've made. We go to my meeting, where she turns out to be surprisingly adept at making posters. I take her back to the house for dinner, introduce her to Bridget and Krishna in the kitchen, feed her some kind of curry thing that Krishna whipped up on a dare when Bridget bet him he didn't know how to cook a meal. The mood is lighthearted, which I guess means Krish and Bridget are on again.

Bridget sends me a look that says, *What do you think you're doing?*

I send her one back that means, *We'll talk later.*

Krishna teases Frankie until she's laughing so hard she falls out of the chair and makes her lip bleed.

When it gets dark, I drive her back to the farm. The farmhouse is blazing with light, the shapes of people visible through the curtains. She's talked all afternoon about the sculptor, Laurie, and his wife, Rikki, who's also an art professor. Frankie hangs out sometimes in Laurie's shed while he works on his art. It's clear they've got a bond going.

West must know it. He must have arranged it so Frankie has these adults to go to. He wouldn't leave her unprotected and alone.

Except that she obviously needed someone today, and she didn't call her brother.

"About the bus," I say on an impulse. "You didn't miss it, right? You just didn't want to get on."

She's bent over in the seat, zipping her backpack.

"You don't have to tell me what's happening," I say, "but if you want me to pick you up sometime, you can just text. We'll hang out."

Frankie lifts the pack onto her lap, compressing a strap in her hands. "You mean it?"

"Sure. I can't be, like, your personal chauffeur, but if you're having some kind of problem . . ."

She toys with the door handle. "I feel like a freak here."

"How come?"

"The other kids . . . They're just different than the kids back home. I don't fit. And . . . there's this kid on the bus. He looks at me. Says things."

"Mean things?"

She nods. "About the way I look."

Her body, I guess. Her breasts. Man, kids are mean. "Did you try telling the bus driver?"

"She wouldn't do anything."

"You can't know that."

"If I report it, he'll say I'm making it up, and she'll take his side. Then he'll turn it into a thing where I have a crush on him and I'm just trying to get attention."

I wrinkle my nose. We never moved to a new town, but I remember how kids who came to our school from outside the state might as well have arrived from another planet. They had different slang words, accented different syllables. Sometimes they had toys or games we didn't know about, or they wore a brand of jeans we'd never seen before, and these contrasts seemed enormous.

"Did you talk to West about it?"

She shakes her head. "He's mad at me."

"What for?"

"He just is. He acts mad all the time, but like he doesn't want me to know. It's my fault we had to move here."

"I thought you moved so he could come to school."

She shakes her head again, but she doesn't say anything.

I don't know what to tell her. The silence lasts half a minute. There aren't any crickets chirping. The night's cool. Summer's over.

I look at her with her hand on the door handle, her hair in her eyes.

This kid.

The thing is, I love this kid. Not the way West does, but my own way, because she's so young and sweet. Because she tries so hard to be tough, and because her mouth and her stubborn jaw are the same as her brother's.

I reach out to touch her arm. "When you just can't, call me. I'll come get you."

"You don't have to."

"I want to."

"West won't like it."

"That's his problem. If he doesn't like it, he can talk to me, okay?"

She smiles slightly. "It was fun tonight."

"It was."

"Thanks."

"You're welcome."

The door slams behind her. I watch her climb the steps to the apartment, fish a key out of her backpack, go inside.

I know she's right. West isn't going to like it. But I sit there watching her shut herself into her empty apartment, and the hair stands up on my forearms.

I'm *so* looking forward to it.

———

Every time my phone buzzes after that night, I think it must be West.

Usually, it's Frankie.

Frankie, wanting me to see the earrings she bought on a recent trip to Walmart.

Frankie, wondering whether she should be Dorothy from *The Wizard of Oz* or Catwoman for Halloween.

Frankie saying, hey whats up?

Saying, theres no good pizza in this town.

But it's a week and a half before she texts me to ask if I can pick her up from school again. I'm at the library. The vibration of the phone in front of my face wakes me up from a doze, and my cheek feels overwarm where I propped it in my hand.

I wipe drool from the corner of my mouth, checking to see if anyone's around to notice.

Nope. It's a quiet Friday afternoon in October, a glorious fall day, and I guess most people have the sense to spend it outside.

Sure, I text back. What time?

Now.

10 min.

When I get to her school, she's sitting on a low concrete wall. The buses haven't left yet, but I spot her right away because she's alone, her arms wrapped around her knees, her eyes on her feet. She's wearing black leggings and a dark top. When she shoulders her backpack, I feel a little bit like crying at her bony knees and skinny calves, her breasts too big and too soft, this baby-woman all alone.

I wish I could scoop her up and shelter her from how mean life can be. Especially how mean it is to girls, smart girls, girls with boobs, girls with no boobs.

I can't, so I take her shopping.

Putnam hasn't got any decent stores to shop at, but we go to the Mattingly's outlet. Mattingly's makes athletic uniforms. Their outlet store is full of shiny polyester emblazoned with the names and logos of obscure high-school sports teams. I buy her gigantic two-dollar basketball shorts—black with yellow insets—and a matching shirt that says "Prairieville Hornets."

Then we hit the Salvation Army thrift store and try on all kinds of ridiculous stuff—prom dresses, overalls, a sweater dress from before I was born, T-shirts and low-rise jeans that show our ass cracks.

We go for burgers at the student union and run into Krishna, who hangs out with us for a while. It's a good afternoon for all of us, I think. A nice break from the routine.

When I drive Frankie home, she says she wants me to come in and see her costume.

I agree with indecent haste.

The apartment isn't very big. There's just the kitchen and a living room plus a short hall with two bedrooms and the bathroom in between. The kitchen is divided off from the living room by a half wall topped with those wooden spires you find on a banister. There's a lot of dark wooden cabinets.

The sink is empty, gleaming, and someone's draped a neatly folded dishrag over the faucet.

West.

In the fridge, there's a plate with a homemade burrito on it and a sticky note bearing West's handwriting. *Microwave about 2 min. Salsa & sour cream after.*

There's a carton of cigarettes in the freezer next to a half gallon of fudge ripple ice cream.

I dish out two bowls when Frankie comes back, and then I make her get out her homework.

The kitchen clock ticks. Ticks. Ticks. It seems to slow down with every passing minute.

When I was thirteen or so, I used to babysit a lot, and I remember this sense of anticipation—this greediness for the moment I got the kids to bed and I could roam through the house, eat frosting from the plastic tub in the fridge, open and close closet doors, bedside table drawers, bathroom cabinets.

Frankie keeps asking me to stay a little longer.

"Sure," I tell her. "Just until you've taken your bath."

"Sure, I'll help you pick out an outfit for school tomorrow."

"I'll sit by your bed and talk for a few minutes."

"I'll rub your back until you fall asleep."

"Sure. I'll do that."

And then she's snoring softly, and I'm walking on tiptoe across the hallway to West's bedroom.

There's a T-shirt thrown carelessly onto the unmade bed.

A stack of books on his desk—a different desk than he had last year, a bigger mattress, an ivy-green comforter with huge pink roses that must have come with the other furnishings in this apartment because he would never buy such a thing.

Condoms in the drawer by the bed.

Lotion on top of the table, a box of tissues.

In his closet, a half-full basket of laundry, which I lift out in one big scoop and press to my face.

West's detergent. West's scent overlaid with sawdust and sweat, musty dirty laundry smell.

I run my finger along the line of shirts hung up in his closet, clothes I've seen him wear, clothes I've taken off him.

I open every drawer, rummage under the bed, and I don't

know what I'm looking for until I find it at the bottom of a
stack, tucked inside a manila folder.

A note I left him one morning. A snapshot of the two of
us that I liked enough to get it printed and give him a copy—
me and West at the bakery, goofing around, flour on his nose
and on my cheekbone, light in our eyes.

A printout of an email I sent him after he left Putnam.

*I love you, and I'll miss you, and I want everything good
for you, West. Everything wonderful. I want you to be
happy. I want you to be whole.*

Two hundred dollars in twenties, tucked inside a Christmas card.

I close the folder and put it away.

I stand in his dark bedroom feeling elated and guilty.

The next thing I know, I'm in the kitchen. I take the carton of cigarettes out of the freezer and methodically open
every package and empty them out into a pile on the kitchen
table.

I break them open, roll them between my fingers, empty-
ing the loose tobacco into a mound.

I don't know why. I just do it. I do it and keep doing it,
swallowing over the ache in my heart and the numb cold I'm
rolling between my fingers until it's done and I can't take it
back.

Then I return to his room, dig out that note I wrote him,
and put it on the table. At the bottom of the page, I write a
new message.

*If you eat enough tobacco, it's poisonous. Hell of a lot
quicker than smoking them.*

I put a fork next to the pile I've made, sweep all the empty papers and filters and cellophane wrappers into the garbage can that I find beneath the sink, and then look at the little scene I've created.

I'm losing it.

But I feel curiously detached from having to care about what's normal and what isn't. Curiously entitled to my behavior, my stalking, whatever displays of emotion I feel like directing at him.

I don't know if what he did to me is what entitles me, or if it's that folder in his bedroom. My name on Frankie's school form. Every sweet moment that ever passed between us.

Either way.

I gather up my books, find the porch light, and flip it off before I let myself out.

I sit on the top step beside the front door and look at the sky.

There's a wilderness of stars up there. I lay back and let myself wander through them until I'm lost—even more lost than I already was.

I trace the shapes of those lights with my fingertip, looking for patterns, and I think about the first time West kissed me on the roof of the house where I grew up. How we went up there to look at the stars. How we were stoned, and I loved him so much, his mouth on mine, his body and his heat and his beautiful face.

The tears that fall down my temples and soak into my hair are hot, but I don't brush them away. It feels good to cry.

It feels good to be here, waiting for West in this forest of stars.

When I hear his truck in the driveway I'll get up and go, seal myself inside my own car before I have to talk to him, because tonight's not the night. Tonight, I made him something to find, and that's as far as I'm going to push it. For now.

Until he drives up, I'll be here, waiting for guidance.

Waiting for a light to follow, for peace to help me find my way.

On Monday morning, a few days after I killed West's cigarettes, I walk to my seminar with Bridget.

When we pass the art building, he's there, of course. Standing by himself. Smoking.

Bridget is talking, telling me about a movie she went to see with Krishna over the weekend, but I'm veering away from her. I'm walking right up to West, plucking the cigarette from his fingers, and grinding it out in the bare dirt at his feet.

His eyes look green next to the pale green glass of the art building, the white of his teeth when he smiles.

"There's more where that came from," he says.

His voice is so soft, I can feel it moving over my skin like the pads of his fingers, trailing over my nipples. "I figured."

I feel soft. My face, my eyes, my mouth. I want to press against him. Let his hard edges sink into me. Reshape me. Change me.

I'll bounce back after he's gone. I always do.

He shakes his head. Pulls out his pack of cigarettes and extracts another one. Taps it against the cellophane wrapper and lights it up.

He blows smoke over the top of my head and says, "Expensive habit to break."

"Me or the cigarettes?"

He squints as he inhales. "You should stop it with Frankie."

"Maybe we should get together sometime," I suggest. "Have a meal. Talk things over."

"You should stop it with that, too."

"With what?"

He points at me. Points at his chest.

I guess I'm supposed to be discouraged.

This time, I take the cigarette from his lips.

I put my mouth where his mouth was, and I inhale carefully, letting the taste of him move through me. Pulling West into my body, through the chambers of my heart.

He watches me exhale.

I drop this cigarette, too, and grind it out.

Bridget touches my wrist and says we're going to be late, we're already late, but I don't stop watching West until we turn a corner and he disappears from sight.

Hands in his back pockets. Elbows out to the sides.

His smile fading as he watches me go.

I start to notice music. Not like I'm hearing music in my head, but like I'm just now tuning in to the music that's already everywhere, all the time.

The last week of classes before fall break—the week after I destroyed West's cigarettes, the week I pick Frankie up from school three times, the week I ace two midterms and set the curve on my Latin exam—I hear sad ballads at the coffee shop.

I hear pop songs on the radio.

I hear a low drone of sound that floats down the hall to my room from Krishna's.

It draws me to his doorway, where I find Bridget sitting crossways on his bed, feet propped up on the backs of his thighs, book in her lap. Krishna lying on his stomach, a book open by his head, a chunky calculator resting by his left hand, his pencil scrawling over a notebook page making notations I can't understand.

He's tuned in to those numbers and symbols, but it's the music that catches me.

Krishna plays this album a lot. I never noticed before that all the songs are love songs.

I go out for a run with Bridget, long sleeves and long tights on a cold morning as we jog in a rectangle around Putnam's campus, turning left, left, always to the left. She runs slow for me, because I'm not as good a runner as she is, and because my pace falters every time I hear some new lyric, a fresh tilt to a tune I've never paid attention to.

I find myself waving her ahead, *Go on, I'll see you at home,* because I need to listen hard, cupping my hands over my earbuds. I've just discovered—yes. This one, too. Another love song.

Angry love songs. Plaintive ones. Complaining ones, ecstatic ones, sexy moaning ones, cute ones, smug ones, turbulent bleeding aching disastrous ones.

Everywhere I go.

I stand by the side of the road on a cold morning, frost on the stalks in the ditch beside me, a crow on the telephone pole, a cloudless sky, listening to a woman pleading over a line of throbbing drums, *Take me back, take me back, take me back, baby, take me back.*

At home, Krishna's music pulls me down the hall another time.

No Bridget today. They argued about something after dinner, and I haven't seen her since.

"You okay?" he asks me.

I'm not sure what to tell him.

I'm in love.

Sometimes it feels like a terminal condition. Killing stupidity. Dangerous to my well-being. It makes me do dumb shit like fly to Oregon on a moment's notice, and shred a hundred cigarettes to nothing.

Krish and Bridget are in love. It makes them do dumb shit like lie to each other about how they feel, pretend not to feel it, fuck and touch and kiss and then run, run, run.

Am I okay?

Is love like this okay?

It doesn't feel okay. It feels necessary.

In the daytime I hear music, and I start to think that whatever is wrong with me might actually be what's wrong with everybody.

I start to think it might be *normal,* because if it's not, then what does it mean that all the songs are love songs?

What does it mean that I hear them now, everywhere I go?

Fall break is the last full week of October before Halloween. I spend a few days of it at home with my dad.

Home is like a thrift store shoe—I love the way it looks, but when I put it on, it feels stiff, creased in weird places. I can pretend it fits if I need it bad enough, but when I'm honest with myself I know it never will.

"You okay?" he asks.

Everybody asks. The other morning I caught sight of myself in the mirror coming out of the shower. I'm too thin, and I look like I haven't slept through the night in about a year.

I haven't.

"Sure."

I'm fine. It's just that I feel some days like I'm moving through liquid, and I have trouble sleeping. When I do sleep,

I dream about burning alive. I dream about alien pregnancies. I dream about losing all my teeth, losing a baby I didn't know I had and searching all over campus for it, in every classroom, in the post office, under every table at the library.

I sit in class and think about West's arms, West's hands, West's smile.

West.

"You seem kind of down," my dad says. "Are you worried about the case?"

Nate's attorney responded to our petition with across-the-board denial and a request for summary judgment. This was what we expected, and in the two days I've been home, Dad's told me no less than four times that there's no way the judge will go for it. We have a strong enough claim that the case will keep moving forward toward trial, gliding along on well-greased wheels, until the money runs out or something dramatic happens to stop it.

I'm not worried about the case.

I think he'd be surprised to learn how little I actually think about it, except when he brings it up.

I haven't told him that Nate is living in a house two hundred feet from the one I'm renting, or that I pass him on my way to class sometimes and we both look down and away, like strangers.

"I'm okay," I tell him.

"You sure?"

"Yeah."

"I picked up bananas and ice cream for dessert. Want to do the honors?"

"Sure."

I build banana splits: a scoop of each stripe of Neapolitan ice cream, a banana cut neatly in half, hot fudge, caramel, whipped cream, and nuts. An old ritual with my dad and me. As I'm swirling whipped cream on top, he comes up beside me.

"Hey, Dad?" I ask.

"Mmm-hmm?"

"Are we not going on vacation at Christmas because of the lawsuit?"

He sighs. "We already talked about this."

Money, he means. We talked about how I was supposed to handle my side and he was supposed to handle the money side, and I didn't need to worry about it. But why shouldn't I know what my revenge costs?

"*You* talked about it. I still don't understand why it has to be a secret. And if we can't afford it, then maybe it isn't worth it."

"We've put so much into this already. We have to see it through."

"But as much as it's already cost, it's just going to get bigger, and I start thinking, you know, what are we doing this for? Because what Nate took from me—I already can't get it back."

"Caroline, we *talked* about this."

We've talked about all of it, every possible facet, every conceivable approach. We've more than made up for all the talking we didn't do in the months after Nate first posted the pictures. We've talked until my jaw hurt.

"But don't you ever wonder if we're making a mistake?" I ask.

"No."

Which, actually, yeah, I knew that already. My dad's idea of a life philosophy is that you figure out what you want, and then you go after it. He believes in ambition and its relentless pursuit.

No giving up. No compromising.

He plucks a cherry from the jar on the counter. "Don't give up on this," he says. "It's going to be hard work, but it'll be worth it."

Maybe it *is* going to be worth it, but if the goal is to make Nate pay, my will might be starting to flag. I pass him on the sidewalk, and he seems untouchable.

I pass him on the sidewalk, and I don't really care.

I have other things on my mind.

Frankie texts me on Wednesday afternoon of fall break week. I drive back to Putnam to pick her up from school. After she falls asleep that night, I sit out on the steps and wait for West.

I hear him before I see him. The drone of an engine coming up the road, changing pitch and volume as he slows to make the turn.

The rocks under his truck's wheels. Light cutting across the garage.

I hear his boots on the steps, but I can't see his face. It's dark by the door, and his headlights messed with my night vision.

I see the cherry-red tip of his cigarette as he flicks it to the ground and grinds it out, then leans down to pick up the butt.

When he's two steps below me, he stops. "Is Frankie okay?"

"She's asleep." I stand up, a few feet separating us, dozens of cubic inches of darkness. "I wanted to ask you, did she tell you she's having trouble on the bus?"

"What kind of trouble?"

"The kind of trouble girls have."

I'm not sure how else to put it or how much to tell him. I

don't know a lot myself—just that Frankie is increasingly reluctant to ride the bus home, and it seems pretty likely that the boy who's harassing her has stepped it up a notch or two.

I can't decide if it's for me or for Frankie to tell him that. I'm wary of stepping between West and his sister. "You should find out from her."

He exhales—a soft whoosh of breath. "I don't want you babysitting Frankie."

"I'm not babysitting," I tell him. "We're friends."

"You can't be friends with a ten-year-old."

"I can if you'll let me."

"What if I won't?"

"Why wouldn't you? Your sister deserves a friend, don't you think?"

"Maybe a friend her age."

"What if she made one at school? She couldn't bring her friend over here. She couldn't go to the friend's house for a playdate, not with your work schedule the way it is. She's stuck hanging out alone for hours every day."

"Laurie keeps her company sometimes."

"He's got to be fifty, though. Are you honestly saying it's better for her to be with him than to do stuff with me?"

Begrudgingly, he says, "No."

"Good. Because I'm good for your sister, and I think you know it."

West turns his head away to look out over the drive. My vision is better now, sharp enough to pick out the shape of his profile against the sky. His Adam's apple.

I can feel how tired he is. His tiredness is tangible, a statement his body makes to mine, and my arms want to reach out and touch him. My heavy head wants to find his shoulder.

He used to feel this way after a Wednesday-night shift at the bakery—dead on his feet by the time we stumbled through the door to his apartment. He'd flop back on the bed still kicking his boots off, pull me against his side, nudge his face into my hair, and fall asleep in his clothes.

There was something so trusting in it, so precious about being that close to him at his most vulnerable.

He taps the toe of his boot against the step. "I don't get what you're doing here."

"I think I'm helping."

"I don't see why you'd want to."

"Yeah, you do."

"I told you I'd keep away from you," he says. "I meant it."

"Is that really what you want?"

I hear him swallow. I wonder if his throat is as sticky as mine. If his heart is beating as fast.

"Yeah."

"Why?"

He doesn't answer for so long, I think he won't. But when he does, I wish he hadn't, because all he says is, "What I did to you . . ."

Like fingers snapping—those words ignite my anger in an instant. "I already told you what I thought about what you did."

"Right," he says. "And it's because of what you said that I knew to keep away from you when I came back here."

"I never imagined you *would* come back here."

"It doesn't change anything."

"For fuck's sake, West, it changes *everything*!"

"It doesn't have to, though."

"What if I want it to?"

"Caro . . ." He leans closer. I think he's going to touch me.

All he has to do is reach out his hand—find my waist or my shoulder—but he doesn't. He sighs. Descends a step. "It's better this way."

"I don't believe that. For me, nothing is better."

He crosses his arms. "It'll get better."

"You're so full of shit."

Then he's quiet for a long time.

He looks at me hard and long, so I look right back at him. I wonder if my face is any easier to read in the dark than his.

I wonder if he misses me in his bed at night the way I miss him in mine.

I don't understand what's in his head anymore. What he thinks he's doing and why he thinks he's doing it. He pushed me away as hard as he could, but now he's come back to Putnam, so why doesn't he come back to me?

What I did to you . . .

That memory, so raw for me. I avoid thinking about it.

It must be the same for him.

But if it's just that memory that keeps him from me—if it's his sense of honor, as if I'm a princess in a tower and he's soiled my gown so that's the end of it—fuck that.

Fuck that with a tire iron, is my feeling. If he's going to deny himself what he wants, deny me what I want, there's nothing honorable in that. It's just pigheaded stubborn idiocy, and I won't stand for it.

Which is the sort of thing it's easy enough to think. But what do you do?

West and I, we look at each other.

It's heartbreaking. His pretty cheekbones, the scar in his eyebrow, his nose slightly off center, his ears too small, his mouth so wide and expressive and perfect.

It's heartbreaking, knowing there was a time when I

could've taken him inside and put him to bed, given him some ease, given him something. But that time came and went, and this is the time we're in now.

The waste of it makes my throat tight.

"I feel guilty," he says. "Like I'm taking advantage of you when you're watching Frankie, only I can't stop taking advantage because I never fucking *asked* you to watch her, and when I tell you to quit, you don't."

"That must be tough for you."

He laughs. "Fuck you, Caro."

"Wish you would."

"Christ Jesus." His hand comes up to brush over his hair and hang up at the back of his neck. He exhales, rough, and I love it. Love getting under his skin.

I love the confirmation and the hit of truth, lust spiking like nicotine through my blood.

It feels like a game, although I know for West it's dead serious. It's just that we've played this way before. The Caroline who played this game last year was scared and damaged and cautious, but I'm not any of those things anymore. I'm winning, and we've barely even started.

"Keep it to once or twice a week, all right?" he says. "You've got your own shit to be taking care of. And I don't want you spending money on her. Leave me your receipts and I'll pay you back."

"Really? We're going to do accounting on this?"

"Cut me some minuscule fucking piece of slack. You're getting your way on everything else."

"Not hardly."

"Caroline." He recrosses his arms.

"West." I cross mine.

"What do you want me to say?" he asks.

"I'm going to be around. You're going to have to deal with it. Deal with me. Stop pretending I don't exist or that everything's going to be fine if you say so."

He makes me wait for his reply. It drags out of his chest, rumbling and low. "Fine."

I lean down to pick up my bag. My knees threaten to buckle. I'm a cocktail of adrenaline and desire, my body dangerous and stupid.

When I return to standing, he's still looking, and it's worse. Better-worse.

Always better-worse, with West.

"What?" I ask.

"I'm trying to figure out your strategy."

"Who, me? Why would you think I have a strategy?"

"You're a politician, Caro. You've always got a strategy."

"You make me sound so sneaky."

"No, not sneaky. But you gotta admit, you're not always direct."

"Maybe that's because you're not so amenable to the direct approach."

"Amenable, huh?" His smile races through me.

"Don't even pretend not to know what it means."

He shakes his head, slow and weary. "I'm not the one who's pretending."

"Being indirect isn't the same as pretending. Especially when you know if you ask straight up, you'll get shot down."

"Why don't you try it and find out?"

"Not tonight."

"You already got what you wanted tonight."

I readjust the strap of my bag on my shoulder. Rise up on my toes, bringing my face a little closer to his. My mouth a little closer. "Not even close."

The breath explodes out of him. He turns his head away.

"There's no reason you have to hang around till I'm home, you know."

"I can't lock the door behind me."

That gets me another smile, slower and wider, though he still won't look my way. "Now you're gonna tell me you need a key."

"I don't mind hanging around until you get back."

"Some nights I'm on till two."

"I know. Frankie said."

Now he looks me over, head to toe. "You sleeping bad again?"

"Sometimes." Most of the time. I stay up late, sleep a few hours, wake up and work, take a nap late in the day if I don't have meetings.

My vampire schedule. It was one thing West and I used to have in common.

Still do, I guess.

"I'll get you a key," he says. "You can leave when you want."

"Thanks."

I brush past him, hyper-aware of his body and the narrowness of the staircase. Conscious that he could reach out, put his hands on me, touch me anywhere, and I'd let him.

Does he feel that, too? He must. It's right here between us, that knowledge, that love song our bodies never stopped singing.

Even mad at him, I'd kill to be able to go with him to his room, help him get his boots off. I'd die to be able to crawl into the crook of his arm so he could sleep and I could keep him safe.

Keep vigil over him.

"Goodnight, West."

" 'Night, Caro."

I hold that image of us in my head when I get into the car and start driving through the tunnel of my headlights down the deserted country road. Me and West in his bed together.

Me and West, wandering through a wilderness of stars with our hands clasped.

Me leading him out.

PATHFINDER

The morning after Caroline told me she was back in my life whether I liked it or not, I quit smoking.

She was just going to keep hounding me if I didn't.

I missed the hit I got from those cigarettes, though, and the way the smoke went all the way down to the bottom of my lungs and made it possible for me to breathe when it felt like I couldn't get a full breath in Putnam any other way.

After she left that night, I stared after her taillights until they winked around the corner and disappeared. I locked up the apartment and ate leftovers from the dinner I'd made my sister.

I thought about Caroline spending afternoons and evenings with Frankie.

Thought about her in my place, in my kitchen, in my life.

I pulled the rest of my cigarettes out of the freezer, opened every pack, broke them apart, and threw them away.

Then I leaned a hip against the counter and sparked my lighter in the dark.

Spark. Spark. Flame.

The whole time, I was trying to convince myself that the flame didn't look like hope, didn't feel like it, but I've never been any good at that kind of self-deception.

That spark in the dark, that wavering flicker—Caroline. Hope.

For me, they were always the same thing.

Impossible girl. That's what I thought when I first met her. She was exactly what I wanted, everything I wanted, and she was impossible.

What made her impossible was only my fear.

Last time I came to Putnam, I fell in love with her. I claimed a life for myself, then lost it. I didn't want to take that kind of risk again—not with my sister, and not with my own heart.

But Caroline lost her future once. She lost everything she believed about herself when her ex put her pictures online. Then she fought to reclaim it. She bit and clawed and scrabbled and took it back. It was the most beautiful thing I ever witnessed.

So how stupid was I to think after what I did to her, she would just let me go? Caroline doesn't let things go. I was the last person on earth she should have wanted anything to do with, but try telling that woman what she's supposed to want.

Just try it. I'll be over here laughing.

She wanted me, so there she was on my porch. There she was with my sister.

There she was destroying my cigarettes and pissing me off, telling me I was going to give myself cancer like I didn't fucking know it already. Like I was supposed to care.

She was trying to make me care, and I resisted for no reason.

Except that's not true.

I resisted because I was afraid.

What if I couldn't fix what I'd done to her?

What if I fixed it and lost her anyway, and I found I couldn't come back from losing her a second time?

What if I claimed Caroline and discovered all over again that hope is a luxury I don't get to claim?

I was afraid.

But it didn't matter.

Me and Caroline—it was going to happen anyway. I was going to let it. That last week of September, that first week of October, I tried to keep my distance, stalling, when all the while I was trying to remember how I'd ever done it in the first place.

How I'd given myself permission to take what I wanted.

It sounds easy—telling yourself you deserve good things. Letting yourself want them. Letting yourself claim them.

It sounds easy, but it's not. For a guy like me, it's right next door to impossible.

I was stuck in Silt. Not just the Silt on the map, but the Silt in my head. The Silt that made me, trained me to survive, and taught me my life was worth precisely nothing.

The path that led out of Silt was the one that took me back to Caroline. Once I found it, it was easy.

All I had to do was follow the flame.

Halfway through the next week, I stand outside the art building before class.

I lean against the windows, listening to the smokers talking, joking around. I chew gum to keep my mouth busy, shove my fists in my pockets so I won't bum a smoke off anyone.

Half the class is out here.

There's a guy named Raffe, short for Rafael. He's got dark skin and wild black hair like an afro except it comes to all these points, and he wears a motorcycle jacket but he doesn't seem like a poser.

He and this blond girl named Annie smoke and argue about art.

Surrealism. Dadaism. Warhol. Avedon. Turner. People I've never heard of.

I listen to them talking about some exhibit in Chicago, realize they actually drove all the way to the city, six hours in the car so they could see this exhibit at a gallery, six hours back, and they're still fucking arguing about it.

Off across the quad, I see Caroline coming. She angles my direction and fetches up in front of me as though the wind just blew her here by accident.

She's picked my sister up twice already since the last time I talked to her.

I've talked myself out of buying cigarettes six times.

"What do you think about art?" I ask.

"I don't think that's a question I can answer in one sentence."

"You ever been to Chicago?"

"Sure. Lots of times."

"Maybe I'll take Frankie sometime. Show her that bean. Go to a baseball game in the spring, or take her by the Art Institute to look at the paintings. She's never seen anything like that."

Caroline's gaze sharpens. "Have you?"

"No." I'm embarrassed to admit it.

"You should go, then," she says.

Raffe and Annie are looking at us. I glance down and realize Caroline's standing close. We're talking low. She's rubbing her hands over her arms in her sweater. It's long and bulky, tied at the waist. It looks warm, but obviously it's not warm enough for the chill.

"You should get going," I tell her.

She looks at her watch. "I should. See you."

She waves goodbye to Raffe and Annie. Calls them by name. Caroline knows all kinds of people. Everybody likes her.

I watch her cross the quad. The wind blows her hair around and catches the panels of her sweater, whipping it open with every stride.

If I ever learned to paint, I'd paint her just like that.

Halloween's on Friday. When I get home from work, Caroline's in my kitchen, asleep at my table at three in the morning.

Next to her elbow is a case of Monster energy drinks like the ones she used to bring me at the bakery.

"Rise and shine," I say.

When she lifts her head, she smiles. All the way, like the sun coming up. *Rise and shine.*

Then her elbow bumps the Monsters, and a cloud drifts over her expression.

"Sorry," she says.

"Nothing to be sorry about. Unless you destroyed some other property of mine?"

Her nose wrinkles. "Yeah. I was feeling bad about that."

"Really?"

"Well, the money part. Krish told me how much a carton of cigarettes costs. I brought you these to make up for it. I figured if you're going to get addicted to a stimulant because you're running yourself ragged, energy drinks are a better choice."

"Thanks."

She gets to her feet. I don't want her to leave. "What'd you and Franks do today?"

"I took her to the Student Senate meeting."

"You on the senate now?"

"Yeah."

"How is it?"

"Scintillating."

She tosses her hair behind her shoulder. It's a lot longer than it was last year, almost halfway down her back. I want to gather it up in my hands and feel if it's heavier. Feel if it's different.

She's too skinny, I know that much. And in this light, the circles under her eyes are obvious.

When she was with me, I'd help her get back to sleep if she woke in the night.

"You talk to her yet?" she asks.

"Who, Franks?"

"About the bus."

"No."

I need to. It's not just Caroline saying so—I get these emails from the counselor at Frankie's school, who's got her coming in to his office once a week so he can make sure she's "settling in." He keeps suggesting we get together for a little chat, but I can't imagine anything good coming out of that.

Bottom line, I go in to see him, he'll find out something I don't want him to know. Something about murder and mayhem, something about my work schedule leaving Frankie alone for hours on end, something about me being twenty-one years old, too young to have complete responsibility for a ten-year-old kid.

I read his emails, then delete them.

Caroline's frowning. "She's having a hard time at school."

"Everybody has a hard time at school."

That makes the little V-shape between her eyebrows

deepen. "No, this is worse than that. Something shitty happened today. She was crying in my car after I picked her up."

"What about?"

"She wouldn't tell me."

"Fuck." I shove my hands in my pockets, rocking back on my heels. "I'll see what I can do."

"If you want me to try to talk to her, I could—"

"Let me deal with my own shit."

I say it too harsh, then wish there was a way to take it back.

"God forbid anyone should try to help you with your shit, West."

"I don't see why you'd want to."

"Yeah, so you've said. Forget it."

"I'm trying."

She shoots me a glare, which I deserve, and starts packing up her stuff. The light gleams in her hair. I soak up the green of her sweater, the way her jeans hug her ass.

I'm a dick.

I'm a dick for ogling Caroline's ass, but mostly I'm a dick because I haven't talked to Frankie. I don't want to know what's going on with the bus because I haven't got an alternative. Either she takes the bus or I quit my job.

I should quit the job.

The hours are convenient, though, and the pay is good, so instead I'm a dick to Caroline, whose car my sister's crying in.

I don't know how to do this. Any of it. Not Frankie and school, not work and having a kid and keeping up with classes, not Caroline in my kitchen in the middle of the night trying to help me when I can't hardly look at her without wanting to apologize to her or kiss her or both.

Most of the time, both.

I wind the new spare key off my key ring and hold it out. "So you can lock up."

"Thanks." She steps closer to take it. "Are you all right?"

I'm drowning. I'm exhausted. I miss you.

I'm such a fucking mess, I feel like people can smell it on me—incompetent panic, guilt, worthlessness—and then she's here, and I don't get it.

I can't make her leave.

I can't figure out what to say.

"I'm fine."

Caroline takes another step toward me.

I shove my hands into my back pockets and look at the floor, because if I don't—

"All right," she says.

All right.

After she leaves, I heat up lasagna in the microwave. I check the heat before I go to bed.

Even under the covers, I can't seem to get warm.

At breakfast the next morning, Frankie tells me, "I need different clothes."

"We just got you different clothes in September."

"They don't fit me anymore."

I look her over, trying to figure out if that can possibly be true. It hasn't even been two months, but maybe she's changing without me noticing.

"What doesn't fit, your pants? Shirts?"

"All of it."

"You've got nothing that fits."

She nods her agreement.

"This wouldn't have anything to do with Caroline telling me you had a real shitty Halloween, would it?"

"No."

"Because she says—"

"I just need new clothes," Frankie insists. "I'm too fat for all the clothes you bought me."

Then she dumps what's left of her breakfast in the trash, sets the plate in the sink, and walks out.

I watch her go. Her pants fit just fine. The shirt's maybe a little shorter than it was when we bought it? She's got hips now. Boobs I try not to look at, because I can't get used to them on my kid sister.

"Where do you want to go?" I call to her back.

"The thrift store."

"I can buy you new clothes," I say, exasperated. "It's not a problem, only I'm trying to understand—"

"Just drive me to the thrift store, okay?"

"Fine."

"Great."

I have reading to plow through for Russian history first. Frankie spends the morning on the couch watching cartoons and drawing pictures of horses.

After lunch, we go shopping. She piles my arms high with jeans and sweatshirts. Everything she picks out is huge. Leggings she has to roll at the waistband, Putnam College hoodies that come down below her butt.

"This shit doesn't fit you," I say.

"You're the one who's always telling me my clothes are too slutty."

"I never said that."

"You said I couldn't wear my costume without a coat over it."

"That was a costume, not your clothes," I tell her. "And it wasn't your fault—all the costumes are like that now. I should've looked before we bought it."

She pushes a sweatshirt into my arms. "This is what I want."

I'm trying to make eye contact. Trying to connect with her. "If something's going on with you at school, we should talk about it."

"Nothing's going on."

"Don't treat me like I'm dumb. You cry in Caroline's car, you tell me out of the blue you need all new clothes that cover you up like a tent, something's going on."

"Why don't you mind your own business?"

"Why don't you tell me what happened at school?"

"Nothing happened."

"I don't believe you."

"I don't give a shit if you believe me."

"Franks, look, whatever's going on, changing your wardrobe is probably not going to fix it. Think about it. You're too smart for this."

"Yeah, well maybe I don't want to be smart."

Hearing her say she doesn't want to be smart—it lights a fuse.

I want to shake her, tell her smart's all we've got. Smart is what's going to save her ass from Silt, keep her from turning into Mom, keep her from turning into *me*.

"What's that supposed to mean?" I ask.

She huffs an exhale. "God. Never *mind*."

I grip her arm. "Don't take that tone with me. I should be writing a paper right now, but I'm here with you, and I think you owe me—"

"I don't owe you anything!" She pulls away and shoves me

hard enough to rock me back on my heels. "Buy them or don't. I'll be in the truck."

I stand between the racks of clothes in the aisle of the Salvation Army with no idea what I'm supposed to do next.

Wishing I could ask Caroline.

Monday morning, I stop at the student cafe in the Forum for some coffee and see Caroline alone at a table with a book in front of her and a doughnut on a napkin, untouched.

Chocolate cake doughnut, glazed. Her favorite.

I sit down across from her, pick it up, take a big bite.

"Dick," she says.

Without looking up, she kicks me in the shin.

Sitting there, I eat the whole doughnut. The sun's shining in the windows across the front of the Forum, bathing her in light. She reads with her mouth slightly open, pushing her tongue into the gap between her teeth. She's switching from her book to a stack of note cards covered in highlighter, and I recognize the format. She's got a Latin quiz.

"Want me to help with your verbs?"

"No. Quit distracting me. I only have ten minutes."

I walk up to the counter and buy her a replacement doughnut.

She doesn't say another word to me, and it's still the best fifteen minutes of my day.

When I come home at two a.m. after my shift that night, I find her pecking away at her laptop in my kitchen.

"You know the library's open, right?" I ask.

"Mmm-hmm."

I open a bag of corn chips. Put some in a bowl so she can share if she wants.

She plucks out a chip. "What's your job like?"

"Boring."

"What do you do?"

"Whatever they tell me."

"What'd you do tonight?"

"Measured stuff. They won't let me cut yet."

"Is cutting more fun?"

"It would be different. I've never used a miter saw, but you can do tricky cuts, like when you've got to cut 30 degrees on the X axis and 45 on the Y—I want to see how that works. Or I'd like to drive the forklift."

"When do you get to do that stuff?"

"Not for fucking ages. What are you writing about?"

"Victorian periodicals."

"Fascinating."

"No, it's good. We had to pick a topic that there were lots of articles about and read a bunch of different journals. I picked the Irish problem."

"What's the problem?"

"Basically, they wanted independence."

"Such a fucking hassle, those Irish."

She smiles.

"You want a beer?"

I ask without thinking about it. I don't want to think tonight. I'm sick of it—sick of everything being difficult all the time. I want to do something easy. Beer, couch, Caroline.

"At two in the morning?"

"I'm all jacked up. Probably won't sleep for a while."

"Why are you jacked up if work was so boring?"

"Those Monsters you bought me."

It's only partly true. I'm jacked up on her being here, and I'm jacked up because Frankie still won't talk to me.

I stayed up all last night writing the last of my final projects to clear my incompletes. I'm so far behind on sleep, I don't feel like I need it at all.

"You want a beer or not?" I ask.

"Sure. I'm about out of brilliant thoughts for the night anyway." She rolls her shoulders.

I snag two beers from the fridge and find a napkin to spit the gum I've been chewing into so I can eat. She's raising an eyebrow at me when I turn around. "What's with the gum?"

"Helps with not smoking," I admit.

"You really quit?"

"Trying." I open the beers and hand her one. "I need to sit." I grab the chips and head for the couch, where I turn the TV on to an infomercial for some kind of food chopper. She follows me in and takes a seat on the other end.

We watch this skinny, hyped-up sales guy try to convince us we'll fucking die if we don't have his chopper.

I can smell her, her hair and her skin, her detergent, the deodorant she wears that's oranges and spices.

"Do you think I'm fucking up?" I ask.

"Yes."

"You want to wait a sec and find out what it is I'm asking about?"

That makes her smile. "No."

"Because I was asking about Frankie."

"Hmm." Her grin is self-satisfied. Knowing.

I've seen her smile like that when she had my balls in her palm and she was trying to decide just how she wanted to suck my dick to most effectively drive me out of my mind.

"You think I'm fucking up with Frankie, or you think I'm fucking up in general?" I ask.

She just looks at me with her eyes big and round, like, *Go on*.

"What else?" I ask. "I'm fucking up with you, too? Fucking up my whole future? Fucking up with school, and—and just more or less everything, huh?"

She's inclined her head, like she wants to nod along with every question I'm asking. It's patronizing, but I don't mind. She's got on jeans and this soft shirt with buttons partway down the front, and it looks like it's been through the wash a thousand times, except I've never seen it before. I think she must have bought it that way. It's unbuttoned so low that the way she's sitting just now, I can see the middle part of her bra. There's a useless little bow there, sewed onto that spot. Her jeans are tight and faded across her thighs, and everything about her clothes and her hair falling down out of the knot she tied it up in makes me want to rumple her.

Makes me want to test the texture of those jeans, find out if her shirt is soft against my face, if it's softer than her breasts, even though I know nothing is.

It doesn't help that her shirt is the exact color of her pussy.

"Just say whatever you want," I tell her. "You look like you're gonna die if you don't."

She shakes her head. "I'm not saying anything until you do."

"What am I supposed to say?"

She sips her beer. "Something about how you're doing."

"I'm doing fine."

That gets me a huff of laughter. "Something *true* about how you're doing."

"You say that like I'm lying all the time."

She considers this. "No, you're not lying. You're bullshitting me. Which is funny, since I know exactly how you feel about bullshit."

The first real conversation I had with her, I gave her a hard time for telling me she was fine when she wasn't. It was bullshit, I told her. The way people went around all the time suffering and claiming to be fine—why couldn't they just say what they felt? Why did everyone have to be so fucking polite when they were dying inside?

That was the night she told me that every day she lived through since her pictures turned up online was the worst day of her life.

I understand what she meant better than I did a year ago.

I drain my beer and set it on the coffee table. I'm tired, buzzing, confused about why she's dressed so touchable, sitting relaxed on my couch, sipping her beer, watching me like she can see inside my head. Like she knows exactly how fucked-up it is in there, but she doesn't mind it one bit.

"You want me to tell you something true?" I ask.

She nods.

"I want to kiss you."

I watch the heat rise up her throat, turning her skin the same color as her shirt.

"Then why don't you?" she asks.

I can't remember.

Swear to God, I can't fucking remember. Maybe there's no reason at all.

Maybe I never had a good reason, and I'm just a moron. Maybe I've always been a moron. Which raises the question why she'd go to all this trouble to get me back in her life.

She's looking over my shoulder at the closed blinds. Her forehead's wrinkled, her eyes out of focus the way they get when she's thinking.

"I had to read this story for class," she says. "It was one I already knew—O. Henry, 'The Gift of the Magi.' Have you ever read it?"

"I don't think so."

"I bet you know it—it's that story about the couple, they're really poor, and the woman wants to buy something nice for her husband for Christmas, so she cuts off her hair and sells it to buy him a chain for his watch. Only he wants to do something for her, too, and he sells his watch to buy her combs for her hair." She glances at me. "What?"

"I never liked that story."

"Me, neither. But tell me why you don't."

"It's supposed to be romantic, right? This big sacrifice they make, you go, 'Aw, true spirit of Christmas.' But it's not."

"How so?"

"You can tell me they're happy under their Christmas tree because they've got their love, but they had love in the first place, right? Love was never the question. The question was what's he got to give her other than love? He can't keep the house warm. He can't buy her a cruise to the Caribbean or whatever the fuck. All he's got is a watch, and he decides, *Okay, I'm gonna sell the watch and give her something that makes her feel beautiful.* Only it doesn't work, because now she's bald, and that probably makes her even more miserable than she already was. It's a depressing fucking story."

I run my hand over the back of my neck, self-conscious. I don't know where all those words came from.

She just watches me.

It's more than I can take. The way she looks on my couch. The way she engages with me like I'm important, like everything I say is interesting, like I deserve to be talking to her after what I did when I don't.

I fucking don't.

There's my reason why I can't kiss her. Whether it's adequate—I haven't got a clue.

"I was just surprised," she says, "by how much more complicated it was than I expected."

"How so?"

She looks at the beer in her hands. Looks at my face.

"It's supposed to be about sacrifice," she says. "The beauty of sacrifice, because he makes this sacrifice for her, and she makes it for him, and it's a disaster, like you said. It's depressing. But look what they were willing to do for each other."

"They already knew what they were willing to do, though—that's my point. They were trying to feel different for one day, just *one day*, get away from being starving pathetic losers, and they ended up looking like assholes. You know who really made out? The guy who sold her the watch, and the guy who sold him the combs. I bet those two had a happy fucking Christmas. I bet those two think it's a *fantastic* story."

She's smiling at me. Drinking me up with her eyes.

She's eating away at me, making the black ache inside me bigger and louder.

I wish I had a cigarette.

I wish I could smack myself over the head with a bottle of booze, put an end to this pressure I feel around her, this longing I can't get rid of.

"It was just one Christmas," she says. "I mean, you have to figure he could go out the next day, sell the watch chain to buy her a nice warm hat to cover her bald head. She could sell the combs and buy him a sweater. It's not *over*."

"Yeah, but how's he gonna feel next time he goes to buy

her a present? Not good. He'll remember that fuckup with the combs and say to himself, *Shit, I'll just buy her a gift certificate, and she can get what she wants with it.* They blew all the romance on that one big gesture, and they're not getting it back."

"None of that is in the story."

"No?"

"No. It's in your head."

She puts her beer down and pulls her feet up to tuck them underneath herself. Rests her arm on the back of the couch, her cheek on her arm, and looks at me with her eyes all gentle.

I just wish she'd quit fucking *looking* at me that way, like I'm the baby Moses in a basket, some precious discovery she can't ever get enough of.

"I wouldn't cut off my hair to buy you a watch chain," she says.

I break out in a sweat.

"I really wouldn't. I think my dad thinks I would, and Bridget and Krishna, too. They think I'm like that woman in the story but worse, because I wouldn't stop at my hair. I'd sell the furniture, my clothes, my dignity, all to have something to give you. But it's not true. I mean, it's just hair, and I'd probably give you my *hair* if you wanted it, because whatever. But her hair in the story is her pride. It's the thing that makes her feel beautiful and worthy, and you can't have that. I won't give it to you. I would never give it to you."

I try to say, *I know that,* but the words come out raspy and impossible.

"I think what you don't know," she says, "is that you can't *take* it from me, either. Even if you sell your watch."

I can't ruin her. That's what she means.

I can fuck up, but I can't ruin her.

My hands are trembling. I forgot that she does this. Sees right into me and picks me right the fuck apart.

Maybe this is what I've been afraid of. That she'd pick me into pieces, and there won't be anything left of me when she does.

"And you know," she says, "the other thing about the story is that her hair will grow back, and she can keep the combs. He can get another watch. They're really good gifts. Like, if you gave me some pearl combs, I'd probably think, 'Wow, these are gorgeous. West must have saved up for a long time to pay for them.' I wouldn't even think about my hair—not right away."

"Jesus, *I* would."

"I know you would." She rises to her knees and moves to my side. Takes my chin in her fingers until we're so close together, closer than we've been since that moment by the grave when I shut myself off from her and told myself it needed to end. That I would have to be the one to end it.

"You'd sell your watch for me, West," she says. "You'd give me those combs and see my bald head and it would break your heart. But what I'm trying to tell you is that it doesn't have to be like that. The *world* isn't like that."

"Like what?"

I'm staring at her lips. Drinking in her face. It all feels so important, but I can't get a grip on it. I'm too tired, my eyes stinging like I could fucking cry.

I wish I could. What a relief that would be.

I'm not someone who can do that, but I can't remember why. If I was made like this, or if I chose it.

"The world's not black and white," she tells me. "Life doesn't have good guys and bad guys or a beginning, middle, and end. Not while you're living it. It's just people doing stuff that's beautiful or stupid or somewhere in the middle."

She cups my face in her hands. Strokes her thumbs over my eyebrows, making me close my eyes and listen hard to what she's saying.

"So anytime you catch yourself writing a story over top of us—anytime you tell yourself you're the bad guy, or you destroyed us, the end, it's over—think about that."

She leans in and touches her lips to my forehead.

It hurts not to take her mouth. To stop myself from pressing her down into the couch, into the soft cushions, touching her and kissing her because I need her and I want her, and because she could make me forget.

It wouldn't be fair to use her like that.

God, I want to, though.

When she moves back and touches her fingers to my lips, I can see that she knows it.

"Just think about it," she says.

I don't have words to give her, so I say, "All right."

After she leaves, I stay up thinking half the night.

Friday morning. Art class. A hundred bucks.

The stack of colored paper on the table in front of me cost a hundred bucks, and I'm supposed to "experiment" with it.

Try things, Rikki told the class.

Rikki's my studio art professor. She's dressed today like the world's tiniest pirate—boots that go up to her thighs and then flare out and fold over at the top, a glittery sash across one shoulder. She's from the Netherlands, married to Laurie, which means she's my landlady in addition to my art teacher.

She's also an art therapist, whatever the fuck that is.

"The idea," Rikki is telling the student sitting in front of me, "is to play with how the colors are in a relationship.

Work with large and small fields of color to create illusions of difference where there is similarity, illusions of similarity where there is difference."

The package of paper contains a hundred and fifty sheets, none of them the same. Sixty-six cents a color. The girl at the next table is going crazy with her scissors, snipping chunks out of one sheet after another. Turning money into confetti.

I can't bring myself to take scissors to a sixty-six-cent piece of paper unless I've got some reason to think it's going to amount to something, so I just push the papers around, laying one on top of another, until Rikki chucks me on the shoulder as she walks past and says, *"Play."*

I pick up the scissors and open and close the blades a few times.

Drop them and shuffle the colors around some more.

This is me in Studio Art.

I've never taken an art class before, and probably wouldn't have, but it was so late when I registered that I had to take whatever I could get into, which was nothing I would have picked. In addition to art, I've got Modern Russian History, Intro to Spanish, and this bizarre African-American lit class where all we've done so far is read philosophy about music.

Back before I started my first year, Dr. T told me the point of Putnam isn't to specialize or get ready for grad school, it's to learn how to learn.

Try everything, he said. *Keep trying things until you find something that clicks. Learn how to think, ask questions, decide for yourself.*

I didn't do that, because I wanted to be a doctor—although looking back, I wonder what the fuck ever made me think that would work out. Four years of undergrad, four years of med school, then residency, loans, studying, no chance even for part-time jobs—whoever's life that was, it wasn't ever going to be mine.

Now I'm trying things. Burning money. Feeling like an asshole most of the time, trying to wrap my tongue around rolling an *R* in Spanish, reading a memoir by this Russian woman who was imprisoned under Stalin.

I've been doing this kind of shit for eight weeks now, but I'm not sure what any of it is contributing to my well-roundedness. I don't know what cutting up colored bits of paper is going to do for me that I need, either, but I pick up a sheet of deep, dark red and snip a triangle off one corner.

Lay it against a bright blue.

Lay it against orange.

I find a lemony yellow and cut a corner off it. Try again.

"Play," Rikki says to Raffe on the other side of the room.

Playing makes me feel like a dipshit.

And besides, this isn't even art. It's math. The textbook makes it sound mysterious, like colors have these properties, and *Oh, hey, what do you know? That one looks this way next to that one and this other way next to that other one.*

When actually, you can assign numbers to hue and value, and they'll follow predictable patterns. Bright pink looks like it's vibrating on top of bright green. The pink square looks bigger on the black square and smaller on the white one.

It isn't magic. It's just numbers and common sense.

Rikki leans over my shoulder. She touches a brown triangle that I'd laid over a pale pink one and reverses the order. "Nice, this one. But work with bigger pieces, hmm? It's hard to see with such small triangles that you have made."

"I don't want to waste paper."

"Always I have one student who is afraid to waste. We will do paintings and you will choose the smallest canvas, or we will make sculpture and you will make something so tiny."

She cups her hands in space, showing me the size of my imaginary sculpture. "Wasting is what the paper is for."

"Maybe I just don't like throwing money away."

"Or maybe you are afraid to take up too much space in the world," she says. "I think for my class, you should be as wasteful as you can be. Cut up *all* the paper. Make the biggest paintings. Then we will see what you can do, hmm?"

She leaves me alone after that. I push my triangles around, searching for the best arrangements. In the sketchpad I'm required to keep, I jot down some guesses for number values and use them to predict which colors will be the best matches. I'll try them out on Frankie later, see if I can trick her with them. Then I'll do bigger versions of the best ones for my portfolio.

It's a better approach, more logical than Rikki's.

It doesn't have anything to do with how much space I want to take up in the world.

Outside after class, I'm thinking about whether all studio art classes come with a side of psychoanalysis or if it's just Rikki's art-therapist thing, when I almost walk into Krishna.

I try to go around him. He blocks me.

I feint to the other side, spin, and head off in a different direction, annoyed because I don't want to be this guy, but I *am* this guy, and I wish he'd let me alone.

"In case you're wondering," he says, jogging up behind me, "I'm not giving up."

"I've got class."

"That was your last one. Now you're going home to study, and then you've got work."

"What are you, stalking me?"

"I asked Caroline."

He runs a few steps to catch up. There's a lot of foot traffic on the path because class just let out, and in order for Krishna and me to walk side by side, everybody who's coming the other way has to step off into the snowbank and get their ankles wet.

Krishna clearly doesn't give a fuck.

I kind of like that about him.

"I'm having a party," he says. "For my birthday. I want you to come."

"I can't."

"You're supposed to ask when it is in order to make your excuse more plausible."

"When is it?"

"Tomorrow night."

"Oh, tomorrow night. I can't."

He tries out a signature my-shit-doesn't-stink Krishna grin on me. The wind's gusty, blowing his black hair around, making him look like some kind of Desi movie star. "Sure you can."

"Fine. I don't want to."

"How come?"

"I'm busy."

"You're always busy. Think of some other excuse, because I'm never going to take that one from you."

"I hate parties."

"Yeah, but this is my birthday. You've got to make sacrifices for your friends on their birthdays."

"I don't have to do anything."

"There's a party at Minnehan at eight, so we're going to kick ours off at ten. It's at the house—you know where I'm living?"

Where Caroline's living. Of course I know.

"I can't make it. Sorry."

"Try."

I glance at him. He's not smiling now. He's got his hands shoved in his pockets, his dark eyebrows drawn in against the wind and maybe against whatever it is he's feeling right now, which is strange because Krishna usually makes out like he doesn't feel anything.

"I can't leave my sister to go to a house party."

"Can't you find someone to watch her?"

Laurie and Rikki have offered more than once. "Even if I could, what am I going to tell her, 'Look, I know you hardly see me and you haven't got any friends or anything, but I'm going to be at this house party tonight for some guy you've never met's birthday, don't wait up'?"

"I've met your sister."

"When?"

"Caroline brings her by. She's cute."

Irrational jealousy grips me. Jealousy of Frankie for having seen Caroline's place. Of Krishna for hanging out with my sister while I'm at work.

"Look, I don't think it's gonna happen. But happy birthday, all right?"

He stops. Just stops walking right in the middle of the path, and I keep going for a few steps, but it turns out I can't leave him there like that.

I've been trying to leave him since I left Putnam last spring, and every time I cut him out of my life I feel crueler, but I'm accomplishing nothing. It's like he's impervious.

Except I know he's not impervious.

Krishna hasn't got that many friends. Not *real* friends. The number of guys Krishna has ever spent a night at home with, drinking and watching basketball and doing more or less nothing—I'm pretty sure it's just one.

The number of guys who know what his home life is like,

his asshole father who thinks if he doesn't take over the family company in India he's a complete failure as a human being—also one.

I stop moving.

"It's not all right," he tells me.

"I know."

"I'm not sure you do. You've been back in town two months, and it's not fucking all right, the way you're acting."

"I *know*."

"Then why don't you do something about it?"

"You think I wouldn't, if I could see some way to? You think I'm enjoying myself? I'm raising a ten-year-old, working thirty hours at the fucking window factory, taking classes, and trying to clear all my incompletes from last semester, and I can't put things back the way they were, okay? I can't. It's not possible."

His face is grave. "Caroline seems to think it's possible."

"Yeah."

He rocks up and down on the balls of his feet. "That's all you have to say? 'Yeah'?"

"What do you want me to say, that I have some kind of grand plan where I've got me and Caroline figured out?"

He closes the space between us and gets right up in my face, madder than I've ever seen him. "I want you to say you're going to get your head out of your ass and take her back."

"I don't deserve her back."

His gaze lowers to the ground. He kicks a chunk of snow, sending it sailing over the frozen lawn.

When he looks up, meets my eyes, I feel the cold seep through my coat and into my bones. "I owe you something," he says. "You took a fall for me with the cops. You didn't have to do that, and you didn't even hesitate. It fucked me up, and then Bridget told me, look, you're friends. This is what friends do for each other. But then the way you cut me off, cut Caroline off, did whatever it is you did to her that she won't tell me—that's not how friends act. So, you know, I can't say what you deserve. I don't know if you're the person I thought you were or somebody else. But fucking hell, West, cut me some slack and come to the goddamn party. Make it possible for me to fucking *like* you again."

"I can't."

"I know you can't. Bring your sister and do it anyway. To-morrow night. For my birthday. I'll make dinner."

"You cook?"

"Bridget's been teaching me."

I think I must smile at that, because he smirks, and then he reaches up and shoves off my hat, running his hand all over my hair. "You should shave it off," he says. "Go the extra badass mile."

"Tattoo 'fuck your mother' on my forehead."

"That would be sweet."

"Maybe I'll do that for tomorrow."

"I'll live in suspense."

He's grinning. It's a sham—the banter, the smile—but a sham smile is better than nothing.

It was never all that hard to make Krishna happy. I just had to let him hang around me. Talk to him. Throw him a bone every now and then.

I never thought much before about whether he was doing the same thing for me.

"Is Caroline gonna be there?" I ask.

"She lives there."

He spins around and saunters away.

I go to study, and then I go to work, heading into a whole afternoon and evening of the same shit I always do at the factory. Counting things. Measuring and marking. Loading and unloading. But I notice that the plant smells like cut wood, sawdust, and that's what I'm thinking about—how much I like that smell.

How I like the sound of the factory floor, this vast concrete space filled with echoes and the swirling lights on top of the forklifts, the beep of the backup alarm, the clang of metal against stone.

I feel like I'm waking up. I've stopped craving cigarettes beyond the occasional random impulse, and in the space where the craving was are sounds and smells, color and numbers, Frankie, Krishna, Caroline.

I think about the rest of the week and how, tomorrow morning, I can tell Frankie about dinner at Caroline's place.

I'm looking forward to it.

It's been so long since I looked forward to something, I forgot what it was like. It feels good. Dangerous, but good.

When my phone rings, I see that Caroline's calling me, and that feels pretty fucking good, too, until I hear what it is she's got to say.

The school counselor's my age.

He's leading me down a hall. Frankie follows, and Caroline brings up the rear. I don't know where we're going.

When I got here, these three were waiting outside the office, Caroline in the middle of a conversation with the counselor that died as soon as I walked up.

The school's deserted. They've been here awhile—talking, I guess, dealing with whatever this is. Waiting on me while I told my boss I needed an emergency day off and tore across town to get to the school.

"Here we are," the counselor says.

His name's Jeff. He can't be my age—not for real. He's got to be old enough to have a bachelor's. But he doesn't *look* any older than me, and between the pleasant smile, the soft handshake, and his purple tie, I can't bring myself to trust him.

"Why don't you three take a few minutes in here to talk privately?" he asks. "And Mr. Leavitt, when you're ready, I'd like to have a brief word before you leave."

The door closes, and then it's just the three of us standing around a table in a room the size of a walk-in closet. It smells like janitorial supplies—sweet and woodsy, laced with chemicals.

Caroline pulls out a chair for Frankie and takes the seat next to her. Frankie reaches out for her hand.

"Want to tell me what happened?" I ask.

My sister shakes her head no.

"Great. That's just fucking perfect."

What I know from Caroline's phone call is that Frankie launched herself over a desk in an apparently unprovoked attack, sat on some kid named Clint, and hit him repeatedly in the face until the teacher and an aide pulled her off.

Frankie's never done anything like that. Not once in her whole life.

"Caroline?" I ask.

"It's better if she tells you."

Frankie's staring at her feet like someone nailed them to the floor.

I pace back and forth behind the chairs. Every time I walk behind my sister, her shoulders draw tighter until they're up by her ears. She looks like she's afraid I'm going to hurt her, but I'm the one who holds her when she wakes up from nightmares. She's got no fucking reason to be scared of me, not one.

"Start talking," I bark.

Frankie scoots her chair away from where I'm standing, burying her face in Caroline's armpit.

"West," Caroline says.

"*What?*"

"Calm down."

"*How?*"

It's an honest fucking question. I wish she'd tell me where the handbook is for this. I'd memorize the whole thing if I thought it might help me out here.

I squat down next to Frankie. Pitch my voice as low as I can, as calm as I can manage. "In a few minutes, that counselor's coming back in here. He's going to ask me what happened, and I'm supposed to tell him you're catatonic? You think that's going to go over well?"

"I don't know what that means," she mumbles.

"It means you're practically in a coma."

"I'm not catatonic. I just don't want to talk to you."

"Well, who do you want to talk to, huh? The social workers who show up at the apartment when they decide I'm not fit to take care of my sister who's beating kids up at school? Unless I missed something, we're on the same team, Franks."

She doesn't say anything. My eyes rise to Caroline's, and there's softness there. Faith in me that eases some of the sharpness off my temper.

I put a hand on Frankie's leg and try again. Try to keep my voice level, try to keep from sounding like my dad, from *being* like him.

"We have to stick together," I say. "I can't help you if you won't talk to me. What's going on right now—this is actually *dangerous*. I could *lose* you."

Frankie's trembling.

"You're scaring her," Caroline says.

"I'm sorry, but this is a scary situation. Scarier than you understand, I think."

Frankie starts to cry.

My fists keep closing, clenching tight, my forearms pumped up with blood and violence that won't do any good here. Not in a school, not in Putnam. I can't fight my way out of this. Can't yell my way to a solution.

"You have any suggestions?" I ask Caroline.

She ducks her head and whispers a question to Frankie. Frankie whispers something back. They go on like that for a few seconds, and then Caroline says, "She wants me to tell you for her. Would that be all right?"

"Yes."

"Let's do it over there." She leads me to the opposite side of the closet-room, as far from Frankie as we can get, and refuses to start talking until I sit. I straddle a chair, fold my arms across the back, wondering why she's going to so much trouble to get me ready for this.

Then she tells me, and it's worse than anything I could have guessed.

I thought Frankie missed her friends back home, and that maybe she was embarrassed of her boobs, uncomfortable with her body—but what Caroline tells me is there's a kid, this slimy little Clint fucker, who's been giving Frankie a hard time on the bus every morning and every afternoon. He's been saying perverted shit about how she looks, her body, sexual stuff that no ten-year-old should be thinking about.

On Halloween, the teacher moved the kids' desks into a new arrangement with groups of four desks clumped together, and now Clint's is right next to Frankie's, so she's been hearing his shit all day long, day in and day out.

She took it and took it until she couldn't take it anymore. Then she attacked.

I run sweaty palms down my thighs. "I'm going to kill him," I say.

Caroline's hands are on my shoulders. She's right behind me, talking soft. "No, you're not."

Frankie's huddled into a ball on the seat of her chair.

I can't breathe right. It's not Clint I want to kill. I did this to her. Me.

The whole time she was a baby, I was afraid. If she slept longer than usual, I worried she'd died in her sleep. I wouldn't be able to make myself look in on her because I was so sure it would come true.

I worried she wasn't eating enough, wasn't eating right, wasn't growing the way she should be.

I worried she wouldn't have anything to wear to school, and when she had a fever I worried that her brain would fry and it would make her stupid. I worried when I found out about all that recalled Tylenol that I'd given her too much and she was going to get asthma or seizures or whatever.

When I was in middle school, Frankie was a toddler. Mom would leave her at the neighbor's, Mrs. Dieks, and I would come off the bus and straight to Mrs. Dieks's place to pick her up. Most of the time I'd find Frankie in nothing but a diaper, slapping her fat little palms on the coffee table, wreathed in smoke and babbling at the TV.

She's a terror, Mrs. Dieks would tell me, and I knew even when I was twelve years old that Frankie wasn't. She was normal. Curious. It was Mrs. Dieks who was too old to be watching her.

I could tell from the way she looked at me—like I might be carrying a disease—that Mrs. Dieks didn't like me. I could guess from the bruises on the softest parts of Frankie's thighs that Mrs. Dieks didn't like my sister, either.

But there was nothing I could do about it but tell my

mom, who blew it off. *She falls down,* my mom said. *I'm sure they're from accidents.*

I remember being so upset, I threw up. Wiped my eyes, rinsed out my mouth from the bathroom tap, and swore it was the last time I'd count on my mom for anything.

You're going to have to fix this, I told myself. *You're going to have to make it better for her.*

But what could I do? I was a kid, barely older than Frankie is now. I carried my sister home the second I got off the bus, changed her diaper, rubbed the diaper rash cream in as gently as I could.

Once she was in school during the day, we both got off the bus at the same time. Mom was working. Frankie was mine to worry about.

When I got my driver's license, I could drive her around. I had money of my own to buy some of what she needed—clothes and food and treats. Even when I left her behind to come to Putnam, Frankie was my first priority, my principal worry, my sister, *mine.*

But now she *is* mine, legally my responsibility, and I've failed her. I brought her here where she's vulnerable. I left her alone too much. I knew something was going on, but I didn't want to hear it.

"It's my fault," I say. "All of this is my fault."

"You're wrong," Caroline replies.

"You don't understand."

"I *do* understand, and you're wrong. But we can talk about that later. Right now, you need to focus on constructive solutions to this problem."

"What'll be constructive is if I bash that little fucker's face in."

I don't mean it. I just haven't got anything constructive to offer.

"It won't help if you get yourself arrested," she says. She braces an arm on the chair in front of me and leans close to my back to say, "Everything's going to be fine, West. Trust me. I know this feels huge, but I was already talking to the counselor, and it's really going to be okay."

I grab her arm, wrap it across my chest, forcing her to drop into a seat behind me on the chair, pressed up against my back. When she puts her other arm around me, I cross mine to cover her hands and squeeze tight.

"Breathe," she says.

I breathe in. Breathe out. Drop my head back until it rests against her neck, her shoulder.

I focus on Caroline. How right she feels against me.

I pitch my voice low and tell her, "It's abuse. What he's been saying to Frankie."

"I know."

"That kind of shit messes you up. I can't fix it."

"I know. But West, we'll help her through it. I promise."

I look at my sister, perched on the seat of a blue plastic chair with her knees squeezed in tight to her chest, and I try to make myself believe it.

From where I stand, leaning against the exterior of the school building, Frankie's face is visible in profile.

She's got her head bent, her hair pushed behind her ear and scattered over her shoulder. I told her to brush it this morning, but it looks like she forgot.

She's sitting in my truck, and I'm pressing the back of my head against unyielding brick, letting the rough surface bite into the underside of my fingers.

All I can see is Frankie. The fine little-girl lines of her face. Her thin shoulders and scraggly hair and black sweatshirt.

Ten years old, alone in a cold car.

Caroline pushes my shoulder, a gentle shove. "West. I'm talking to you."

"I heard you."

I didn't, though. I'm not quite inside myself. I'm set apart, noticing the pressure of the brick teeth on my palm, observing my sister, listening to a recording of everything the counselor said without feeling any of it.

Frankie needs enrichment. They haven't got her test scores back, but she's doing work above grade level in every subject.

She's unhappy. She's in his office three or four times a week. She's walking out of her classroom to sit in the chair by his door or across from his desk, and that's okay. She's allowed to do that. He cleared it with her teacher. He gave my sister a safe space to go to when she needs it.

He'd like to see her make more friends.

He'd like to see her talking more at school, would love to give her more opportunities across the board, and he wants to know if I've thought about music or art lessons, because sometimes they help kids who are dealing with grief.

I guess that means she told him about Dad.

What else does she tell him when she goes to sit in the safe space he made for her?

What does she tell Caroline on their long afternoons together?

Obviously a fuck of a lot more than she tells me.

Caroline faces me. "West."

"I'm going to quit at the factory," I say.

"You don't have to. I can pick her up every day. I don't have any classes that late."

"I need to be around."

She reaches out with a fingertip and hooks my sleeve. I watch her rub the cloth between her thumb and her finger like she wants to touch me but she can't get close enough to do it.

"You should go," I say. Never have I felt less like I deserved her loyalty.

She takes my hand.

I let her.

"Last year," I say.

"What about last year?"

"I was pretending."

"Which part?"

"The part where I had a life outside of taking care of Frankie."

"But you *did* have a life here. It wasn't imaginary."

"Look what came from that, though."

"You didn't cause it. You didn't make your mom get back with your dad, you didn't kill him, you didn't make it so Frankie had to see it."

"She told you she saw it?" The knowledge sweeps through me, leaving me cold.

Of course she did.

My mother lied. My sister witnessed a murder.

She told Caroline, but she didn't tell me.

"I'm sorry," Caroline says. "I wasn't sure if I should say anything, or when, or how to tell you—"

"I knew," I interrupt. Because I did. I didn't *want* to know, but I knew.

I think of Dr. Tomlinson then. Of terrible secrets that are never secrets. Not really.

"I'm supposed to keep her safe," I say.

"You're doing a good job. She's a wonderful kid."

"She's fucked-up."

"West, *everybody's* fucked-up."

"I don't want Frankie to be like me."

Caroline's eyes glisten. Her throat works.

I pull her hand until her elbow's against my side and I can put my other arm around her.

We stand there like that.

Past the parking lot, I can see the playground. They've got one of those spiral slides off by itself, and this huge play structure that has a climbing wall part, four different slides that branch off in different directions, a rope bridge, all kinds of shit.

There's dried leaves gathered in the corners and against the fence—red and green and gold.

So much color at this school.

"I never had a counselor like him," I say.

"Jeff?"

"Twenty-four years old. And that picture of his wife and his baby."

"What about them?"

"You heard. He wants to see her settled in better. He wants her to reach her 'full potential for achievement and happiness.'"

Maybe that's a thing people say in Caroline's world. She would've gone to a school like this, with school counselors and teachers and principals who wanted things for her. She has a father who wants the world for her. It's such a foreign country to me.

Nobody ever talked to me about potential and achievement and happiness but Dr. T, and what I did to get what he was offering canceled out any part of me that might have deserved it.

She strokes my arm. "It's good, right? It's all good."

I pull Caroline closer, position her in front of me, take her weight when she sags against me.

We watch my sister. She bends down and disappears,

probably fishing around in her school bag. Takes something out of it, drops her head again. She's writing.

"If Jeff was her dad, he'd know what she was writing," I say.

"Probably not."

"She wouldn't have nightmares. She'd have daydreams. Horses and unicorns, princes and castles, all that shit girls her age draw in their notebooks—that's what Frankie would have."

Caroline turns in my arms and puts her cold hands against my cheeks. "That is such a mountain of crap."

"It's the truth."

"Even if it were true—even if she'd had a different life up to now, some sheltered life with unicorns and rainbows—sooner or later she'd grow up, and she'd get hurt. There's no way around it."

"You didn't see her when she was a baby. There was nothing to her."

She strokes her hands down my neck. "You know who I wish I could've seen? You. I wish I'd seen you when she was born. How old were you, ten?"

I nod.

"I want a time machine," Caroline says, "so I can see you when you were eleven or twelve and she took her first steps. I want to see when she was learning to talk, and when you taught her to read."

"She taught herself to spell first," I say. "Went right from the alphabet song to phonics to spelling everything out loud, and then once she could spell she picked up *Fox in Socks* and read it to me. Didn't miss a single word."

"I bet you were proud of her."

I was. I always have been.

Caroline flattens her hands against my chest and leans back to look me in the eye.

"She doesn't need another father," she says. "She's got you."

"I'm just her brother."

"No, you're not."

"I'm her guardian."

"Jesus, you're stubborn." Caroline steps away, turns to face the car, and points at Frankie. "Look at her," she says. "Look at that girl and tell me you don't know every single thing about her."

"She didn't tell me about Clint."

"She's *ten*," Caroline says. "That's old enough for secrets. But I met your mom, and I saw where you grew up. I've talked to your sister. I've seen her with you. You're her father, whether you like it or not. You've been her father since the day your mom brought her home from the hospital. *Look at her.*"

I look.

I look for what feels like an hour.

I can't tell Caroline she's wrong.

I don't know what Frankie's writing about, but I know the way she nibbles on her lip when she's got a pen in her hand. She gnaws the skin off that lip, and when it's cold and dry out it cracks sometimes and bleeds, and I've got to get after her to put Carmex on it so it'll heal.

I'd give my life for her without hesitating. Anytime. Any day. Under any circumstances.

That's how it is, and Caroline's right that it doesn't matter what some piece of paper says. Me and my sister belong to each other deeper than words on paper, deeper than I can find the words to say out loud.

She's my kid.

I guess that means I'm her father.

What a fucking terrifying thought.

"I don't know what to do for her," I say.

"So you learn."

"I don't know how to start."

"Quit being such a baby. Read a parenting book. Read twenty, if it makes you feel better."

"It's not just parenting, though, it's this stuff." I gesture at the playground. "Enrichment. Art classes. It never crossed my mind to worry about that."

"That's what Jeff's for."

"No, that's my point. I'm saying, we're living here like we lived in Silt. We're *surviving*, because that's all I know how to do. Jeff hears about Clint and the bus and the sick shit that kid said to my sister, and he doesn't think about punching someone. He tells me, *Yeah, that's terrible, but we're gonna handle it. What I'm worried about is how we can make your sister's life richer.* Richer! What the fucking fuck?"

She's frowning at me.

"*Richer,*" I say again, dropping the word like a hammer. "*Fuller.* More *beautiful.* That's not surviving, it's something else. It's *thriving.* I don't know how to do that."

Caroline butts her head into my chest, hard.

Then she does it again.

"What'd I say?"

"West." She slams her head into me a third time. Rolls her forehead back and forth. "You drive me *crazy.*"

"*What?*"

"You don't know how to do it for your sister because you don't know how to do it for *yourself,* okay? But if you'd just fucking *listen* to me sometimes, and if you'd just *let me in,* you might start to figure it out."

I'm as shocked as if she'd smacked me—still reeling from her words—when she lifts her face to mine, rises to her toes, and kisses me.

Really *kisses* me, with tongue and teeth, her hands on my head, body pressing into mine.

I don't even think about resisting. I take her ass in both hands and pull her tight against me, kiss her back, one kiss after another, soft and then hard, a deep stroke of my tongue, scared and confused and glad she's here, because I know what *richer* and *fuller* and *more beautiful* mean, but only when I'm with Caroline.

She breaks away and kisses my chin, my jaw, my cheek, and my temple. "You're going to figure it out," she whispers. "Trust me on this one."

I can't trust myself, but I can trust her. "I'll try."

She hugs me tight, tucks her head against my neck, and says, "You fucking better."

I look down at the top of her head, and then I look at my sister again in the car, miles away, thinking whatever it is she's thinking about.

In between us is Caroline.

Her house is a couple blocks from campus, a big old cedar-shingled place that's impressive from a distance but looks shabby close up. I park in the alley in the back. Krishna lets me into the kitchen. It smells like onions and garlic—warm cooking scents. Bridget and Caroline are at a little table tucked into the corner of the room.

"Where's Frankie?" Caroline asks.

"I left her with Laurie and Rikki."

"Is she okay?"

"Yeah, she just got a better offer. They're doing some kind

of art-film double feature with popcorn and Junior Mints. She seemed excited, so I said go for it."

I want to is what Frankie actually told me. I couldn't say no to that, especially not when it meant a night off for me and a chance to see if I can remember what it's like to have friends.

I'm holding a case of beer and a foot-long sausage. I stopped at the Kum and Go on the way here. "Happy birthday," I say to Krishna. "Legal at last. Must be a thrill."

"Oh, it is. I almost creamed myself when I woke up this morning and realized I could finally drink with the big kids."

"I'll bet."

"That's some present," he says. "You must've killed yourself trying to figure out what to get me."

"I was gonna get you *101 Unsolved Math Problems,* but they were all out at the gas station."

"It's a poorly stocked mart, that's for sure."

"Figured you'd rather have beer and a giant sausage than a copy of *Hustler.*"

Krishna flicks his eyes at Bridget. "You can put the beer in the fridge," he says absently. "Open one for me, though."

"You got it."

"We picked up two kegs for the party later."

"Two? You're not screwing around."

"You only turn twenty-one once."

I set the sausage down, twist off two caps, hand him one.

"Grab a chair," he tells me. "I'm making minestrone."

"You're wearing a fucking apron."

"I know. Trying to look like you, killer. You were always rocking the apron at the bakery last year."

Nostalgia and disappointment, pleasure and pain.

So many times he came by the bakery just to hang out for an hour before he went home to crash.

So many shifts I spent with Caroline sitting on the floor doing her Latin homework, talking through some idea for a paper or highlighting up her textbook.

Gone now. I haven't even walked by the bakery. I didn't ask for my job back because I got myself fucking *arrested* out of the bakery, and I can't look the owner, Bob, in the eye.

I burned all these bridges behind me when I left Putnam, thinking I was going home when there wasn't any home for me to go to. Just work and worry and people fucking things up while I tried to be someone they could count on.

And to be that guy, I betrayed what I had with every single person in this kitchen.

I take the chair next to Caroline.

She's wearing jeans and a T-shirt, just a plain white T-shirt with a pocket on it. Her hair's down, against her back, still damp from the shower. Her feet, in thick gray socks, are hooked over the rungs of her chair.

She looks amazing to me, even with that tilt to her head and that wrinkle between her eyebrows that means she's trying to figure me out.

"Check the garlic bread," Bridget says to Krishna. "The broiler's tricky, and it can burn if you're not paying attention. I think it's been in there long enough—"

Krish talks right over her the way they always do. "I set a timer."

"—timer is a good idea, but it's not smart to rely on it completely, because sometimes the broiler is so hot that—"

"It's fine. The timer's going, so I'm not checking it."

"It's burning, though, I can—"

"It's not burning."

"Krish, I can *smell* it burning. You have to—"

By the time he's found a hot pad, there's smoke coming from under the broiler, and the whole kitchen smells like singed bread. Krishna is swearing, throwing doors open, while Bridget flaps around making a lot of noise.

Caroline and I take it all in, unfazed, and I don't know, it's nice.

It's nice sitting next to Caroline, looking at her thighs in her dark blue jeans, her elbow on the table, listening to Bridget and Krish bitch at each other.

He puts the bread in a basket, a fucking *basket,* and sets it in front of me like I'm the king of France. "It's still going to be a while on the soup. I guess I was supposed to start it sooner and the bread later."

"You know you were," Bridget says. "I sent you that text when you were in class to remind you, and I said I could pick up the Parmesan so you didn't have to waste your time, but you think you know everything—"

"—but really that's you, right?"

And then Krishna smiles at her in this way that completely betrays him.

I've seen him look at her before, but never this obvious. I glance at Caroline, wondering if she sees it, too.

She lifts an eyebrow. *What?*

I glance from Bridget to Krishna and back to Bridget. Mouth the word, *Fucking.*

She nods.

"No shit?"

She makes a circle with her left hand, thrusts into it with the index finger of her right, smiling at me with her eyes.

"No shit what?" Krishna wants to know.

"Nothing," we say in unison, and for a second it's just like it always was between us. Easy.

I pick up a piece of garlic bread and shove it into my mouth.

I'm fucking ravenous.

Ten more minutes, I tell myself.

I have class tomorrow.

I've got work in the afternoon, Frankie to talk to, my whole life to sort out.

Ten more minutes, and then I'll go.

Dinner did something to me, though. The bread was frozen and burned, the soup so salty it about sucked all the moisture out of my body, and for dessert a cheesecake that Bridget made Krishna from scratch.

It was good. The food and the company, the way I could close my eyes and almost pretend I was an ordinary college guy eating dinner with his friends, drinking a few beers, joking around about big sausages and who's gonna do the dishes, talking about nothing.

Ten more minutes. Ten more.

Instead, I take my cup back to the keg and draw another beer.

I have just enough to drink to push my guard down, and the music keeps it there—club music, dance music, loud throbbing anthems, and dark catchy songs that make people want to huddle in corners and talk real close together and put their hands on each other.

The house fills with people. I know a lot of them—people I've sold to, drank with, handed paper bags of muffins at three in the morning. Old lab partners, group project partners, girls whose names I know because Krishna hooked up with them, girls whose names I know because they've tried to hook up with me.

I let it infect me. Noise and heat, girls and sweat. The house gets loud, the music gets louder, everybody's got a red plastic cup and something to say. Every time someone raises a hand and shouts "West!" over the crowd—every time someone presses another cup into my hand—I let myself take it.

I'm drinking and talking, laughing with some dude whose name I can't remember, leaning a palm against the wall, dipping down so I can hear this chick named Sierra who seems to know me though I'd swear I've never talked to her before. I've got a view down her shirt but her tits are just tits and mostly what I'm doing, even when I'm not doing it, is watching Caroline.

I like the way she looks. The way she laughs.

I like the way she moves when she's weaving through bodies with her drink held high, the way she jokes around with Krishna and Bridget and her other housemates, the way that even though she's not all that tall she looks like the tallest girl in the room because she holds herself so straight.

She holds herself like she matters, laughs like she cares, smiles like she's somebody.

Regal. Caroline's *regal*. Always has been.

Always will be, and nothing I do or say to her is going to change that, because she wasn't lying when she said she wouldn't cut off her hair for me.

She knows who she is deep inside herself. I can break her heart, but I can't break her pride. I can't break *her*. She's not ever going to let that happen.

Fuck, I want her.

All the time, like a virus, a disease I caught, except the other way around—like a cure I caught a year ago, and it's inside me, winding through my veins, pumping through my heart.

It's easy to take it.

It's easy to drink more than I'm supposed to, easy to go to her when I see her resting on the arm of the couch.

It's easy to walk up behind her and sweep her hair back over her shoulder and lower my head.

I hold her shoulders, bracket her between my palms, tell her *keep still* with my hands, and I open my mouth there, right at the edge of her jawline. It's the first place I ever put my lips on her, and I know she'll remember.

I act like she's still mine, because I've never stopped being hers. Not for a second.

I step in closer, bending down, pressing against her as I wrap my arms around her front, feel her breathe, feel like I'm home here, now, with her.

"You having fun?" My mouth is so close to her ear I can whisper. I can tell her anything, sneak explicit words beneath the music—tell her every single dirty act I want to carry out on her body, and no one but Caroline will hear.

"Yeah."

I feel her breathing, her back rising and falling against my chest, her heat and her excitement.

"We should go somewhere," I say. "Have some more fun."

"I'm not sure that's a good idea."

But she's got her hands on top of mine, and she's pulling my arms tighter around her.

She's got her ass against my crotch, and she's pushing back into where I'm getting hard, making me harder.

This, we always knew how to do.

My hands are at her ribs, crossed around her. I slide them up until they're just under her breasts. Not quite indecent, but I feel the hitch in her breathing. I know she's getting wet for me, just thinking what I could do with one sweep of my thumbs. "This feels like a good idea."

She twists around, heat in her eyes, color in her cheeks. "How much did you drink?"

"Four beers."

"You're not wasted."

"Buzzed is all. What about you?"

"Two beers, and I switched to water a while ago."

We study each other. Around us there's movement, shouting and laughter, posturing excitement, but it might as well just be me and Caroline, because I could give a fuck about everything else in the room.

She's sober, and I'm close enough. We both know what we're doing. If this happens, it's because we're deciding to let it happen, right now, unimpaired—except I'm never unimpaired around her.

I've been drunk on her since the day we met.

"Come upstairs with me," she says.

"You sure?"

"I'm not sure about anything." She wets her lips, the tip of her tongue flicking out, mesmerizing me. "But yeah," she says. "Come upstairs."

I let go of her so she can stand up.

I grab her hips because I can't help it. I need to grip her. I need to hold her and bite her, lick her and take her, everything I can get from her tonight, all of it, I'm going to store it up, hoard it away.

She covers my hand with hers. Interlaces our fingers together.

She pulls me toward the stairs, up the risers, down the hall to her room.

The framed Putnam Women's Rugby jersey on the wall above Caroline's bed vibrates with the thump of the bass.

I stand in the middle of the rug, not sure where she wants me. I'm in the calm space at the center of a tornado. If I move too far in any direction, it'll fling me out, fling me away from her.

When she takes a step toward me, I grab her at the waist and pull her in.

I get her right up against me, get my hands in all that hair, and I kiss her as if I'd never stopped. As if we can start right up again, right now, and pretend everything in the middle never happened.

She tastes like she always did. Hot and eager, wet and sinuous. Amazing.

Amazing is all I can think as I'm filling my hands with Caroline, breathing her in, licking over her lip and giving her my tongue, taking every eager pant like it belongs to me.

I strum my thumbs over her nipples, the beat of the music inside me, the vibrating bass in my balls, driving intrusive seeking urgency in my dick, in my hands on her ass, my knee between her legs pushing her back to the bed, knocking her down.

I'm going too fast, too eager, but she's keeping up with me, lifting her hips into my hard cock with her legs spread, biting the tendon in my neck and sucking at me like she needs it this way, too. Fast and hard and important.

God, it feels as important as breathing, the way the pressure builds when you're holding your breath underwater, your eyes closed, that urgency for air pounding away at you until you can't take it anymore, you just have to.

I have to.

We have to.

She gets her hands under my shirt and rakes her nails down my back. Grabs my ass so hard I feel the bite of her nails on my taint.

I keep kissing her. It's not a seduction, it's an invasion, an attack, clashing swords, clanging shields, both of us desperate to get at each other, get inside the other, get there.

"Take this off," she demands, and I sit up and whip off my shirt, grab hers by two fistfuls of cotton from the bottom and pull and pull until it's gone.

Her bra is white and lacy.

Her bra is sailing across the room to hit the locked door with a soft tap, and I'm sucking half of her breast into my mouth and flicking my tongue over the tip while I massage the other and she's gasping my name. "West. Jesus. Don't you think—"

I'm not interested in thinking. I kiss the words off of her mouth, push them aside, reach down and jerk at the laces of my boots and somehow miraculously manage to get them untied on one side while I start kissing her again.

The other side gets knotted up.

Whatever. I'm not fucking stopping over boots. She had slip-on shoes that she's already slipped off, so I go up on my knees and work at her button and zipper, shoving her jeans and panties down before she can say anything, because I'm afraid she'll see reason and make me stop.

I get my hand between her thighs, my fingers in where she's slick and hot and soft, swollen, and I'm a safecracker working at Caroline's pussy. I know everything she likes, know it like I know how to spell my own name, so I spell my name all over her cunt, working two fingers inside her, my thumb pressing on her clit, not too much, just the way she likes.

Her cheeks are blazing pink, her eyes closed, forehead wrinkled up like she's going to cry, and she says my name on a sob, "West."

"Don't stop me," I'm pleading, and she says, "No, no,"

which is exactly what I've been afraid of, although part of me recognizes the sanity of it.

I mean, this is stupid. I know it's stupid.

This could ruin everything, ruin it worse than it's already ruined, and until tonight I didn't know there was anywhere we could end up that was worse than where we already were, but there *is*.

There's this. This one thing I haven't fucked up yet.

My hand stills.

My head drops to her neck, and she slaps my shoulder so hard.

"No, West, I meant *don't* stop. Don't, don't." She's fucking herself onto my fingers, lifting and pushing at me, slapping the flat of my shoulder like I'm a balky horse and she wants me to get a move on. "Please."

I never could say no to her.

"You have condoms?" I ask.

"In my desk."

"Can you hold on while I get one? I don't want you to die on me."

Now she's laughing, patting my shoulder where it's got to be red, she hit me so hard. "Hurry."

I'm already up and moving, yanking at the boot laces I've managed to tangle up so bad, but there's no hope for them so I just pull the fucking thing until it comes off, nearly dislocating my ankle in the process.

I take off my socks, and I can feel the music in my bare feet.

The condom's where she said, where I keep mine in my own desk at the apartment, and it strikes me in the chest like it means something, but I don't stop to think about what that might be. I sit down on the edge of the bed, condom in hand, looking at her spread out on top of the covers like every fantasy I ever had.

I jerk myself a few times because it hurts and I can't not.

She sits up, replaces my hand with hers, pulls on me fast and tight so that I lose whatever I had left of a brain and turn into an animal.

"Lie down," I tell her, and it's an order, my voice so low, so violent I barely recognize it. She doesn't object. She seems to know what it means, which is just that I want her so bad I can't talk or think or do anything but roll that condom on fast, get my hands under her ass, push inside her and yank her onto me at the same time, graceless and fast, hard enough to shut her mouth with a snap of teeth.

"Get your arms up," I tell her. "Hold on."

She scoots back, and I keep moving after her, moving my knees up as she's coming to a half-reclined position so she can find a grip on the top of the headboard behind her. Then she's got a hold and I've got her, my arms braced and gripping oak, her legs around me and squeezing into my hips, her pussy clenching, her tits bouncing with every thrust.

I've got her moaning under me, got the smell of her, the sounds of her, like nothing else.

Like no other woman I've known, nothing I've had, no one like Caroline.

I've got her, but I can't stop chasing after her. We fuck fast and rough, and I don't know if it's what she needs, but I can't do it any other way. If I slow down, stop to savor it, stop to think—I can't.

There's no way but this way.

There's no one in the world but me and her, her pink nipples, her pussy, her lips and her eyes and her hair, the creaking bed and her bucking hips.

I'm fixated on her white knuckles lined up next to mine, clenching and releasing in rhythm. That's where I'm looking when she tightens up, and I'm surprised by the sound she makes, the way it breaks over her face.

That's all it takes to push me over—Caroline coming, the most erotic sight I know. Fluttering hot pleasure rushes through me everywhere, wrings me out, wrecks me for anything but her warm, soft body and my forehead against her temple, my mouth on her cheek, on her shoulder, resting on her neck.

Then we're breathing.

Our hearts are racing, bodies cooling, the music pounding into the floorboards but its urgency pointless now, because we're here.

Finally.

Here is where we were going—naked and touching each other everywhere, soft, vulnerable, together.

I'm smiling into her neck, thinking this is the best monumentally stupid thing I've ever done while drunk, when I hear another noise out of Caroline that doesn't sound like laughter.

Sounds like crying.

I don't move. Not until I feel her hands at my shoulders, pushing me.

Shoving me away.

"Get off, okay?" Her eyes are swimming. She shoves me again. "Please, get off, I can't . . ."

"I will, I swear, baby, hold up," I say, because I've got to grab the condom or we'll have a mess on our hands. When I've got it secured, I pull out, sit up.

She turns her back to me.

I can see every bump in her spine.

I wrap the condom in a tissue and throw it into the trash can by her desk, then sit back down next to her and put my hand on her shoulder. "Caroline?"

She shudders. "Don't."

"Talk to me, though."

"I can't. I don't—just give me some space, okay?"

It's not okay, because I don't know what that means. A few feet, a few minutes?

A few miles? A few months?

She was there for me at the school with Frankie. She stuck by me after what I did in Silt, stuck close to me since I came back to Putnam even though I've been standoffish and inconsistent and probably fucking infuriating.

She was with me just now—wasn't she with me?

Christ.

I stand up and dress, jeans and socks and shirt. I kneel over my knotted shoelace and spend an eternity unknotting it while Caroline cries.

Something crashes downstairs.

The sound of crashing and sobbing sends me tripping into dark channels of recrimination.

You've got nothing to give her, no business being here, no right to touch her, no skills to fix this.

You're worthless, you're toxic, you're poison.

I sit down on the bed.

Her crying is as empty as the sound the shovel made when I sank the blade into the dirt and piled up soil and rocks to dump on my old man's corpse. The only thing I'd done in months that felt easy, because I knew that he was gone, and I knew I could put him in the ground and be done with him. There was my past, *there*, six feet deep. I was going to cover it with so much dirt that it could never claw its way out of that hole.

He can never touch me again. That's what I thought. That's what I paid for when I paid for the funeral.

But he's in me. He looked like me, talked like me, probably fucked like me, because I can remember being five years old and hearing my parents fucking and my mom crying after.

You don't ever forget something like that.

And no matter how deep I buried him, there's no way for me to pretend not to know that my father was the kind of man who'd do what I did to Caroline after the funeral.

I sure as fuck didn't enjoy it, but I did it. I closed my eyes and closed a fist way down deep inside myself and bludgeoned my way through it, telling myself I had to because it was the only way. Telling myself I didn't have a decision to make.

Caroline was right when she read me the riot act in Silt. Everything she said, she was absolutely right. Everything she's said to me since.

I'm afraid.

I'm so fucking afraid of making any kind of choice, because ever since Frankie was born I've told myself that thinking of me, of what *I* want, what *I* need, is a luxury I don't get to claim. It's all about Frankie. My life is for Frankie. If I live for *her*, I don't have to think about *me*.

I've been making excuses for inexcusable behavior, acting like the Fates snipped my threads so short that I just have to take whatever life shoves down my throat. I just have to breathe through my nose and swallow it and survive so Frankie will never know what that's like.

But that's not living, is it? Survival isn't life.

Survival is what you do when you don't get to choose.

I'm not going to wake up in the morning in my bed over the garage and pretend to be some kind of a role model for

Frankie, some kind of a parent to her, after I left Caroline naked and crying in her bed.

I survived that man. I won't turn into him.

What I've got to figure out is how to defy him. How to live a life that's rich in everything he never had, fulfilling and beautiful like he couldn't imagine, because he drove all the beauty away from himself.

And it could be that it'll always be harder for me than it would for some normal guy, because I started out the way I did. I'm smart, but there's all this stuff I don't *know*.

I don't know how to be a father to a kid who's safe. I don't know how to be a student just to be a student—how to explore, how to waste paper, how to play. I don't know how to tell Caroline I'm sorry and make her hear how much I mean it, and I don't know how to put what I did behind me and look toward the future.

But I told her I'd try, and I will. Maybe if I try ten times harder than anybody else, that'll be good enough to get the job done.

I lie down beside Caroline and put my hand on her shoulder again, stroking up and down her arm.

I close my eyes, fit my body to hers, and keep touching her, smoothing her, soothing and waiting.

Whatever she needs. Whatever it takes.

I'm not walking away again.

FORGIVEN

Caroline

The night of the party.

The music. The noise.

Half an inch of foam on top of my beer, floating in its red plastic Solo cup.

Half of me wanting to leave, go for a drive, go for a run, get away from what was coming for me.

What was coming for me being West, of course.

West leaning against a wall, sipping his cup and observing.

West bending toward some girl, his head cocked, his lips curving into a smile, listening with half his attention even as his eyes roamed the room to find me.

His gaze like a hand, heavy, stroking.

The intention in that look. Hot enough to brand me if I stood still and let it sink in, which I did. I wanted him to look.

I wanted him.

The night of the party. The night before the party. The night after the party.

Every night, I wanted to get my hands on him, get my mouth

on him, sink my teeth into him, tangle our bodies up, crush our lives together, smash into him and keep doing it. Keep doing it.

Keep doing it because it felt amazing, because I wanted it, because I didn't know how to stop.

We'd found each other last year, edged closer together, closer and closer until we were so close that I couldn't imagine my life without him in it.

We got inside of each other, dug in deep and held on, and when we collided on my bed that night, his body hot on top of mine—when I got his skin under my hands—my fingers remembered how to grip him.

My body remembered how to take him in, twine around him, pull at his pistoning hips.

But I cried when it was over because it hurts to surrender to that kind of violent need.

It hurts to see yourself, your defenses down all around you, your wits scattered.

Everything I'd done since he came back to Putnam was in pursuit of that moment. That joy in my body, our two bodies together.

God. That moment hurt.

There was my truth, broken into pieces small enough to read: He'd hurt me. I hurt.

He'd made me angry. I was angry.

He'd driven me away, and I still felt the distance, even with his cock pushing hard inside me, his face in my neck, his tongue in my mouth.

It wasn't the same. We weren't. Maybe we could never be the same.

I'd told West there are no beginnings, middles, and ends. *Think about it,* I told him, because I wanted him to listen to me.

I said to him that life is complicated, people are complicated, because that's what I believed. That's what I had to believe. But saying that to West—even if it's true—didn't change the fact that he'd written an ending over top of us. Written it with his mouth on another woman's body.

He pushed inside me, crashed into me, loved me and kissed me and fucked me until I came hard enough to see stars, only it turns out that seeing the stars when you're alone in the wilderness doesn't mean you'll know how to follow them to safety.

He was my north star once.

That night of the party, I cried because the skies had changed. There were stars scattered across the black night, bright and gorgeous as jewels, but I couldn't read them.

What I didn't understand right away—what I figured out that winter, trusting my instincts, trusting myself until I could believe it down deep inside—was I didn't need to know the way.

The wilderness is life. There's no way out of it.

That's not important.

The important thing is that from that night, West was with me.

West was with me all the time.

When I come back to awareness of myself, the quality of the sound from downstairs has changed. It's not so raucous now, the music slow-moving and trippy, voices conversing, laughing rather than shouting.

The party is winding down.

I cried myself to sleep, or into some kind of stupor.

West's got one arm over me. It's good—not too heavy,

not too much. Different, though. He's so much bigger than he was in the spring. I can feel the weight of the difference against my breasts, snugged into my ribcage.

From where I lie, I can see out the window to the sky.

He's awake. I can tell by the way he feels against my back.

I turn over, lifting the arm that's between our bodies and letting my wrist drop against my forehead as though it might be some use in shielding me from the sight of his face so close.

It isn't any use.

There's the scar through his eyebrow, the no-color color of his eyes, his hair too short, his ears too small, his mouth so wide, and everything about him just exactly as it should be.

I guess he could say, *That was fun, but I've got to get going.*

I guess it's possible he could act like a douche, like Krishna might act, smiling and chattering while he backs toward the door and makes an exit.

But there isn't any part of me that expects him to.

"Can we talk?" he asks.

That's West. My West.

I reach up on an impulse and slide my hands over his neck. Lift my shoulders off the bed, cool air leaking through the window on my naked shoulder blades as I set my mouth against his.

I do it because he's here. Because I can.

His palm finds my waist under the blanket he must have put over me. It rests there on my skin as he holds still and lets me kiss him.

When I pull away, he says, "Can I do that, too?"

I sink down, nodding, and then it's him kissing me, cushioned in the softness of my pillow, his hands against my head making a hushed space where I can hear my heart and feel his lips.

I think of all the words for kisses. *Hot. Possessive. Questing. Fiery.* This kiss isn't any of those. It's not any of the other things we've been to each other, either—fun or funny or angry or supportive or dangerous.

It's a kiss that says, *Here you are. Here I am.*

Here we are.

Kissing West that way—it makes me feel so much better.

When he stops to breathe, I let out a long breath and tell him, "Okay."

"Okay?"

"Okay, we can talk."

"I was hoping that was what you meant," he says. "And not, you know, *Okay, you can go now.*"

"That's not really my style."

"You didn't seem to want me here a little while ago."

"I clubbed you over the head and dragged you up here by one ear."

"Is that how you remember it?"

"More or less," I admit.

"But there's this." He touches the corner of my eyelid. My lashes dried in clumps, and my cheeks still feel hot.

"That. Yeah. I didn't anticipate that."

"Me, neither." He lowers down and kisses me again, softly. "We probably should've talked first, fucked each other's brains out after."

"Then we might not have fucked each other's brains out at all."

"Right."

We're quiet for a minute, just looking at each other. Thinking about what we did, whether we should have. What it is we're supposed to say now that we've come through months of separation and arrived here in my bed.

West sits up, propping his back against my headboard.

"I'm going to promise you something," he says. "You don't have to promise me back. I don't think it has to work like that. I just want to tell you—I'm not gonna keep anything from you. I'm done pretending that my business isn't your business. I want to be straight with you, Caro, because I'm hoping . . ."

He looks down at me, caution in the lines around his mouth. But his eyes aren't cautious or angry—not the way they've been so much of the time since I landed in Silt.

They're just West. All of him, right there in his face.

"I'm hoping what we did tonight means something to you, the way it does to me," he says. "Even if you think it was a mistake, which, you know, it probably *was* a mistake, but if it was, I made it because I want you back in my life so bad."

I didn't know there was anything inside me left closed to him, but hearing West say he wants me back just throws a door open inside me, and I'm crying again.

He scoots back down to the bed to wipe at my tears with his hand. "Caro."

"No, it's fine. I'm fine. Don't baby me."

"I kind of want to baby you."

"Then baby me, but not because you think I'm pathetic."

"I don't think you're pathetic. I think you're awesome. I'm the one who's—"

I cover his mouth with my hand.

He lifts an eyebrow. I take my hand away.

"Isn't it time?" he says. "Don't you think it's time for me to tell you how sorry I am? What a sorry-ass piece of shit I am, and a coward, and stupid, and—"

I cover his mouth again. "Don't."

He goes quiet, watching me for clues. Like I have a clue. I reach out blindly for the blanket, pull it up to swipe at my tears, exposing one leg to the cold.

Everything feels so close to the surface. Scratch us any-where and see what comes out. West's confession. My anger. West's reasons. My heartache. West's abject apology. My re-grets.

I don't want to hear any of it.

"Tell me if I was wrong," I say. "What I said in the truck on the way to the airport. Which part did I get wrong?"

He shakes his head. Says something against my hand that I can't understand.

I take my palm away.

"No part," he repeats. "You were right. You're always right."

"I'm not, though. I'm guessing all the time, and I screw up. Don't put me on a pedestal."

"You're always right about the stuff that matters."

When he smoothes his hand over my forehead, pushing away a strand of hair that stuck to my temple, I take his wrist and pull it down until his palm is pressing flat over my heart.

I leave it there. Let him feel it beat.

I'm alive. I guess that's what I'm showing him.

I don't want to spend my life staring backward at every-thing that's gone wrong. I want to be *here*.

So I pull him down by the back of his neck until his mouth is on mine and he's kissing me again with his hand over my heart. He's kissing me deeper, moving over me, stroking my tongue with his, letting me feel the heat and the strength in him.

There are things I want to say, blanks in the conversation that the good girl who still lives in me insists I've got to fill up.

She wants to tell him, *I forgive you.*

She wants to say, *I still love you.*

She wants to press her hand over his heart, too, and make him swear never to leave. Never to fuck up like that again.

But I'm not her anymore. I'm not sure if I *do* forgive him.

I know I love him, but I don't want him to have those words. I want him to earn them back.

Convince me, I think, as my blanket falls away. As West's thigh moves between mine, his belt dragging over my hip, his hands so sure of themselves, so good at gliding down my back to my ass, at grabbing and lifting and positioning me just so.

"We're gonna go slower this time," he says, kissing over my collarbone. "So much slower it might just kill me."

"Make sure it's not so slow that I don't notice it's happening."

He grins. It's almost right. Almost West's smile. But he's holding something back.

"Tell me." I put my fingertip at that worry line between his eyebrows that won't quite go away.

"Don't get me wrong," he says. "I like this. I want this. But shouldn't we be talking?"

My hands are sneaking up his back, his smooth tan skin, every bit of him familiar but different, broader, stronger, harder. "We *are* talking," I say.

Because we are. What he means is that we're not following a script.

Only, there is no script. There are no rules for this.

I don't think we're doing it wrong, because I don't believe there's any way to do it wrong or any way to do it right outside of how I feel, how he feels, how we feel between us.

All the songs are love songs. That's what I'm learning.

All the songs are love songs, and this one is ours.

"Are you happy?" I ask. "Right now, this instant?"

He kisses the top of my shoulder. My biceps muscle. "You're naked."

"Does that mean yes?"

"That means fuck yes."

"Me, too."

He kisses the swell of my breast. Cups them both in his hands and drops his head to my cleavage. His back rises under my palms.

"Are you smelling my boobs?"

"I'm smelling you."

"That's a little weird."

"Okay." He roots his nose in there until it touches my breastbone. Kisses that spot. "I can live with weird."

He kisses my ribs, licks down my ribcage, mouths my stomach, smells me at my navel and then between my legs. Looks up with his hands already dug under my ass, his mouth an inch from the stripe of my pubic hair, and says, "You still happy?"

He sounds like he's teasing, but I know what he's asking. All the guidebooks and conventional wisdom in the world say this is where I should snap.

This is the moment when I should be angry, disgusted, cold with him.

I should want vengeance.

I should rain down my vengeance upon him, and the last thing I should ever let him do is what he's about to do right now.

But I'm swollen and aching and I need him.

When I squirm, he smiles and licks a hot line right through the middle of me.

I'm not sure I believe in vengeance.

I know I don't believe in tit-for-tat, this-but-not-that, you-can-until-I-say-you-can't, I-love-you-until-I-decide-I-don't.

With West, I picked deep and then deeper. I picked all the way, hot and cold, good and bad, dark and light.

I picked West in my bed and West on his fire escape in the snow, chicken-soup West and bakery West, drug dealer West and brawler West, West in Silt and West in Putnam. I picked hand jobs and blow jobs and doggy style and missionary and sloppy oral and morning-breath kisses and nights when we're too tired and we just hold hands and go to sleep.

I picked him. *Him.*

This is where we are now. Who we are right now. Us.

I don't know how I'll feel in the morning. I'm not pretending it's all going to be perfect, that it's perfect now, or even that perfect is a real thing that exists in the world. But tonight, there's no bullshit between the two of us. There's just his hand sliding up my thigh. His mouth moving down, his breath on my clit.

What he wants to do. What I want to let him give me.

That's all this is.

I put my hand over the top of his head, rake my nails over his scalp and give him one hard, firm push.

"Easy there, tiger," he says. "We're taking it slow, remember?"

This time when he smiles, it's his real smile. I know, because it hits me down low and deep, makes me shudder, makes me wetter than I already was.

"So slow, Caro. You're gonna hate me for it."

I don't, though.

He tortures me, asks me every now and then, "You happy?"

I keep saying yes even though he's killing me.

Yes, yes, West, God.

He kills me and kills me.

I'm so happy, I could die.

PIONEER

Can I talk to you?

That's what I asked Caroline in her room, in her bed.

Can I talk to you? I asked Frankie the next morning over pancakes.

I called her counselor and set up another meeting. *Can I talk to you?*

I left my boss at the window plant a message, asking him to call me back, giving notice that I'd be quitting as soon as I found work with daylight hours.

I don't think I'd ever talked so much in my life as I talked that November.

You get your mind made up that you know how everything is and so there's no point in talking. You know what you've got to do. You know what the future looks like.

And then you hit some pivot point, some paradigm shift that shows you everything you thought you knew wasn't right, so you start going around all the time saying, *Can we talk? I have to ask you something. I've got things I need to tell you.*

I guess it's because I'm stubborn—because I get set in my ways, pulling the cart through the same ruts day after day—but I always thought when I asked people to talk to me that I knew how the conversation would go. What I'd say. What they'd say back.

It's funny, because I was always wrong.

Those weeks in November and on into December—they were full of surprises. Happy surprises, sad surprises, gutting surprises, frustrating surprises, amazing surprises.

Caroline was sometimes the biggest surprise of all, because she kept coming around. Staying over. Sticking by me. And those were the weeks that everything finally changed.

I stopped thinking I knew how my life was going to go.

I started waking up in the morning thinking how interesting it would be to see what happened next.

And somewhere along the way, I noticed I wasn't asking, *Can I talk to you?* anymore. I was just talking.

Listening.

Getting surprised, and liking it.

The morning after Krishna's party, Frankie's picking at her pancakes, and I'm trying not to care.

She drenched them in syrup. I warned her it was too much, suggested she could put the syrup in a cup and dip the pieces so she'd have the right amount, but she just rolled her eyes like I was the stupidest person on the planet and kept squirting the syrup on.

She ate four bites. Now she's poking at what's left. Lifting the edges up with her fork. Dropping them with a heavy, wet *splat*.

Her hair's a rat's nest at the crown of her head, and she's wearing a nightgown with Tinkerbell on it that pulls too tight across her chest. A kid's nightgown on a teenager's body.

I need to get her new pajamas.

I push my chair back and stand, thinking I'll do the dishes. That way, I don't have to get annoyed at her for wrecking the breakfast I made.

"What are we doing today?" she asks.

The plan is to sort through our shit. Have a heart-to-heart and work it all out.

Frankie isn't aware of the plan yet.

I sit back down.

She's eased one elbow onto the glass top of the table and dropped her head so the pancakes are exactly at eye level. I watch as she lifts up the whole stack of pancakes and drops it down. *Splat.*

"You're gonna get syrup in your eyeballs doing that."

She glances over to check if I'm serious.

"I thought we'd just hang out at home," I say. "If it's okay with you."

"All day?"

"Sure, why not?"

"You're always making me do stuff on the weekends."

"I thought you liked doing stuff."

"Not all the time."

"We don't do stuff *all the time.*"

"Every weekend."

"You don't want to do stuff with me?"

She shrugs. Forks up her pancakes four or five inches. *Splat.*

"Was it fun over with Rikki and Laurie?" I ask.

"Yeah."

"What movies did you guys watch?"

"I don't know what they were called."

"What were they about?"

"There was one with these boys whose dad took them to an island and they killed him by accident."

"For real?"

"No, it was just a *movie*."

Her tone of voice says I could not possibly be more of a moron.

"Was it R-rated?"

"How should I know? It was from Russia. There were subtitles so you could understand what they were saying."

"What was the other movie?"

"It was like . . . I don't know how to describe it. Kind of old-timey, but it wasn't old, and there were boats and stuff? I couldn't figure out what was going on. Rikki said it was non-representational, which means it wasn't really about anything."

"What's the point of a movie like that?"

"It's what they were watching."

"I mean, is it supposed to be pretty to look at it, or some kind of commentary on the human condition, or what?"

She shrugs.

I wait a beat, but that's all I'm getting out of her. "Did you have bad dreams over there?"

"No. Why would I?"

"I don't know. Why wouldn't you?"

"It was nice," she says. "Their guest room has the softest blanket in the whole world, and one of those mattresses like on TV that's made of foam. When you lay down on it you sink in like you're going to sleep in an alien pod."

"I've never slept on one of those."

"It wasn't very comfortable. But it was cool."

Having temporarily forgotten she's supposed to be annoying me with the pancakes, she cuts off a sliver of a bite from the edge. Too sweet. I can tell by the way she chews slow and drinks a lot of water afterward.

"You want me to do the pancakes over?"

"Nah. I'm not that hungry."

"All right."

I get up to do the dishes. I place the stopper, squirt soap into the sink, watch steam rise off the stream of hot water coming from the tap. That was the longest conversation I've had with Frankie in ages, and I don't want to wreck it.

"West?" she says to my back.

"Yeah?"

"What did Mr. Gorham say?"

A real question about a real thing, asked in a civil tone of voice.

I could fucking *cheer*, it feels like such an accomplishment.

"He said he'll take care of things with this Clint kid. You won't have to sit near him on the bus anymore, or in class."

Silence.

"That's good, right?"

"Yeah," she says. "Thanks."

I swallow over a lump in my throat. "I didn't do much, but you're welcome."

While the bubbles rise in the sink, I think about what else there is to talk about. About how to get from surviving to thriving. I haven't got a clue, so I think about what Caroline might say.

"He wants to get you doing more gifted and talented stuff."

"He always says that."

"It sounds like he thinks it's pretty important."

"I don't want to do it."

I turn to look at her, trying not to let on how much

her statement worries me. My sister looks sallow under the kitchen lights. She's sitting with her arms and legs crossed, a stubborn frown fixed on the far wall.

"Sure you do," I say.

"No, I don't."

"Why not?"

"I just don't, okay?"

"No, look—"

And then I stop myself, because I can hear my volume rising, and no.

Not going to be that man.

I recognize the way she looks right now. I've felt that mask on my own face, that hard set to my jaw, that steel in my eyes. All I'm going to accomplish if I keep after her right now is to make her dig in further.

I don't know what her reasons are, but she's *got* them. Me and her—we're alike that way. So instead of giving her grief, I ask, "What *do* you want?"

Her eyes narrow. "What do you mean?"

"You didn't want pancakes for breakfast, you didn't want to move here, you don't want gifted and talented—what do you want, Franks? You want to go back to Silt? You want to take art lessons after school? You want me to find this Clint kid and punch him in the face? What?"

Her eyebrows are drawn in, her face sharp. "I want to go to my room," she says.

I close my eyes and breathe.

This is what I'm getting from her right now, and it's fine. It's not what I want, but I can live with it.

"I'm trying to do right by you," I say. "You know that."

She nods, slowly.

"So think about what I asked, and when you know the answer, tell me."

"Okay."

"Okay." And then, as though it's an afterthought—as though I haven't been thinking about how to tell her all morning—I say, "Caroline's coming over later."

"What for?"

"To study. And she'll probably stay for dinner."

"Good."

Frankie starts down the hall.

"She might stay the night."

Frankie stops on her threshold. "Like, in your room?"

I clear my throat. "Yeah."

"Gross."

Then she disappears, closes the door shut behind her, and I'm standing there like a jackass, unsure whether to count that conversation as a success or a failure.

There's snow flurries that afternoon. It's too early for snow.

I'm watching them fall in fuzzy, lazy swoops when I see Laurie come out of the house and go into his workshop.

Frankie's in her room. She came out a few minutes after our talk, asked me for a ruler and some paper from my art class sketchbook, and then returned to her cave. Later, she emerged again and said her pencils all sucked and she had to use the set I bought for my art class.

I gave her one of them and the sharpener. She disappeared.

Bored with my reading, I text Caroline.

It's snowing, FFS.

She texts back, I noticed.

When are you coming over?

Little while. I'm writing.

You think the roads are slippery?

It's melting, Oregon boy. Too warm for it to stick.

Come over, then.

What are you doing?

Reading about Stalin.

How's Stalin?

Megalomaniac. How are the Irish?

Such a problem.

Come over.

I need to finish this draft.

Come over.

Yeesh.

I grin.

An hour?

Two.

Bah.

You'll survive, darling.

Call me that later when I'm fucking you.

In your dreams.

I know, right?

Quit texting me or I'll never finish.

See you in 1 hr. 58 min.

GOD.

Satisfied, I put the phone down. Frankie comes out with a paper in her hand.

"What?" she says.

"What what?"

"Your face." She points.

I run my hand over my mouth and chin. I'm still smiling. "Caroline's coming over," I report.

"You told me that already."

"Yeah."

She shifts from foot to foot. "So I guess she'll be over a lot now, huh?"

"She might."

"You know, she was my friend first."

"She was my *girlfriend* first."

"But that was a long time ago."

"It was last spring."

"And you fucked it up."

"Who told you I fucked it up?"

She rolls her eyes. "Like anybody needed to tell me."

"Yeah, well, I fixed it, so now we're gonna have to share her."

"Will she still pick me up from school?"

"I think you better ask her that when she gets here."

"She's coming now?"

"In a couple hours."

Frankie waves the paper at me. "I want to run over and give this to Rikki."

"Can I see?"

She flips the paper over and shows it to me. It's a portrait of a woman—glamorous, all hair and lips like a fashion model. It's shaded and intricate, with decent perspective. Fucking impressive. Way better than her other drawings.

"You made that?"

"Rikki showed me how. You just make a grid on the magazine and then you make a bigger grid on the picture, and you draw it one square at a time. It's easy. It's not really like drawing at all."

She hands it to me, and I can see the faint gridlines now and some details that aren't quite right—a squinty eye, the jewelry cartoonish where Frankie drew what she thought it was supposed to look like instead of what it actually looks like. Still. "This is amazing."

"No, it's not."

"Franks—"

"Can I take it over to Rikki's?"

"Yeah, if you get dressed first." I give her the picture back. "Would you make me one next?"

"Why?"

"I don't know. Just to have it."

"I guess so. Sure."

"Great."

She leaves the room, and I hear a dresser drawer open. When she comes out, she's wearing jeans—normal jeans, not huge ones—and a giant sweatshirt. She opens the front door. "You should draw your own," she says. "It's really easy. I could show you how."

I follow her to the door. "After dinner. I'd like that."

She smiles up at me.

"Careful on the steps," I say. "It's snowing."

"Okay, Grandpa."

I watch her make her way down, one hand gliding over the powder on the railing. Then she's off, running across the yard without a coat, snow falling in her hair.

Laurie's moving around in the space outside his workshop. I wanted to talk to him, so I throw on a coat and head down the stairs myself.

I find him buried to the elbows in a big gray metal box on stilts, peering through a small glass window while a compressor hums loud over a low hissing sound that stops and starts, stops and starts.

I don't come out here much, and when I do it's usually because I'm grabbing Frankie for hanging around too long. I don't blame her for wanting to hang around, though. Laurie's workshop is sweet. It's like a barn crossed with a carport. Inside, there's a space like a hayloft full of rusted-out pieces of scrap metal and a row of stalls that makes me think the place was a stable once. Each stall holds a different kind of supplies—wood and metal, ceramics, rubber, glass.

The open-air part under the carport roof is where he does welding. There's a big compressor just inside the door, propane tanks, face shield, huge gloves, I don't know what-all else.

I'm still trying to figure out what the fuck the story is with the gray metal box when the compressor kicks off and he steps back.

"Hey, West," he says.

"Hey, Professor Collins."

"Laurie."

I can't call him Laurie to his face. It's not only because he's a professor—it's also because he's my landlord *and* he's got a Wikipedia page that calls him an *internationally acclaimed multimedia three-dimensional artist*.

"What is that thing?" I ask.

"Sandblaster."

"What are you blasting?"

"Glass."

He withdraws his arms, unscrews the wing nuts on either side of the window he was looking through, and extracts a beige shape.

"That's . . . what is that?"

"It's a hammer."

"A glass hammer." It's almost entirely wrapped in masking tape, like a hammer mummy with just the round surface you hit with and the bottom of the handle showing. "What for?"

"It's a series. Tools. This one's just a study—I have a commission to do a big one. But the logistics are a pain in the ass."

He takes his mummy-hammer inside the barn. I hear water running. I edge closer to the sandblaster, curious what it looks like inside.

There's a brass-colored nozzle attached to a hose laying on top of an open plastic grid. The nozzle must shoot sand at the glass, and then the sand falls off and through the grid to come out the hole in the bottom.

Neat.

Laurie comes back out drying his glass hammer with a paper towel, a roll of masking tape dangling from his fingers. Unwrapped, the hammer is aqua blue, shining, and I want to touch it. I want to wrap my fingers around the handle and pound something with it—which is all wrong, because it would shatter if I did that, and I'd be fucking disappointed.

It reminds me of Studio Art last week, how Rikki was debating with Raffe about what art is. Raffe said art has no purpose—that if something *has* a purpose, it's not art. And Rikki said the opposite. That the purpose of art is to make you feel or think, and a lot of the time both.

Art provokes a response, she told us. *Be provocative.*

"You want to try the sandblaster?" Laurie asks.

"Sure."

"Give me a minute to mask it again." He wraps tape over the polished surface of the hammer, leaving one strip around the handle bare. "So what we're doing is blasting off the polish to give it a frosty surface." The hammer is heavy when he hands it over. I touch the strip, cool glass beneath my fingertip.

"Put it inside there," he says. "Careful with it, though—I had that thing in the kiln more than a week."

"Just to cast it?"

"Yep. You have to bring the temperature up slowly, hold it there, bring it back down just as slow. Otherwise it'll crack, explode, God only knows. Glass is fussy. Took me eleven tries to get that hammer."

Eleven tries. A week in the kiln for each one. This thing is worth a fucking fortune in fuel and labor.

I place it on the grating carefully, close the observation window, and push my hands into the gloves. They're bulky. The nozzle is hard to hold on to. When I first pull the trigger, the hammer jumps from the compressed hit of air, and I almost drop it.

"Good," Laurie says. "Just do that back and forth evenly."

"For how long?"

"Until it's done."

It's meticulous work, satisfying. After I get the hang of it, I relax enough to say, "I wanted to thank you for watching Frankie last night."

"No thanks necessary. It was fun."

"She behaved herself, I hope?"

"Always," he says. "And I was happy to see your truck wasn't out here when I went to bed."

A minute passes. Laurie comments, "Rikki says you're doing well in Studio Art."

"I'm spending three times as long on that class as everything else, just praying to get out of there with a B."

"She says you have an interesting mind."

"I have the least interesting mind in there."

"What makes you say that?"

I tilt my head toward the sandblaster. "This kind of stuff is easy for me. Machines, problems, figuring out one step after the next. But Rikki wants me to be creative, and I'm not."

Laurie seems to accept this. He's quiet for a while. Then he asks, "You ever use a wheel to grind glass?"

"No."

"Want to try?"

I do.

I want to see the kiln, too, and find out what it costs to run it for a week. Ask what happens when you scale it up—what kind of logistics problems does he mean? How's he going to cast a giant hammer? Can he make it in pieces?

"I'd better get back to my reading," I say.

I draw my hands out of the box and turn the art back over to the artist.

He takes the hammer and holds it lightly with his finger-tips, flipping it one way and the other.

"How's the factory?" he asks.

"I'm giving notice. I need to find something where I'll be home more with Frankie."

"You want to work for me?" he asks. "I need an assistant. Flexible hours. Decent money."

"What kind of work?"

"Stuff like this. Finishing. Polishing. Answering email or phone calls. Whatever I don't feel like doing, to be honest. I'm behind on this commission. I could use the help."

"Shouldn't you hire an art major?"

He waves the hammer in dismissal, making me worry he's going to drop it. "I've been trying, but I can't find any who know fuck-all about tools. You seem like you know tools. And like I said, Rikki thinks your mind is interesting."

"I guess—yeah. I would. As long as you know what you're getting. You need references or something?"

He laughs. "You're twenty-one years old, you're raising your kid sister, studying your ass off, doing night shifts at a window factory. You could be an ex-con and I'd still proba-bly hire you. Under the table, though, okay? I don't want to deal with taxes."

He holds out his hand.

I shake it.

I mean, fuck, of course I shake it. Even if the money's only so-so, the job's perfect.

But when his fingers grip mine, I'm not thinking about Frankie or the paycheck. I'm thinking about what's inside that workshop.

Compressors and welders and kilns, polishing equipment, all kinds of shit I don't know the names of. Tools to learn how to use. Systems to work out.

It takes me a minute to figure out why my heart's beating so fast. It's been such a long time.

I'm excited.

That night, Caroline's in my bed.

She sits with her back cushioned by my pillow, her hair down over her shoulders and her arms, tongue toying with her tooth gap, typing on her laptop.

I'm at the desk, supposedly studying for a Spanish quiz, but Spanish is easy. Caroline is right there. *On my bed.*

"Quit looking at me," she says. "I'm trying to think."

"It's late."

"It's only eleven."

"Frankie's sleeping. It's late."

Fingers hovering over the trackpad, she smirks. "I'm almost done."

"You said that an hour ago."

"Maybe I want you to spend some time wanting what you can't have."

"I been wanting what I couldn't have since I went back to Oregon last March."

She takes her hand off the trackpad. "You could've had me, though," she says. "All you had to do was ask."

I drop my feet from the desk and clasp my hands together.

I promised her no bullshit, but it's hard to know how to find explanations without it.

I owe her an explanation.

"I never wanted to leave Silt," I say.

But that's not what I mean.

I take a breath, try again. "I never *wanted* to, because it never seemed possible. When I was a kid, I was too young to aim that high. I wanted to get through the day, the week, whatever. I wanted to get enough to eat, or if my dad was around, to not get beat. Or I wanted my mom and dad to get married, because I had this idea that things would get better if they were married. But then Frankie was born, and by the time I was old enough to think about leaving, I knew I couldn't leave without her. So when I dreamed about what I wanted to happen, it was always about *her* leaving."

Caroline puts her laptop down on the floor by the bed. Pats the spot next to her on the mattress.

"In a minute," I say. "I want to get this out first."

Rubbing my hands together, I reach for the words. "When I came here my first year—I wasn't really here, I think. My body was here, but my head was in Silt, with Frankie, and everything I did my first two years—everything with you— it's like I let myself get close to what I wanted, but I wouldn't really *take* it. I was following this plan for what I was sup- posed to do that was all about what Frankie was going to need me to be. And you—God, I was so fucking hard on you, pushing and pushing you away when you were *all I wanted*. I felt like I had to do that, because I wasn't *here,* right? I had to convince myself I wasn't here so I could be *there,* with her."

"West, come sit by me."

"I'm almost done."

She walks over and knocks at my hands until I move them apart. Then she straddles my lap. She puts her palms on my shoulders, resting comfortably on my thighs. "You were too far away," she says. "Now you can tell me the rest."

I wrap my arms around her and hold her first. Feel how soft she is. Move her hair behind her shoulders and inhale against her neck.

"So you went back to Silt," she says.

"Yeah, but before that, when we got together, those weeks last spring—you have to understand, Caro, then I *was* here. I was with you, and being with you was the only thing I'd done that was just for me in . . ."

"Forever," she says.

"*Ever,*" I reply. "It was the only thing I'd done for me *ever.*"

"And then you went back to Silt."

"You saw what it's like there. There's no place for me to want anything. It's just what I can want for Frankie. At least, that's how it feels. Maybe that's not how it is. Maybe I could've called you up, said, 'Come help me do this,' and we would've been okay there, but it didn't feel like anything I could let myself do."

"Tell me how it felt."

She's stroking my head, my neck. I'm so tense, my back teeth ache.

"It felt like if I tried to do that, I would ruin you. Not even that *I* would be doing it. That Silt would, my family, just the way it is there—where I come from ruins people. Good people. And I'd have to watch it happen. I'd be responsible for it, because I wanted you and drew you to me across all those miles. I *couldn't.*"

I get my hands in her hair and kiss her. "I couldn't."

She smiles, but it's the sad kind, the kind that hurts. "You were ten when Frankie was born."

"Yeah."

"The same age she is now."

"Mmm-hmm."

"Do you ever think about that—your sister with a baby?"

"Christ. No."

"But it's the same, right? If Frankie were in your shoes, if she had a baby brother born and nobody to take care of him but her—"

It gives me chills. "Don't."

She runs her hands up and down my arms, warming away the goose bumps. "It's cruel even to think about, isn't it? She's a kid. She's too young. But so were you."

"I was old enough."

"You were always as old as you had to be. That's the part that breaks my heart." She resettles herself on my lap, pressing closer. "How old were you when you met the Tomlinsons?"

"Sixteen."

"How old the first time? With Mrs. Tomlinson?"

I didn't tell her. She never asked me directly, and I avoided the subject, never wanting her to have to think about me fucking an older woman, a married woman, a woman I gave what she wanted so she'd give me what I needed.

I fucked Mrs. Tomlinson because that was what I had to do to get out of Silt.

Caroline knows it.

She's figured it out. I can see it in her eyes.

"Baby, don't you think—"

"How old?" she repeats.

I blow out a long exhale. "Sixteen."

"Did you want her?"

"She was pretty. I wasn't a virgin."

"But she was the one who initiated it."

"Yeah, I wouldn't have . . ."

I'm forced to stop, the memory choking me hard for a second. How fucking terrified I was the first time in her car, when she sucked me off in the parking lot of the golf course and I watched out the window for Dr. T to drive up. How scared I was to say no, how furious that I had to say yes.

Furious at how I responded to her when I knew even at sixteen that she couldn't be right in the head. That what she wanted from me wasn't sex—it was something else. Some hit of power, of danger.

I was so furious at Dr. T for not knowing about it. For never putting a stop to it. It would've ruined my chance at Putnam, but there were times I still wished to fuck he'd figure it out.

Resting my head against Caroline's shoulder, I breathe in the scent of her hair. "She was his wife," I say. "And I already knew he could be my ticket out of there if I played it right."

"It's illegal what she did to you."

"I consented."

"Sixteen-year-olds can't consent to sex with adults. You were indebted to her, afraid of her husband and what you would lose if you told her no."

Something in her tone tells me it's a question, and she needs the answer. Not for herself, but for me. She needs *me* to acknowledge that what she's saying, this story she's telling—it's my story.

It is.

But I never saw it that way. I never let myself see it that way. I just thought about it as what I had to do, and I didn't let myself wonder why Rita Tomlinson wanted to fuck a minor or what it meant for me that I was the minor she decided to fuck.

"Yes," I whisper.

"West?"

I lift my head and say it again. "Yes."

"If that happened to your sister in six years—"

Rage. Shame. All over me. God, this is why I don't do this, why I never wanted to do this, because it's too fucking awful. "Please don't."

"I want to make sure you hear me."

"I hear you. But don't go there. Please."

She strokes her hands over my head, down my neck, across my shoulders, along my arms. My chest. My back. Everywhere she can reach.

She holds me, and it helps. Slows me down. Brings me back into my body.

Even though my life before her isn't something she can fix, it helps.

"That's why I don't want to hear it," she says. "I don't want to hear you tell me how worthless you are, or why you're sorry for what you did to me with that woman. I know what you did and what it meant. I *know*. And it wasn't about sex. It was about—God, I don't even have the word for it. Hopelessness. Despair."

"I used sex to make you leave me. It was . . . that was something special between us. Sacred, even. And I turned it into a weapon. Turned it on you."

"What else did you have to use?" she asks.

It's like thawing from a freeze. It *burns*. It takes my breath away, and I have to drop my head again and breathe.

It's harder than I thought it would be.

Harder still when she says, "It hurt me so bad, West. I don't want you to think I'm being Mother Teresa here, pretending it didn't."

I'm shaking. "Caro."

"No, I should say this. I should level with you, because it hasn't stopped hurting. Sometimes I think about it and I can't stand it, like I really can't *stand* it, and I have to do something to get out of my head or I'll just be so full of hate. So mad at you. I don't know if I was ever as mad at Nate, even, because what he did was nasty, but what you did was so fucking *personal*."

I expect her to draw farther away from me.

She puts her arms around me instead. Her hot cheek presses against my neck.

"What helps," she says, "is when I'm looking out the window of the truck and seeing you with her, sometimes I can flip that. So I'm looking *in* it, at me. Imagining what you were feeling to make you do that. And you know, West, it's fucking awful from that direction, too. It *hurts*. I almost can't stand it, because it means I have to accept how badly I failed *you* when you went home to Silt. How badly everyone failed you."

"I wasn't your responsibility."

"You were," she says. "You were, and you still are. And the good thing is, when I put myself outside the truck, after I do it, I'm not . . . I'm still mad, but I'm mad at the whole world, you know? I'm just as mad *for* you as I'm mad *at* you, and I can kind of see how it will be easier to feel that way next time. That eventually, it's the only way I'll feel. That Silt was this awful thing that happened to both of us together, instead of something you did to me." She kind of laughs. "I mean, I'm not quite there yet. But I'm trying."

"I'm sorry," I tell her. "More sorry than you'll ever know."

"I know you are," she says. "I'm sorry, too. But now you're here."

"I'm trying to be here. I'm trying so hard."

She holds me. We stay like that until I can breathe again, and I start to feel more than just guilt and shame.

Until I can feel her warmth and smell her body.

Caroline on my lap. My dick wakes up.

It seems fucked-up that it's even possible for me to want her after what we just talked about, but I do. And she wiggles against me, letting me know she wants me, too.

"So tell me something, West," she says. "What do you want?"

No way Caroline can know I asked Frankie the same thing over pancakes this morning.

No way can she know that nobody ever asks me that. Nobody but her.

She kisses along my jaw. "What do you want, West?" she whispers.

She kisses my eyebrows and my forehead and the tip of my nose. "What do you want?"

I take her chin and guide her mouth to mine. I grab hold of her sweater.

I'm going to show her.

The sweater is long—down below her hips when she's standing up—and I pull it off over her head because I like the contrast of the waistband of her black leggings against the pale skin of her stomach. Her bare breasts and her soft cotton-covered thighs.

"I thought about you like this in Silt," I say.

"Oh, yeah?"

"When you were staying at my grandma's. That time I was over for dinner, sitting by you on the couch, it was all I could fucking think of—getting just enough of your clothes off to put my mouth on you. Slide my fingers inside you."

"We were in a room full of people."

"I know. All day at work, you were texting me, trying to get under my skin, and I was thinking about getting you upstairs alone at Joan's on those mismatched pieces of carpet. She still have those?"

"Yeah. You had a lot of plans."

Not plans. Urges. Needs.

Impulses I kept shutting down, because I was so sure I had to.

"At the airport, I saw you before you even came outside," I confess. "You were fussing with your bag behind the glass, and I wanted you to stay right there so I could watch you. You looked amazing. You looked like . . ."

Like water in the desert. Like color in a black-and-white movie.

Stupid clichés. She looked like Caroline. Like herself.

I could hardly believe she was real.

"I drove twenty miles over the limit all the way to Eugene," I say.

She drops her forehead onto mine. "You idiot."

"I knew as soon as you came through the door, I'd ruin it. There wasn't any way not to ruin it, and it made me so fucking angry, so that's what you ended up seeing when you did come outside. How angry I was at the world for making me and you impossible."

"We're not impossible." She tilts her hips into me. "We're right here."

I smooth my hands over her ass. "I should've just told you how bad I wanted you. How I wanted you in the truck on the way from the airport. At the funeral home in that family room with the door locked. How I couldn't stop thinking how you'd bite your wrist if I bent you over the back of the couch. Bite my shoulder if I lifted you up against the inside of the bathroom door."

Her pupils are huge. "You looked at me sometimes like . . . but you wouldn't *talk* to me."

"I felt so black. So *dark*. And it wasn't right, you know? It was sick to want you like that, to want some quick fuck when you were trying to help me."

"Maybe it would have made you feel better."

"It would have made me feel like complete shit. And that sounded good, too—getting something I wanted that much, then getting punished for it."

She kisses me. Sinks down onto me, grinds herself against me, licks over my lip, and bites it. "What do you want?" she whispers.

This time it's a taunt. A tease.

This is all I want. Just this.

This is the only thing I ever wanted for myself.

"Let your hair down," I say. She unwraps the elastic she's got it bundled up in. It falls down over her back and shoulders, and I gather it in my hands. "It's so long."

"I've been thinking of cutting it."

"I like your hair."

"You want me to leave it long?"

"I'll buy you some pearl combs."

She smiles, resting her hands on my shoulders.

I lift the hair away from her neck and kiss where it makes her shiver. Kiss her throat. Cup her breasts.

She feels so good against me. I'm too full, and touching her helps—just the weight of her pushing my thighs down, the sight of her bare tits and her skin, her big brown eyes right on me. "What else do you want?" This time when she asks, it feels bigger, and my throat gets full and tight because I don't have any way to know.

Other guys my age—they've been figuring out the answer to that question for years. They've got interests and hobbies and talents and goals. They've got fantasies, ambitions, resentment when the world doesn't fall at their feet.

I have no idea what I want, not beyond this moment, but this moment is expanding around us. This moment is endless. It ripples out, broadening with every movement of her hips as she rises and settles, rocking against my thighs.

"I want you to look at me," I tell her.

She brushes her lips over mine. "I'm looking at you."

"Right at me," I say, gathering up her hair again, brushing the feathered ends up and down her shoulder blades, the column of her spine, making her arch and shiver. "The whole time."

Her smile is shy, her cheek warm against the back of my hand. " 'The whole time' implies duration."

"Mmm-hmm."

That smile. "Duration of what?"

"The whole time I'm fucking you."

She lifts her breasts in her palms and rubs her thumbs over the nipples, offering them to me. "All right."

"Stand up."

I peel off her socks and her tights. I ease my fingers beneath the elastic of her panties at each hip bone and slide them around and down, following the curve of her ass, tickling across the top of her upper thighs.

Her pupils are bottomless black. She watches as I kiss her navel. As I lift her hands off my shoulders, link our fingers together, pull her arms behind, and capture her wrists loosely at the small of her back in one fist while I work her panties down to the floor.

I stop wherever I want to test her flesh against my tongue. Firm and lean over muscle, stretched over bone, soft and yielding at her inner thighs.

Her ribcage lifts under my hands, her nipples harden under my palms. I love her body, her face, her smile, the breath moving in and out of her—love her heartbeat and the way it quickens, the way she gasps when I lick over her nipple.

I love her. Caroline Piasecki.

I always will.

"Keep your hands there."

Her mouth is slack, her gaze soft, her hair falling all around her. I pull it forward from the back to make a curtain around my head. Kiss her stomach. I hold her ass in my hands, wrists brushing her knuckles, suck her nipple into my mouth and draw on it, flick my tongue over it, rhythmic and fast, relentless.

I can smell what I do to her.

If I weren't in the shadow of her hair, I could see the desire in her eyes on mine, the warm pink spreading across her upper chest, the flush on her thighs. I grip the backs of them. Move my head into the light so I can lick into the heat and the wet and the mess I've made of her.

Lick into the heart of her, thinking she's mine, she wants to be mine, and whatever it is she sees in me, that's who I want to be. The best in me. The version of me that deserves a woman like her, fierce and strong and smart and loyal.

I could make her come, but I stop short of it, her hamstrings trembling. If I let her, she'd buckle at the knees, drop her hands to my shoulders, slump into me.

If I asked her to, she'd lie back on the carpet. She'd move to all fours and turn around and present.

She'd suck me. Pull me tight and hard until I came against her belly.

She'd let me take her from behind with a tight grip on her hips even though she never comes that way, not unless I touch her clit. She'd let me shoot over her low back, striping over her spine, her ass, the whitest skin of her body.

Thinking of everything Caroline would give me, I think of Rita Tomlinson. How she would direct me. Talk dirty to me, talk down to me, like I belonged to her—my fingers and my mouth her tools, the same muscles I used to carry her husband's golf bag available for her pleasure.

Do it, she would say. *Touch me. Take me. Harder. Faster. Now.*

I was never a person to her.

The first girl I ever fucked took me in a shed behind the trailer park laundry. She stuck her hand into my shorts, and her palm was clammy-hot. Her breath smelled like watermelon gum.

I was hard and willing, but it wasn't like this.

I liked it, what that girl did to me. What Rita did, I hated it, and I liked it, but I didn't *choose* it. Later, when I did choose, it was always fast and hard and impersonal.

Caroline's the only woman I've ever touched like this. The only one who's been my choice.

I don't want to see myself as the loser of a series of battles, all the odds stacked against me from day one, but it's hard not to wish I'd had more of this along the way.

More love. More touch.

More people who looked at me the way Caroline does, saw me like she does, asked me what I want.

I touch the loose fists of her fingers, and she grips my hands tight.

"Bed," I say, barely audible. "Get on the bed."

She does as I ask, clearing away the books. I turn on the closet light and flip the overhead switch off so it's quiet and dark and we can be just the two of us.

She watches me strip. Watches me crawl up over her, strokes my arms and my shoulders as I lower down to my elbows to kiss her.

"How come you're so much bigger?" she asks me.

"Landscaping. And lifting weights in Bo's garage." Burning off frustration and hatred. Trying to get rid of the habit of her, the knack for hope I'd picked up in Putnam.

"When I got off the plane and saw you," she says, "I thought you were scary."

"I felt scary."

She widens her thighs to bring me between them. Lifts her hips to rub hot swollen slickness over my cock. "You feel good to me now."

"That's all I want. To be good to you."

Her hand curls over the back of my neck. "Be good to me forever."

"I hope I get to."

She lifts her knees. Tips up her hips. Invites me inside. "We decide. You and me."

I kiss her, my tongue delving into her mouth, my boundaries dissolving. She kisses me, her fingertips digging into my shoulder blades, nails biting crescent moons into my back.

When I can stand to pull away, I back off so I can tell her, "I don't think I ever made a decision on you. It got made for me when we met."

"Same here. You'll recall I fainted."

"Oh, I recall."

"You were over top of me, just like this."

"Thinking dirty thoughts."

"Mutual dirty thoughts."

"Even while you were passing out?"

"I think I passed out from how dirty my thoughts were." I rest my forehead against hers, resisting the urgent message of my cock to make this happen now, now, now. She lifts her hips again. "You said you wanted to get inside me."

"It was hot out. I said I wanted to get you inside."

"It sounded like the same thing." Another hint from her hips. "Would you?"

"Get inside you?"

"Yes."

"We need a condom."

"Not really. I'm on birth control."

"I didn't . . . It wasn't like I tried to make you think. I wasn't fucking other women."

"Because you love me," she whispers.

"Because I love you."

It's the first time I've ever told her.

She already knew, though. She's known forever.

"I love you, too, West."

"After all that."

"You know I do." She tightens her arms around me. "Come inside me now."

She lifts.

I thrust.

Gliding, sinking, easy and hard at the same time, but perfect, because me and Caroline—that's who we are. That's the way we're going to be.

Deep, deeper.

Hard, harder.

Fast, faster.

Clutching, gripping, grabbing, pulling, kissing, holding on. There's nowhere to go and nowhere else we have to be.

This is what I want.

The first thing, the main thing—this woman in my arms, in my life. This woman next to me. As long as I've got her, I can figure out the rest of it.

I can do whatever I've got to do and be whoever I need to be to keep her.

TRUE GRIT

There's a reason they call it *falling* in love—because of the way it tips you ass over teakettle and then shakes your life up, hard.

Don't get me wrong. There's nothing like it. No better drug. No adventure more fantastic.

But it changes things.

It changes you.

I got West back that November and fell in love with him all over again. It was like that Gravitron carnival ride where you stand against a wall and they spin you and spin you until the floor drops away and you're stuck there by centrifugal force.

I never could stop myself from laughing on that ride. I'd try so hard to peel my hand off the side, lift my arm, wave at my sisters across the way. My oldest sister, Janelle, always tried fancy stuff, walking her feet up, posing kind of silly. Alison would be white-faced, scared.

I would laugh until my cheeks hurt, slain by the hilarity of my own helplessness.

It snowed early and often that winter, and West and I laughed so much. Talked so much. Fucked all the time, everywhere, completely helpless against the urge to put our hands on each other.

School. Sleep. Food. Sex. West.

I didn't have the strength for anything else. I was falling, swooping, drifting, whirling around.

Laughing.

When I finally hit the ground, I hadn't braced for the impact, but I was too dizzy, laughing too hard to care.

I wouldn't have changed the ride for anything.

When the phone rings, I'm on West's couch. I've got a library book in one hand, Frankie's head in my lap, and no way to reach my cell.

"Can you get that?" I ask.

She glances at the screen as she hands it to me. "It's your dad."

"Oh." My stomach sinks, and I'm hitting the answer button with my thumb when it occurs to me that the response has become ingrained.

When my dad calls, it's because he wants to talk about the case, and talking about the case makes me queasy.

I drive to Des Moines and my pulse picks up on the interstate.

I walk past my attorney's receptionist and start to sweat.

"Hey, Dad."

"Hi," he says. "I wanted to warn you, you're going to get a call in the next day or two from a staffer at State Senator Carlisle's office. They're interested—"

"You guys want to get Chinese for dinner?" West has wandered in from the kitchen.

"I thought you were making Sloppy Joe's," Frankie says.

"We're out of ketchup."

"I hate Chinese."

"You like those crispy things. Crab rangoon."

"Nuh-uh."

"You liked them last week."

My dad's still talking. "—bill might come out of it, and she thought—"

"Well, what *do* you want?" West asks.

"I want Sloppy Joe's."

"I already said we don't have ketchup."

"So go get some."

"By the time I got back from the store, it'd be—"

"Sorry, can you hang on a second?" I slide out from under Frankie's head and take my call into the bedroom.

As I pass by West, he finally notices the phone in my hand and mouths the word *Sorry*. I shake my head to indicate it's no big deal. As I step into his bedroom, I can hear him and Frankie resume their bickering.

"—say she was talking on the phone?"

"I thought you saw."

"Obviously I didn't. Who's she talking to?"

"Her dad."

"Jesus, Franks, and you didn't think maybe we should—"

The closing door cuts off the sound of their voices. I sit on the edge of the mattress.

"Okay," I say. "Repeat that last thing you were telling me?"

"Where are you?" my dad asks.

"At West's."

"Again?"

"Again." I scoot on the mattress until my back hits the wall, and then I stick my legs underneath the hideous comforter. I've slept here so many times now that it's beginning to feel like *my* hideous comforter. My room. Cozy and familiar.

"Caroline." My father packs a million admonitions into the three syllables of my name.

"Let's not start this, okay?"

Some days, I wish I'd never told him I was back together with West, because he *will not let it go*. West has always been and apparently will always be "that boy" to my dad. As in, *That boy is all wrong for you, That boy is trouble, That boy is going to break your heart,* and, lately, *That boy is a distraction you don't need.*

"The sister is there?" he asks.

"Her name is Frankie, Dad. She *lives* here."

"I'm not comfortable with it."

"You don't actually have to be."

"I was talking to Janelle, and—"

"Stop right there," I tell him. "Return to the reason you called. Or I will hang up."

That earns me another sigh, but it works.

Dad tells me there's gossip on the judge grapevine that Senator Carlisle is looking at introducing a law to criminalize revenge porn. Someone told someone who told my dad that I might be contacted as an expert witness.

Expert witness. The phrase gives me goose bumps.

I *want* to be an expert witness.

"I know your instinct is going to be to help with this," he says. "Normally, I'd support that, but we're in a delicate position with the case, and any testimony you share even informally might come back to bite us in the ass. If they find out that the Jane Doe in the suit is you—"

"I get it."

"Anything you say right now, Caroline—anything that might become public—" he warns.

"No, right, I get it. If they call, I'll be careful."

This is how lawsuits work: they limit your options, choke off your freedom to speak and act and be who you want, because you always have to be thinking about the jury in your future and how they might see your behavior.

"I'm not sure who gave them your name, even," he says. "We have to be cautious about your profile. This issue's starting to get a lot of attention, and if you become a spokesperson, get known as an activist, that affects our options down the road. We want to—"

"Dad, I *get* it. Thanks for the warning. You can stop now."

I can see him in my mind's eye. He's in his study at home, I'm sure, feet propped up on his desk, fingertips pressing into one temple, forehead creased in a frown.

Sighing.

"Okay," he says. "How's everything going with your classes?"

"Classes are fine."

"You have everything you need?"

"Yep."

"You should come down this weekend," he says. "We could see a movie."

"I can't." It's the truth, but I probably would have said the same thing even if it weren't. "I've got plans here. Thanks, though."

"All right. Well, call me if you hear from these people. Or . . . You know. If you need me for anything."

"I will."

West cracks the door open, looks in to see if I'm still on the phone.

"I've got to go, Dad," I say.

"Okay. Goodnight, sweetheart."

"Goodnight."

I hear him say, "I love you" as I'm hanging up, but it's too late to say it back.

West sits down next to me. He slides his hand down my blanket-covered leg and squeezes my toes. I wiggle them in his grip, relieved for no good reason that he's here.

"Everything okay?" he asks.

"Yeah. He just wanted to warn me about a phone call he thought I couldn't be trusted to handle without his advice."

"You sound testy."

"I *am* testy." I thought I'd established boundaries with my dad last year. I thought we had an understanding, but every time I turn around I have to remind him once more that I'm a grown-up now.

And then there were those two words: *expert witness.*

West drags his hand up my thigh. "Me, too. Frankie's driving me fucking nuts."

"Sorry. She doesn't do that with me."

"Because she worships the ground you walk on."

"It's a girl thing. I remember when I was her age, I was completely in love with my music teacher. She had long blond hair and wore silver jewelry and diamond studs, and she smelled like spicy perfume. I couldn't decide if I wanted her to be my mom or my girlfriend. She lived down the street from us and hired me to feed her cats when she was out of town."

"You don't even like cats."

"I know. But I spent hours in her house looking at all her stuff and thinking how I was going to have a place decorated exactly like hers someday, and I would dress like her and act like her. It would be impossibly glamorous."

West gives me a once-over. I'm wearing jeans and a ratty sweatshirt. I put my hair in a loose ponytail right after I showered this morning and left it there. Some of it's probably still wet.

"Impossibly glamorous, huh?"

"Shut up. Your sister thinks I'm glamorous."

"We both do. We can't help it. You're the most glamorous creature either of us has ever met."

I lean forward and shove his shoulder. He catches me under the arms and drags me over his body as he lies down. We end up crossways on the bed, laughing.

When he tries to pull me close enough to kiss, I resist.

"C'mon, princess," he whispers. "Cheer me up."

"In thirty seconds, your sister's going to be all, 'What are you guys doing in there? Eew! Gross! Knock it off!'"

"I know. We have to hurry up and do something really gross before she notices."

He tugs again, and I let him kiss me. His mouth is soft, his tongue hot and demanding. It takes about four seconds for me to forget why I'm supposed to be resisting his demands. Four more to get over my grumpiness.

I feel a slackening around my breasts and his hot palms move beneath the bra he's just unfastened. He cups my breasts, making my nipples ache.

The damp surge of need that follows makes me moan.

When Frankie knocks on the door, I'm far enough gone to be startled. I jump, and West pinches one nipple hard, which makes me hiss.

"Shh," he says. His other hand tightens on my ass, fingers digging low and deep and dirty, making the ache between my legs worse.

"West?" Frankie calls. "Are you ordering Chinese or not? I'm hungry."

"She's evil," I whisper. I tilt my hips and grind against his erection. He's so hard. If his sister weren't here . . .

But his sister's always going to be here.

"I know," he whispers back. "I'm a complete failure as a parent."

Frankie bangs on the door again. "You better not be doing anything gross in there!"

"Do you want Chinese?" he asks me.

"I'm fine with it."

"Yeah, but what do you *want*?"

I smile down at him. Rub myself against his erection. "That."

Grinning, he asks, "What do you want that you can actually have before Franks goes to bed?"

"To finish my reading."

"You want me to keep her out of your hair?"

"Nope."

"You'll tell me if she is."

"I'll tell *her* if she is. Remember? I deal with Frankie and me. You deal with Frankie and the rest of the world."

She pounds on the door again. "West? I'm starving."

"Lay off, will you?" he calls. "We'll be out in a second."

"What are you doing in there?"

"Putting away laundry."

"And I'm the Queen of Sheba."

He lifts an eyebrow and whispers, "Queen of Sheba? Where does she get this shit?"

"School?"

He takes me by the hips and lifts me off him. "I better order. You want chicken fried rice and an egg roll?"

"Yep. And an orgasm." He sits up quick and kisses me hard. By the time he's done, I'm breathless. "Make that two orgasms."

West flops down on the bed again, raking his hand through his hair. It's long enough now that it sticks up when he pushes his fingers through it, which means it's pretty much always sticking up. "You and me both."

"How many hours until bedtime?"

"Four."

I look at the clock. "Five, I bet. She hasn't been to sleep before ten all week."

He looks at the door.

He looks at my shirt.

Specifically, he looks at my nipples, then rubs his thumb back and forth over one. Back and forth, until I feel as though I'm turning to lava between my thighs.

"You're killing me," I whisper.

"No," he says. "I'm killing *me*."

Then I'm on my back again, and he's over me. "Keep quiet, and I'll give you that first orgasm right now."

I'm about to tell him it's not happening—not with his sister hovering out there—when he pulls my knee up and rocks into me, hard.

Oh. God. It's *so* happening.

"If you're not out in five minutes, I'm going to eat at Rikki and Laurie's," Frankie says through the door. "I'll tell them you starved me. I'll say you're locked in the bedroom making dirty noises, and—"

West picks up a book off the nightstand and throws it at the door.

"Hey!" Frankie shouts.

"We'll be out when we're done with the laundry," he says.

"Fine."

I hear her footsteps retreating down the hall.

"We really should go," I say, but it's completely half-hearted. I can't make myself mean it, because his eyes are blue in this light, dark and intent, and his hand is moving under my shirt.

"In a minute."

"One minute?"

"Maybe two."

"You can't make me come in two minutes."

"Watch me."

His thumb finds my nipple again. My eyelids droop. I can't keep them open—not when he's touching me like this. Kissing me this way. Not when he's unsnapping my jeans, lowering the zipper, finding me hot and wet and making me hotter and wetter.

He whispers dirty promises in my ear, licks and sucks me. He finds all my weak spots and exploits them.

"Ninety seconds," he says after I come. There's laughter in his voice. "Easy."

"Don't call me easy," I rasp.

I sound so weak and soft, exhausted as though I've run a marathon when all I've actually done is breathe hard, tighten up against West's fingers, and bite down on the noise while he makes my body sing.

West chuckles, clasping my wrists in his hands and collapsing on top of me.

We've only got thirty seconds left before Frankie's back at the door, but they're sweet.

So sweet.

By the time I get off the phone with the senator's aide, I'm smiling. This is the third time I've talked to him this week and the first call when I felt like I was making solid progress.

"How are my toes coming along?" I ask Frankie.

"I'm doing the second clear coat."

"Sweet."

She concentrates on the motions of the little black nail-polish brush. I look up at the kitchen ceiling, walking back through the conversation.

I forgot to talk to him about fraud. All those sites that take customers' money with the promise of wiping their reputations online—someone needs to stop that. I lost a bucketload of West's money to one of them. And I need to see if—

"Who's Jane Doe?" Frankie asks.

"Hmm?"

"Who's Jane Doe?"

It takes a minute for my attention to settle on the question. "It depends. It's a name the government uses when they don't know who someone is. Like, if you find a dead body and can't identify it, if it's a man, it's John Doe, and if it's a woman, you call her Jane Doe. But in legal cases, you use those names for when the victim wants to keep her identity a secret."

"You told that man on the phone not to use the word *victim*."

"I did. I like the word *target* better. But usually when we talk about crime, we talk about perpetrators and victims."

Carefully, she brushes polish over my big toe. "So you were a victim, but you don't want anyone to know?"

"Well, not exactly."

"But you're Jane Doe. That's what West said."

"For me it's just a strategy," I tell her. "It's a way of keeping the records of the case sealed."

Frankie puts the brush back into the bottle and twists the cap closed. "I wish I could do that."

"Do what?"

"Make it so no one knows about Clint."

"Is he still bothering you?"

"No, he stays away from me now. He has to. But when Mr. Gorham came to our class to talk about bullying, I think it was kind of like Jane Doe? Because he didn't use my name or anything, only everyone knew he was talking about me anyway. I wish I could just . . . I don't know. Erase what happened. Start over."

"I know how you feel." So much of last year, I wanted to erase what happened to me. "But you know," I say carefully, "when bad stuff like that happens, sometimes it can be good, too. Like, last year, this guy I used to care about, he wanted me to feel like I didn't matter—like I was a bad person, and I deserved bad things to happen to me. So he did something to embarrass me online. And it worked. I felt awful. But then I figured out that he was wrong about me, and that *he* was the one who had a problem, not me. And it made me stronger."

"How?"

"It's hard to explain. I guess it's that I don't think anyone's ever going to be able to do to me again what that guy did. I'm sure I'll get hurt other ways, but not *that* way."

I don't realize until after the words are out of my mouth that I'm not just talking about Nate. I'm talking about West, too.

If it weren't for Nate's attack, I wouldn't have been able to deal with what West did to me in Silt. But I *can* deal with it. Because I'm stronger.

I'm different.

And I'm glad for it.

"You know what I figured out?" I ask. "That only *I* get to decide what my actions mean. Only *I* get to choose how I feel about who I am and what I did. *I* get to define what I'll accept and what I won't. And that goes for you, too. You're in charge of your life."

She wrinkles her nose. "West is in charge of my life."

"He's in charge of keeping you alive and fed and all that, and making sure you have a chance to learn stuff and become a good person. You're in charge of everything else. And you know, what Clint did, that sucks. It should never have happened. I'm sorry it *did* happen. But the thing to remember is, he was the one with the problem, not you. You were the one who fought back. Not in the most constructive way possible, I think we can agree . . ."

She cuts me a glance. Smiles when she sees I'm smiling.

". . . but you know you have it in you. You can stand up for yourself and take down the guy who's threatening you. And that has to feel pretty good, right?"

Frankie nods. "He's afraid of me now."

"Awesome. Just so long as you don't use your mighty fists again, right?"

"Right." Frankie tilts her head, thinking. "Is the guy who tried to hurt you afraid of you?"

I see it in my head—Nate passing me on my way home from class. Glancing to the side so he doesn't have to meet my eyes.

"I think he kind of is, actually. But what matters to me even more is that *I'm* not afraid of *him*." I wiggle my toes. "Are these done?"

"Yeah, but you can't walk around for a while."

"You want to make some popcorn?"

"Movie style?"

"Is there any other way?"

"No."

"You'll have to do the hard work, though," I say. "Since I can't move."

"I know how."

Frankie skips over to the cabinet to get out the air popper.

Skips.

I wish West could see her. I'll tell him later tonight, when he gets back from working with Laurie.

I'll tell him all of this, because it will help remind him that even though she's struggling, his sister is amazing and resilient.

So am I.

Bridget uses tongs to pick four hard-boiled eggs out of the bowl on the salad bar.

"Can you make some for me?" I ask.

"Sure." She adds three more eggs. "Are you going to do a sandwich?"

"Maybe just on crackers."

"Okay. Pick me up some bread, and I'll get the mayo."

It's halfway through December, and we're in the dining hall, grabbing lunch between classes. This has been our Wednesday thing since freshman year, and even though we're both off the meal plan, eating most of our meals at the house, we still do Wednesdays.

Or we try to. I missed last Wednesday because I had to go to Iowa City for depositions with my lawyer in the afternoon. Those weren't too bad, but this morning I had to get up at the ass-crack of dawn and drive to Iowa City again, this time to be deposed by Nate's legal team.

November belonged to West, although I spent a couple days with my dad at Thanksgiving.

December belongs to the case.

"You want me to get your drinks?" Bridget's scooping low-fat mayo into a bowl.

"Yeah, maybe two waters and a skim milk?" The dining

hall uses these tiny glasses, so you have to take three or four to get enough liquid.

I carry the drinks, bread, crackers, and the bowl of soup I got on the line over to the table by the window where Bridget and I like to sit. She's already there, mashing up hard-boiled eggs with a fork. There's a pile of finely diced dill pickle on a plate. I slide into my seat and reach for the celery stalk.

I dice with a butter knife, remembering the first time I saw her make egg salad with ingredients off the salad bar. It was just a few days into first-year orientation. I was so glad, then, to have been assigned to Bridget by the housing gods, because here was a girl with ideas.

Here was a friend who was smart and kind and matched to me in every way that mattered.

She finishes mixing mayonnaise into the bowl of eggs. "I can take that celery."

I pass her the plate, and she tips the diced celery in, along with the pickle, salt, and pepper.

"How was your lawyer thing?" she asks.

"Horrible."

"What was it like?"

"They asked me every question fourteen times, and most of the time I wasn't allowed to answer. When I was, I had to say whatever one thing I'd rehearsed with the lawyer, and then Nate's lawyer would say something to make it sound like I was a crazy slut."

"God."

"I know. But it was exactly the way my dad told me it would be, so I knew what to expect."

"Does that help?"

"What?"

"Knowing what to expect?"

I shrug, because the cry-pressure is building behind my eyes, and I should be tougher than this. I *am* tougher than this. "It just turns out that when smart, rich guys in suits spend hours asking you questions designed to make you feel like a crazy slut, it's really hard not to start feeling like a crazy slut."

"You're not a crazy slut. We don't even *believe* in sluts."

"I know. But it's still hard. It's, like, *superhuman* difficult."

"Did you cry?"

"In the car on the way home."

"But not in front of the lawyers?"

"No, but only because we took two breaks so I could pull myself together."

"Can't you get out of doing this?"

"Only if we withdraw the suit."

"But you're not thinking about that."

"I don't know. I don't know if I'm thinking about it."

I haven't let myself think about it.

But I keep hearing what Frankie asked me. *So you were a victim, but you don't want anyone to know?*

It feels wrong.

I've always believed I could do whatever I put my mind to, but if I want to get into law school with my sex pictures on the Internet—if I want to get *through* law school and out the other side, to practice and advocate for social justice, to run for office and become a legislator and change the world for the better—what do I have to do to make that happen?

My dad says this is what I have to do. Push through the suit. Wear the Jane Doe straitjacket.

I'm not so sure anymore.

At the long table to our left, a big group of students bursts into laughter.

I have to swallow, because my throat hurts. I wonder if I'm coming down with something.

"Caroline?" Bridget reaches across the table to cover my hand with hers. "Why are you doing this when it makes you so unhappy?"

I swallow again.

My throat aches, and my eyes fill with tears.

I don't have an answer.

I wake up in the dark. The clock reads 2:48 a.m.

West is plastered against me, and he's way too hot. The air in his bedroom is dry from the space heater running in the corner. I have one nostril that's completely blocked, and the other is so desiccated I can only inhale a thin stream of over-warm oxygen.

There's no way I'm getting back to sleep.

When I try to wiggle out from under his arm, it tightens for a second. "Where you going?" His voice is husky with sleep.

"Just out to the living room."

"You need me to rub your head?"

It's my favorite way to fall asleep—West's fingers rubbing circles over my scalp. "Maybe later. I have to pee anyway."

"Come back soon."

"I will."

After I visit the bathroom, I stop in the kitchen for a glass of water, then pad out to the sofa. I wrap myself in the ratty afghan on the couch and sit in the dark.

Untethered, my mind wanders.

I pluck at the holes in the ratty old blanket, which I suspect West's grandma must have knit in the 90s. It's got the color palette—maroon and forest green.

In the bedroom, I hear West turn over, rustling the covers.

I think about the depositions. How terrible they made me feel.

I curl into a ball under the blanket and close my eyes.

A spring creaks.

Seconds later, a telltale floorboard groans, and then I hear water running in the bathroom.

By the time he comes into view, I'm sitting up again.

He's got nothing but boxers on, which seems crazy for December, but West's internal furnace runs hotter than mine.

He scratches his stomach. "Scoot over."

When I do, he sits down sideways and positions me between his outstretched legs.

"Pillow."

I hand him one. He sticks it behind his head, wraps me in his arms, and leans back, pulling me down with him, my body wedged between the couch and his skin, my head resting in the nook beneath his shoulder.

He feels good.

He smells good.

It's so good being with West.

I wish I could explain to my dad—to anyone who thinks I don't belong with this man—how I feel in moments like this one. Moments when the *rightness* of the two of us expands inside me, pushing out against the walls of my chest until what I'm experiencing is so much more than I can put in words.

Gratitude. Satisfaction. Contentment.

I don't know how to say it. There isn't any way. There's just this big, blissful feeling that I want to spend the rest of my life in.

West kisses the top of my head. "Pull that blanket up, would you?"

I raise it to cover my shoulders and his stomach, and then

from underneath I tuck it in along his side, pushing a few inches of blanket beneath his thigh, his stomach, his upper arm. I like to fuss over him, but not too much. Just a little bit, where he might not notice and get spoiled.

"Sorry I woke you up," I say.

"S'okay. What's going on in your brain?"

"Too much, apparently."

"Yep." He shifts his shoulders, settling us deeper into the couch. "Tell me."

"I talked to Paul again today," I say.

"Remind me who's Paul?"

"The senator's aide."

"Oh, right."

"So, I don't know. I was just thinking about it. Not about him, but more about what it's like when I'm talking to him. I feel like . . . like there are things I can tell him that no one else is going to. Things he doesn't get—doesn't understand properly—but I can change his mind."

"About revenge porn?"

"For starters, yeah. I think it's getting so I could change almost anyone's mind on that, if I had a clear shot at it. If they aren't, you know, a prejudiced jerk or whatever."

"I bet you could."

"And this is going to sound dumb, but I feel a little bit like I was *born* to do that."

His reaction is an exhale across the top of my head—a huff of pleasure and amusement. "Maybe you were."

I twist so I can see his face. "Maybe I was, West."

His eyes hold mine, steady and calm. There's no mocking in them.

He runs his hand up and down my back beneath my T-shirt. His palm is warm on my bare skin, but his eyes are warmer. So sure of me.

"He wants me to talk to the media," I confess.

"Who, the aide?"

"I guess the senator. They think their best shot at getting this passed is to start with a public education phase, and they want to set up interviews with major newspapers and some of the morning shows on local news in Des Moines and Iowa City, the Quad Cities . . . They want to put a face on revenge porn in Iowa."

"Your face."

"My face."

"Makes sense to me. You've got a beautiful face."

"My dad would shit a brick if I said yes."

"Yep."

"But I was thinking . . ."

"You were thinking you were gonna say yes."

I smile a little. I can't help it—it's nice to be known. I love that he knows me.

"I *want* to. What's the point of suing Nate, spending all this money trying to destroy *Nate,* if it means I can't do any of the other stuff I want to do? There's no point, right?"

"Right."

He squeezes me tighter. We lie there like that for a while, just breathing. West's hand warms the base of my spine.

"What do you want, baby?" he asks.

"Right now?"

"No. Down the road. Ten years, twenty years . . . what do you *want*?"

I hitch my leg up over his stomach and snuggle closer until I've got my face in his neck. I tell his throat, his pulse, "I want to be president."

His heart beats, steady and strong. I can feel him, alive against my lips.

"I've never said that out loud before," I admit. "Not since

I was a little girl and Janelle told me women don't get to be president, and that even if they did, I would never be the president because just how special did I think I was anyway? And she was right. I get it, how impossible it is. Even then, I got it. So I stopped saying it out loud, and I kind of stopped letting myself think that far ahead. I just think about, you know, law school, getting a job after, working my way into local office."

"But that's not where you want to end up."

"No, I want to end up in the White House. And I know I don't have a great shot at it, because nobody does. No woman does. And even if every other star in the universe lined up for me, with what happened last year, it's probably impossible. The way the world is—"

"Caro," he says.

"Yeah."

"Stop telling me why you can't have what you want."

My cheeks are hot. I'm breathing fast, just from admitting such a deep, foolish hope to him. From trusting him with that. "There are a lot of reasons why I can't have it."

"Well, yeah. But if you want Pennsylvania Avenue, baby, you should go for it."

"You think?"

"Fuck yeah, I think. You're smart and strong and gorgeous and talented. You're a leader—I always believed that. You need to do your leader thing, and that means you take what happened to you last year and you use it to change the world. Beat people over the head with it if you have to. Talk and talk until the world's got to listen. And then if you want to be president, what you have on your record is what happened to you and what you did about it. Nothing to be ashamed of."

His words wash over me like warm water. They wipe me

clean, leave me pure and righteous. Because what he said—
that's just exactly what I want to do. Just exactly how I want
my future to be.

"It's so big," I say. "It scares me."

"There's nothing wrong with being scared. Being scared
keeps you sharp. And anyway, you can break it down to one
ballot at a time. You've got my vote."

"That's good. Only 126 million to go."

"I have faith in you."

I wriggle up and kiss his jaw. "You're sweet."

He takes my cheek in his hand and traps me with his eyes.
He's so solemn. I can see how much he wants me to hear him
when he says, "I'm not doing you a favor, Caro."

My heart is full and my lungs feel bound up tight with
love and gratitude, fear and promise.

"I'm glad you told me," he says.

"I am, too."

I am, because now I know what comes next, and it doesn't
seem to matter that it will be hard. It's just the thing I've got
to do.

"I have to settle the lawsuit," I say. "It makes me feel like
shit, and it sucks up all this time and resources. I don't think
there's any point to it. When I go home for Christmas, I'm
going to tell my dad."

He smooths his hands over my hair. "Okay."

"And I'm going to call Paul back and tell him I'll do the
media stuff. Maybe I can do an interview for the school
paper and the paper in town. I could write some pieces for
online, too. Salon, or HuffPo? I'll have to look around at
where I might be able to do a personal essay kind of thing.
Or else—"

He pushes on the back of my head, brings me down to his
mouth, and kisses the words off my lips.

"What was that for?" I ask.

"You were getting loud. I don't want you to wake Franks up."

"I wasn't getting—"

He kisses me again, and he does it so well that I'm smiling when I stop to breathe. "Liar."

"Not to you," he says.

"You just wanted to kiss me."

That makes him smile. "Got me there."

This time, it's me who kisses him. My excitement becomes our excitement, the kiss sinuous and liberating, like running fast and falling down in the grass and looking up at the spinning sky.

I want to tell him more. Tell him everything I ever hoped for. All the ways I've let my ambition be taken from me, yanked from my fingers like so many papers flung onto the floor, scattered around my feet.

Sooner or later, I'll tell him everything.

He lifts me and carries me down the hall to our room. The blanket falls to the floor when he locks the door, but I'm not cold. Not with his body over me, his eyes on mine, his words inside me. *You've got my vote.*

I think, fleetingly, that the reason I don't need vengeance is that I have love.

Vengeance doesn't give you anything. It doesn't fill you up or soothe you, satisfy you or change you.

And even if it did, I don't need that, because my heart is already full. West's hands are on my ass, his lips on my neck, at my throat, on my collarbones, moving down. He's teasing me, smiling and calling me "Madam President," pulling my shirt off over my head and licking his way down my chest.

"President Piasecki," he says to my breastbone. "That's got a nice ring to it."

I close my eyes.

I'm twenty years old. I have a year and a half of college left. I'm supposed to be drinking too much, partying too much, playing rugby, studying abroad and sleeping around and figuring out what I want to do with my life.

I'm not supposed to know, already, that I want to spend the rest of my life with him.

But I do know that.

I know a lot of things.

"President Leavitt's got a nice ring to it, too," I say.

His eyes come up, a question in them. "You're not talking about me."

"President Caroline Leavitt," I say slowly.

I watch him get it. Understanding shows up on his mouth first—always his mouth—and creeps upward, over his cheek-bones, into his eyes. A surprised happiness he couldn't hide from me if he tried.

He doesn't try. He just grins and glides his hand down my stomach, right past the waistband of my pajama pants and into the wet heat of me, making me gasp.

"You'd make a hot first lady," I say, before he scatters what's left of my marbles.

"Bite your lip, baby."

I do. As he works his fingers inside me, I bite it hard enough that in the morning it'll be swollen, but that's fine. That little twinge of pain—that taste of blood—only height-ens the pleasure.

He makes me come with his hand, and then he moves in-side me and makes love to me so slow, so quiet, for so long that I feel another orgasm begin to build. That dragging sweaty sweetness swelling between us. When it's rising up, starting to sharpen, he draws me to my knees and pushes inside me from behind.

He pulls my hair off my neck and whispers in my ear, "I'm going to fuck you like this in the Oval Office."

Swear to God. West.

Head in my hands, my ass in the air, I'm trying not to laugh when he makes me come again, and this time he goes over the edge with me.

I drop with my face into the pillow, heavy and exhausted, drowsy. He's so hot and heavy and all over me, his sweaty, familiar weight, the scents of our bodies. Nothing can touch us.

I've never lost sight of my happiness.

Not for one minute.

THE BEGINNING

It snowed a ton that December.

The first week of Putnam's winter break was supposed to be Frankie's last week of school, but it dumped so much on Putnam County that all the schools were closed.

Caroline had planned to spend the few days before Christmas with her dad, but she ended up stuck at our place.

The temperature hovered around thirty degrees. The garage roof creaked and groaned under the weight of the snow.

We ate grilled cheese with tomato soup and watched Christmas movies.

When we were starting to get restless, Laurie and Rikki loaned us a thousand-piece puzzle of the earth made up of hundreds of tiny pictures, and we spread it out on the coffee table and worked on it together for most of the morning and the early afternoon of Christmas Eve.

After a while, Caroline and Frankie wandered off. Frankie borrowed my art pencils and fussed with a drawing she wanted to give Mom for Christmas. Caroline sat on the couch researching media opportunities on her laptop, gearing up to become Iowa's revenge porn poster girl once the holidays were over.

I stayed with the puzzle, identifying one piece after another. Matching them to their neighbors by color, shape, content, and slotting them into place.

Piece by piece, the satisfaction built until I'd finished the whole thing.

I looked at what I'd made and realized I'd spent the entire day absorbed in a metaphor.

The puzzle was the future—formless, confusing. A thousand tiny decisions I'd have to make. A thousand things to figure out without anything much to guide me but some idea of where I wanted to end up.

That night, with snow blanketing the fields and the roof of Laurie and Rikki's house—with snow on the roads and over the stair rail and blown up into the corners of every window—we made a huge bowl of popcorn and watched *The Grinch Who Stole Christmas*. I sat between Frankie and Caroline, my arms spread behind them on the couch, my feet up on the coffee table, lights winking on the little artificial Christmas tree that Frankie and I had picked up at Walmart.

After my sister went to bed, Caroline helped me put the presents out, and we turned off the overhead lights and soaked up the glow of the tree, watching the snow fall.

We didn't say anything.

We didn't have to say anything. We were here.

And as for what came next—it would be like the puzzle. Complicated, but I could take it one piece at a time.

Even though I came from a fucked-up family in a fucked-up place, and even though I'd been through a lot of fucked-up shit that didn't teach me the right things to live a normal life, I had clear eyes, curiosity, and perseverance.

I had Caroline with me.

The future would slot into place one piece at a time.

"No, I know."

It's lunchtime on Christmas Day.

Caroline is pacing from the front door of the apartment to the back of the kitchen. She's got her dad on a headset, her hands sunk into the back pockets of her jeans. She's wearing a dark green sweater with a drapey neck that looks soft and open and inviting.

She means it to be festive, and it is, but it's so fucking sexy, too. There's a shadow under her collarbone where I'd love to put my mouth.

"Yeah, I know," she tells her dad. "Sorry not to be there. I wanted to. If it clears up in an hour or two, I'll see if I can make it tonight."

I must be frowning, because when she passes and catches sight of me, she lifts her eyebrows and her shoulders at once, like, *What do you want me to tell him? It's Christmas.*

"I-80's gonna be too slippery," I say.

"It might be," she tells her dad, who must have said the exact same thing I did. "I'll keep an eye on the weather and—"

She pauses.

Then, "Yeah. If you think that's the best way to handle it, all right."

"Handle what?" Frankie asks. She's sitting at the kitchen table, drawing in her new sketchbook with the pencils I gave her for Christmas.

"Don't eavesdrop," I tell her. "It's bad manners."

"*You* are."

"True."

She rolls her eyes. "Hypocrite."

She's learning all these big words from the gifted-and-talented teacher. She's been reading a ton, too—the teacher hooked her up with a librarian at the Putnam Public Library who saves out books just for her. Frankie is blowing through a book every day or two. She doesn't want to talk to me about them, but Jeff Gorham tells me it's good for her.

Enriching.

"He's going to reschedule the family Christmas dinner," Caroline tells us both. "Since they're not sure when I'll be able to get there."

Frankie gives me a pointed glance and sticks out her tongue.

A moment later, Caroline's saying, "I need to talk to you about that, actually," as she walks down the hall toward the bedroom.

She closes the door behind her.

"What's she need to talk to him about?" Frankie asks.

"None of your business, Little Miss Nosy."

"You don't even know, I bet."

I'm pretty sure I do, though.

More sure when Caroline's end of the conversation gets loud enough for me to register that she's angry, though I can't quite make out the words through the door.

Then I can make them out just fine.

"For the fifth time, I'm not *asking* you, I'm *telling* you. I've already made a decision, and I'm not going to just wait and see how I feel in a few days. I already know how I feel. That's why I'm *informing* you of my feelings."

"Stay here," I say to Frankie.

I find Caroline sprawled on the bed, hands and legs flung wide, scowling at the ceiling. "No," she says. "No! I don't accept that. I knew you'd say it, and I hear where you're coming from, but I don't accept it."

I sit down on the bed, prop my back against the head-board, and extend my legs over top of hers.

She reaches out to find my hand.

The conversation takes a nasty turn, and every time she raises her voice, she squeezes my hand tighter.

"Not listening to me."

"No, Dad, I hear you, but no."

"Damn it, Dad, it's got nothing to do with him!"

She doesn't say anything too ugly to take back, but she's upset enough that her voice cracks, and I can tell she's not getting anywhere with her old man.

Eventually, they start cooling down. I've never heard any-one argue loud enough to be audible through a closed door and then, ten minutes later, work back around to, "Merry Christmas, Daddy . . . . I love you, too."

Caroline hangs up and shifts onto her side. I lie beside her. She turns her face into the bedspread, letting her hair con-ceal her expression.

"Are you crying?" I ask.

She sniffles. "No."

"It's okay if you're crying."

"I'm not. I'm gathering my strength to fight another day."

"Okay. Does you gathering your strength but not crying mean that now would be a bad time to give you your Christ-mas present?"

Slowly, she sits up. Her eyes aren't red, but her throat and cheeks are flushed.

I think if she's going to be president, we'll have to work on her poker face at some point.

"You already gave me a bunch of presents," she says.

"Those were from Frankie."

"Since you paid for them, they were from you. I love my scarf."

She wore it earlier over her pajama T-shirt—orange and blue and red, with silvery threads shot through it. It looked good.

Felt good, seeing her wear something I'd bought her.

I release her hand so I can get up and dig around on the top shelf of my closet. The jewelry store box is dense as a rock in my hand. The leather bracelet seems stiff and clumsy when I hold it out to her, a symbol I'm not sure about.

What if she doesn't want the reminder? Maybe I should have buried it in the backyard.

But Caroline extends her wrist and lets me put it on her. My name pressed into leather, snugged around her skin.

She traces the letters with one finger. Smiles at me.

"It's okay?" I ask.

"It's good."

She draws close and kisses me, and it *feels* good. Like I've righted a wrong, restored something that was out of balance.

When she eases away, I press the jewelry box into her hand. She takes it with eyes so huge, I wonder for a second what the fuck I did wrong. Then I figure it out and laugh. "It's not a ring. But good to know it's too soon for that."

"It's not—I didn't mean—"

"It's fine, Caro. Open it."

Inside are the heavy silver links I bought her.

"Pretty," she says, lifting the bracelet out. "What's this on it?"

The light catches the charm when she lifts it to the light. She answers her own question. "It's a comb. West—"

"I thought I'd give you both," I say. "The comb, and the watch chain. It's . . . maybe that's not a good present, but I thought—"

And then her arms are around me, so I don't have to say the rest of it.

"West."

She's crying for real now.

"I didn't mean to make you cry. It just reminded me, is all."

I've thought so many times of her telling me not to write a story over us. Not to give myself a role—good guy or bad guy, sheriff or villain, because life's more complicated than that.

That conversation was never about the story she read in English. It was about me.

It was Caroline telling me I fucked up, but I could have another chance.

When I went to the jewelry store, I was going to see about silver combs to give her. I thought she should have a keepsake of the moment she offered me what I most needed—what I didn't even know I needed.

But then I thought, *No, I don't want her to have half. I want her to have everything.*

She kisses me. "It's perfect."

When I kiss her back, she drags me on top of her, the cool silver links dripping down my neck from where she's clutched her fingers around them. "You're perfect," she says.

"I'm so fucking far from perfect."

She kisses my lips, my cheeks, my closed eyes. "Close enough for me."

I roll to my side, and we lie there for a few minutes, legs intertwined, looking at each other.

Close enough.

———

"Frankie."

I tap her door again. "Open up."

"Leave me alone!" she shouts.

"Franks, honey, it's Christmas. You're crying. I'm not leaving you alone."

"I'm not *crying!*"

She throws something at the door that hits hard enough to make me take a step back. Caroline's behind me, hands cupping her elbows.

"You want me to try?"

Twenty minutes. Twenty lousy minutes on the phone with my mom on fucking *Christmas Day,* and me in the next room the whole time monitoring the call, but it still ends up this way—with my sister flinging the phone down, busting out in sobs, and running from the room.

Mom didn't even call until right before Frankie's bedtime. I tried her earlier, hoping to get it over with, but she answers the phone when she feels like it, and Christmas is no exception.

Usually, we get her when she's on her way somewhere in the car and she wants to fill ten minutes with pointless chatter.

How are you guys doing? she'll ask, but she doesn't want to know.

Frankie has a harder time than I do with the calls. Some afternoons I'll come in from working with Laurie to find her shut in her room, her hand-drawn STAY OUT sign taped to the door, and I'll look at Caroline and mouth, *Mom called?*

Yeah, she'll mouth in response.

Then she'll make cookies, or I'll download an episode of a show Frankie likes and use it to pry her out of her isolation.

Tonight, Mom was more emotional than I felt like dealing with. "I *miss* you guys, oh my *gosh,*" she said when I was on the phone with her. "Like fucking *crazy.*"

There was a looseness to her speech, the way it spilled out of her, that made me reluctant to turn the call over to Frankie, but I figured, it was Christmas. I couldn't really say no.

I should've said no.

"I don't know what to do," I say.

"You could give her a minute to cool off."

"She's not mad, though. Not really. She's hurt, and I don't want to leave her be."

I tap at the door again. "Frankie. Open up, or I'll take the knob off the door and let myself in."

"You can't do that."

"I can, actually."

"You're not my dad!"

"I'm your brother and the guy who's paying the rent around here, so open the door, Franks. I'm serious."

"No."

"For fuck's sake."

"West—" Caroline says.

I turn around, put my back to the door, and slide down it.

"I don't know how to be her father," I say.

"You're doing great."

"I've been at it for weeks. Asking her questions. Being here, trying to let her know I'm listening, talking to the fucking counselor, talking to the gifted-and-talented teacher, filling out the fucking paperwork, but I'm not getting anywhere."

Caroline slides down next to me. Touches my arm. "You are."

"She won't even let me in the fucking *room.*"

"It's just the holiday," Caroline says. "Talking to your mom. Her feelings are running high, but she's going to come around."

"She's pissed at me for taking that top away from her."

"It was the right thing to do."

The top was from Mom, low-cut and completely wrong for a ten-year-old.

We sent Mom a photo book. It was Caroline's idea. We picked out the best snapshots of Frankie and took some more of Iowa, the farm and the sculptures, me with Laurie, Caroline with Frankie, and put them together in an album.

So she'll see what she's missing, Frankie said.

When I asked if she got it, Mom said, "It's nice," then changed the subject.

She's back with Bo, fighting with my uncle Jack, on the outs with most of the Leavitts. She told me Leavitts have no loyalty.

I guess she forgot I'm a Leavitt. That her daughter is, too.

I just don't want her in my life anymore—for my own sake and for Frankie's. I don't want her carelessness, her gusts of passion, her brief forays into thoughtfulness that leave you feeling like shit when she forgets all about you. I want Frankie to have more.

Through the door, I can hear the soft sound of her crying.

I stand up. Tap the door again. "Frankie, look. I need you to open this door. I'm going to count to ten. That's all you get. Ready? Ten—"

Caroline interrupts, "Are you sure you don't want me to try?"

"Nine."

"West?"

"I'm sure. Eight. Seven."

"Can I do anything?" Caroline asks.

"Yeah. Go get me the screwdriver out of the junk drawer in the kitchen. Six."

"Flathead or Phillips?"

"Five. Phillips."

She rises to her toes, presses her lips against mine, and says, "I love you."

"Four. Love you, too, baby. Three."

Frankie cracks the door open on *two*. Her eyes are red. "What do you *want*?"

"To borrow your new purse. Jesus, Franks, what do you think I want? To talk to you. Let me in." Gently, I push her shoulder so she'll move aside, and then I walk into her room and close the door.

There's a neat pile on her desk of everything she got for Christmas today, stacked up and organized in a kind of display that she's put on for herself. It's such a kid thing to do, such a *Frankie* thing, it makes me feel too much at once.

Proud I could give her that stuff so she could have a good Christmas, the kind of Christmas kids are supposed to have.

Pissed at whatever my mom said to ruin it.

But over all that, just this pure hit of love for my girl.

I sit on the unmade bed.

"What?" she says.

"I didn't say anything."

"You're looking at me funny."

"I was just thinking how much I love you," I confess.

Her eyes dart away, guilty.

This is how it is with us now. I keep reaching for her, but I never seem to catch her. She doesn't want me to. "What'd Mom say?" I ask.

"Nothing."

"It wasn't nothing. You talked for a long time."

"We just talked about Christmas and presents and stuff. She's living with Bo again."

"I know. She told me."

"She asked did I want to come home."

"No." The word is out of me before I know what's happening. I'm standing, towering over Frankie. "No fucking way."

She shrinks back. I have to calm down, I know I do, but what the fucking fuck? What kind of person would do that— just ask Frankie does she want to come home, a casual question dropped into a Christmas phone call without checking with me first, without fucking asking whether I thought it would be a good idea?

Who does she think she is?

That I know the answer only makes me angrier. She's Frankie's mom. I'm just a fraud.

"Tell me what she said," I demand. "Every word."

Frankie eyes me skittishly. "She said I could come home if I wanted. She said she misses me, and you probably . . ."

"I probably what?"

Frankie shrugs at the floor. "You have Caroline."

"And that means what, exactly?"

Another shrug. "You don't want me anymore."

"Did I say that? Did I ever fucking say that?"

"No, but you don't have to. You hate me!"

"I don't hate you!"

"You're yelling at me. You're mad, you get mad, you never used to but you do now, and I hate you! I want to go home. I miss Mom. I miss Dad."

"You don't fucking miss Dad."

"I do, too! He loves me!"

"Loved you," I say. "He's dead."

It's nasty. Such a nasty thing to say, but he was a bastard

and she wants him more than me. It's the worst thing she could say, the starkest evidence of my failure.

She wants to go back to Silt, and I would rather die than go with her.

I would rather die than send her.

Her face crumples. "I hate you!"

And then she's facedown on the bed, crying again.

Caroline's in the open doorway, saying my name. Her hand lands on my arm. I come back into my body, the aching tension, the bitter taste in my throat.

I hear myself. Everything I said.

I'm not a good parent. Not a good person.

I can't become one—I don't know how. Because Caroline's wrong. It's not about parenting books, patience, trying harder. It's about *me*. I'm short-tempered and angry and violent because I was born this way, *born* to it. Fucking cursed from the start.

Both of us. Me and Franks.

When I try to touch my sister, she smacks my hand away. "Leave me alone."

There's nothing I can do.

"West," Caroline says again.

"Can you sit with her?" I ask.

Because at least I can give Frankie that much. Someone who knows how to love her.

Someone who will say the right things when I can't.

Because of the snowstorm and how everything happened with Christmas, Caroline decides not to stay over at her dad's even for the few nights of break she'd originally planned. What she really wants, she says, is to drive down for dinner with her family and come back the same night.

She wants me and Frankie to come with her.

I have a feeling she's scared to leave the two of us alone. She dragged us out the day after Christmas to shop sales and spend gift cards at the mall in Des Moines. Frankie hasn't said anything more about moving home to Silt.

I'm trying not to think about it.

I'm not even angry. I just feel hollow, knowing I can't give my sister what I want her to have. Not if she won't let me.

Not if I don't know how.

Caroline says I'm overreacting. She says my mom's trouble, but we already knew that. She says I'm a good father, a good man, that everybody's got flaws.

Caroline points out that I raised my voice, but I didn't attack my sister physically, didn't insult her verbally, didn't bad-mouth my mother, didn't hit anyone or throw anything, didn't get drunk or high or shoot anybody.

This is supposed to help, I guess. Counting all the ways I didn't fuck up.

It doesn't help. It makes me grateful she's willing to talk to me at all when I'm such a truculent pain in the ass, but it doesn't alter my conviction that I don't have what it takes to be a parent.

But Caroline gets what Caroline wants, so off we all go two days after Christmas to the Piasecki homestead.

Caroline's from the kind of family with a dining room, and a dining room table, and a tablecloth that's old, with a lace strip down the middle and candles and dishes that match.

I get through dinner by saying either *please* or *thank you* at the end of every sentence and otherwise keeping my mouth shut.

Frankie does good. She's completely baffled by the gravy boat, and she drops cranberry sauce on her lap, but she's ten, so nobody minds. Caroline braided her hair and picked out her clothes. She's shiny and bright in the candlelight, pretty as a picture in a book.

When Caroline sits beside her sisters and her dad, I can see her face reflected in theirs—her eyes from her dad, nose and chin probably her mother's legacy.

Janelle is the loudest, and kind of bossy. Alison's just home from a stint in the Peace Corps. She's thin and quiet, overwhelmed-looking.

Caroline's dad is like a band director at the top of the table, big gestures and big hands waving around, jowls and disapproving eyebrows that would be intimidating except that when he smiles at his girls, he looks like Santa Claus— all soft belly and sparkling eyes.

He smiles at Frankie that way, too, so I can't make myself dislike him no matter how many suspicious looks he sends my way.

I've met him exactly twice. The first time, I did the best I could to come across as a moronic horndog. The second time, I was in jail. If it takes him a decade to warm up to me, it's no worse than I deserve.

Caroline doesn't like it, though. Every time he gives me some tiny measure of shit, she gives it right back to him, and the conversational temperature rises degree by degree, until the both of them are a little hot.

Everywhere I look, I see something to remind me what kind of childhood Caroline had. School pictures on the wall. Framed kid drawings. A bedraggled brown paper football-looking thing in the center of the table that Caroline says is supposed to be a turkey Janelle made in kindergarten.

I can't get worked up about her dad's disapproval because I'm too busy looking around this place, thinking, *This is what safe looks like.*

Not the size of the house. Not the neighborhood or the leather sectional sofa or the turkey on the table, but the way these people *are* together, familiar and affectionate, tuned in to one another, telling Frankie funny stories from when the three girls were little whose punchlines don't depend on anybody getting hurt or humiliated.

I can't send my sister back to Silt.

I won't. Not if there's any chance she could have this instead.

After dinner, everybody's got presents to exchange, which is awkward because Frankie and I didn't have enough warning to buy anything, but they've got stuff for us. Nice stuff—a pair of leather gloves with fur in them for me, a set of birthstone earrings and a cashmere scarf for Frankie.

I can't sit still through it. I end up ducking out to use the bathroom, then pass by the kitchen, where all that dirty china's stacked up by the sink just begging to be washed.

I'm about halfway through the dishes when Caroline comes in, picks up a towel, and gets to work drying.

"You okay?" she asks.

"Yeah. Frankie being good?"

"She's great. She went out with Janelle to get butter so they can make Christmas shortbread."

"She wasn't begging, was she?"

"It was Janelle's idea. And you know it's fine if she's not perfectly polite. Everybody understands."

Caroline's dad comes in. He stops short when he sees us by the sink.

"Coffee?" Caroline asks.

"Yeah."

"I'll make it," she says. "You can dry the dishes."

To me, she notes, "It's actually his job. I'm usually the one who washes. I can't get the dishes dried well enough to meet his exacting specifications."

So then it's me and Mr. Piasecki, side by side at the sink, and Caroline bustling around the kitchen grinding beans and measuring.

"When are you going back?" her dad asks her.

"Probably in a few hours. After the shortbread, if that's okay with West."

"Why wouldn't it be okay?" I ask.

"If we stay that long, Frankie will be up past her bedtime."

"It's fine. She'll fall asleep in the car."

"You could stay over," her dad says. "We've got two rooms empty upstairs even with Alison here, and that air mattress we could put up in the finished part of the basement—"

"Three rooms, Dad?" Caroline asks. "Really? You're going to go with that?" She hops up on the countertop next to my left elbow, putting me right in the line of fire between the two of them.

Her dad glances at me. "Is this how it is, West?"

"I'm not sure what you mean."

"She's living with you, taking care of your sister for you, and now you won't even let her visit overnight for Christmas unless I let you share a room?"

"No, sir," I say. "That's not how it is."

"That's sure what it sounds like."

I clear my throat. Try to think of some way to say it that's tactful, but fuck it. I'm not tactful. "Caroline's in charge. I just go by whatever she wants."

He looks at me for a minute. Makes this *hmph* kind of noise. "That's the first intelligent thing I've heard you say."

Caroline reaches across me and punches him in the shoulder, hard.

"Hey," he says. But it's mild, and he's looking at her with affection as he rubs his arm and asks, "What about what *I* want?"

"You're not the one who has to sleep in the bed," she says.

"I'm not talking about beds anymore."

"Fine, then let's talk about what you're really talking about—you're not the one who has to live with it, Dad. I am. So I'm going to make the decisions, and you get to decide whether you support them or don't, but that's the extent of it."

"When you're making decisions with my money, going to school on my dime, it's not the extent of it. I get a say. You owe me a real conversation, not just this garbage about I support it or not but that's all. I'm already living with it. I didn't get a choice on that, but we've got a choice on this lawsuit."

"You don't have to live with it the way *I* do," Caroline says. "You're not getting deposed. You're not taking calls from the state senate and telling them, *Yeah, you're right, I could help you, but I won't, because I've got this vendetta I'm in the middle of, so no.*"

"We talked about this. We knew it was going to be hard, that's just the way these things go. It's normal to get discouraged at this point in the proceedings, but when you start something, you see it through—that's what I taught you."

"I'm not quitting, Dad."

"What you do is you put your finger on what you want, and then you go after it. If you think you can just give up at the first sign of trouble—"

"I'm not giving up!"

If I were her dad, I'd back the fuck off, but I guess the two of them are too much alike, because he sounds just as pissed when he replies, "What do you call it, then? Halfway to trial, and you're going to walk away? We could nail this kid, Caroline! We get a judgment against him, that gives us a lien on his future salary. We'll make it so he can't take a step for the rest of his life without this breathing down his neck. Make him *pay*."

I've been washing the same plate for a solid minute. The water is running, steam rising off it, and you could cut the tension with a knife.

Caroline cuts it with one question. "What if I don't want him to pay?"

Her dad sets down the plate he was drying and leans his hip into the counter. I might as well be invisible, standing here between them. "Why wouldn't you want that?"

"Because there isn't any justice in it," she says. "It's not a scale I can balance. He puts my naked body online, sends his dogs after me, makes my life scary—"

"Makes your life hell," her father says.

"—and I decide, *Hey, then I'm going to do it back to him*? That's your solution? That's not justice. It's vengeance, and it's petty."

"You don't understand how the system works."

"I *do* understand," she says. "You raised me to understand. And what I'm telling you is, the system is broken on this. I don't need Nate's money for the rest of his life, I need for what Nate did to me to not be *allowed* anymore. I want that law on the books. I want a bunch of changes to the laws so that assholes can't post photos without consent and websites can't hide behind the Copyright Act with impunity. I want people's attitudes to change so I don't get called a slut just because I had sex with my boyfriend and he took some pictures. I want to help make sure nobody else goes through what I did—that *Frankie* and girls like Frankie won't ever have to endure that—

and what we're doing, throwing money into a pit with this civil suit, hiding behind Jane Doe—that's not going to change a thing. So don't talk to me about justice unless you really want to *talk* to me about *justice,* because there are nonprofits you could give the money we're paying the lawyer that would use it to bring about a lot more justice than this lawsuit that *you seem to think I need your permission to walk away from.*"

When she's finished, the whole house is quiet.

The whole world feels quiet, with Caroline's words just echoing around.

This is what it sounds like, I think, *to know exactly what you want.*

This is what it sounds like to thrive.

I've heard her before like this. Every time, it wrecks me, because I'm so fucking proud of her.

Her dad doesn't say anything. I watch him, looking for some sign that he's got pride in her, too.

What he does surprises me: he sits down at the kitchen table and thinks. You can tell he's thinking because he looks so much like Caroline, his forehead furrowed and his eyes gone far away.

Coffee burbles and drips into the pot. Caroline picks up the dish towel and angrily dries what's left of the dishes in the sink. At a loss, I start washing again. We finish up. Caroline puts the dishes away.

I lean back against the sink with my arms crossed, trying to understand what this even is.

Where I'm from, men are only good for two things. We learn how to fight, and we learn how to fuck. There isn't anything much else for us—no jobs you can raise a family on, no other ways to live unless you go looking for them, and even then there's no guarantee you're going to find something better.

I found Evan and Rita Tomlinson. They were enough to get me out of Silt, but not enough to teach me some better way of life.

I've never watched anybody do what Caroline and her dad are in the middle of doing. They're arguing, but she's *safe*.

This house where she grew up looks like a temple to me, and it's not the money, it's that there's love all over the walls, and good food, and Christmas presents for people they barely know, and shortbread cookies for my sister.

They can do all that and still argue with each other.

They can argue without fucking up their love.

They raised their voices, just like I did. Lost their tempers. But then her dad sat down at the table and shut the fuck up and *thought* about what Caroline said to him.

He's still considering it.

And I think, hell, Caroline's got to be right. She's so fucking smart, and she brought me here and had this argument right in front of me, so she has to be showing me what she thinks I need to see.

Showing me how to do this.

It's not impossible. It's just something I have to learn.

I'm good at learning, even if I'm complete shit at everything else.

Out of the blue, Caroline's dad asks me, "What do you think?"

"About what?"

"Nate."

"I'd like to see him get what's coming to him. But to be honest, short of the death penalty, I'm not sure there's anything that could happen to him that I'd think would be as bad as what he deserves. And I figure, even before the pictures, he already screwed up and lost Caroline, so he's got a lifetime of regretting that ahead of him."

Caroline's giving me an *oh-please* kind of look.

"What? He does. He had you, and he lost you. Stupidest move of his life. You'll be in the White House someday, and he'll be telling his sad drinking buddies at the lonely bar where he wastes his time, *She was mine once, but I fucked it up.*" I glance at Caroline's dad. "Sorry."

"For what?"

"He said *fuck*," Caroline explains.

He blinks. "Oh. That." He waves his hand. "The White House?"

Color climbs her cheeks. "West wasn't supposed to say."

"Why not?"

"Because it's—"

I can just about hear the words that come next. *Childish. Stupid. Impossible.*

Not for me.

And right then, that's when I get it. I really finally *get* it—how we box ourselves in.

How we take something that's hard and make it harder for no good reason.

When I think about what kind of life I want my sister to have—who I want her to be like, what I want her to see, what I want to model for her so she'll have a clue how to flourish, to thrive—I can't think of any better model than the woman I love, lecturing her dad on what justice is.

Caroline is going after what she *wants.*

I've got to be the same way. Both of us do. It's the only way to live that makes any sense.

Go after deep and make it deeper.

Accept that life is going to be hard—that everything worth having is worth fighting for—but don't fucking make it harder than it has to be.

Don't put yourself in between the life you've got and the one you want.

I walk straight to her, pull her close, and look down into those deep brown eyes of hers. I say, "Caro, it's *not*. Whatever it is you're thinking about saying, it's not true. And even if it turns out to be true down the road, if you go after it but you can't get there—let it happen when it happens. Don't write the end over the beginning."

The gap between her teeth peeks out when she smiles. "I've heard that before."

"A smart woman said it to me."

She comes up on her toes and gives me a kiss—chaste but full of feeling.

Her dad clears his throat.

She stops kissing me, but she doesn't unwind her arms from around my neck, and I don't step away from the feel of her body pressed against mine.

He can fucking get used to it.

"All right, kids," he says.

He wipes his hands down his face. I've seen him do that once before, when he came to talk to me at the jail in Putnam.

It's what he looks like, I'm guessing, when he's giving in to Caroline's way of doing things.

"We'll have to draw up an ironclad settlement agreement," he says. "Make sure you get assigned copyright over all those pictures, nondisclosure . . . I guess we can let go of admission of guilt. He'll sign if he doesn't have to admit he did it."

"Everybody already knows he did it," she says. "Everybody who counts."

She's looking at me when she says it.

I hear the front door open, Frankie chattering, footsteps

heading our way. She sounds happy, and it occurs to me that I gave her that.

I gave her this Christmas. This family. Caroline.

As far as I'm concerned, everybody who counts is right here, exactly where I want them.

If I have to fight to keep my sister here, I will.

Late that night, I wake up to the sound of Frankie screaming.

"Daddy!" she's saying. "Bo!"

And then, "Don't!"

I peel back the covers and tuck Caroline in.

I walk to my sister's room and stand in the open doorway. "Frankie. Frankie. Franks, it's okay."

After half a minute, she stops thrashing. Then I can hear her sniffling and rummaging around for the box of tissues we keep on the floor by her bed.

I grab her a tissue and sit by her waist. Hand it over. Rub my hand up and down her back.

"You're okay," I tell her. "You're safe. I'm here."

She quiets.

I run my fingers through her hair.

"Tell me what happened," I say. It's the first time I've asked.

Maybe I didn't really want to know.

Maybe I was afraid of what I'd hear.

Frankie draws a deep breath. "I was at a sleepover."

"At whose house?"

"Keisha's."

"Where's Keisha live?"

"Bandon."

"How'd you get home?"

She's quiet.

"Don't lie to me."

She's so quiet.

I miss my chattering girl who never shut up. My Frankie from before, who ran to me when I came in a door, who hassled me for piggyback rides and never got sick of sucking up as much of my time and attention as I could spare.

I left that girl to come here, and I never got her back.

What I've got now is this new Frankie, who sasses me, hassles me, ignores me, but never tells me what's in her heart.

I want my sister back, and the only way I can think to get to her is to wade through all this mess between us. This story she doesn't want to tell, these changes in her life she's afraid to talk to me about, the reality she doesn't want to face: that we're not ever going back to Silt.

We're refugees.

"Tell me what really happened."

"I was asleep," she says.

Just like that.

"Dad was gone, he'd been gone a couple days, and I guess Bo knew that because he never came around, but he came around that night. It woke me up when Mom answered the door. I heard them talking. She let him in."

Frankie sits up suddenly. She crisscrosses her legs. Her knee overlaps my thigh.

"They weren't doing anything," she says. "They were just talking. But Dad came home, and he was on something, I think."

"On what?"

"I don't know. He was almost always on something."

"Fuck." The word comes out of me, not a curse but a prayer. Months too late to do any good. *Don't let him hurt her. Don't let anything hurt her.*

"He was talking too fast, super angry, and they were all

yelling. I think Dad hit Mom, because I heard her kind of yelp, and then Bo said something and they were fighting. I hid under the covers. They were crashing around until . . . until it was too quiet. And Mom said, 'Wyatt, don't.'"

The hair on the back of my neck stands up at the way she delivers those words, straight out of her nightmare.

"That's when I went out there."

I'm clutching my knees. I want to keep her from seeing whatever she's about to see, and even though I know distantly that it's happened already, it doesn't seem to matter.

Don't go out there, Franks. You're gonna get hurt.

"Bo was on the floor, wiping blood off his mouth. Dad had—"

She shudders and leans into me hard. I put my arm around her. When she speaks again, her voice is high, forced. "Dad had a gun. He was pointing it at Mom, right at her head."

I pull her onto my lap. She twines her arms around my neck and drops her head on my shoulder, so much like the baby she used to be that I can remember viscerally the heavy, damp weight of her. Holding her, jiggling her until she was drowsy, putting her down in the middle of mom's bed for a nap, and then peeling carefully away, chilled from the loss of her body heat. Her lips slack and open to any of a thousand kinds of harm.

"Have you told anyone this?" I ask.

She nods. "Aunt Stephanie. And Caroline. But I didn't tell them all of it."

I hold her tight. "I'm glad you told Caroline. You can tell her anything you need to. But now I want you to tell me."

After a minute, she begins again. "Mom tried to send me back in. But Dad said, 'No, stay, you should see this, you should see what happens to—'"

She stops.

"It's okay. Tell me the parts that matter."

"I was so scared. I wanted to be brave, like you would've been if you were there, but I was so scared and I didn't know what to do. I told him to put the gun away. He pointed it at me. *Don't talk back to me, Francine.* Mom was crying, and Bo was moving, but I wasn't paying attention with the gun on me. I was looking at Dad. And then Dad—"

She chokes on another sob.

"It was so *loud,* West. And red, bright bright red, everywhere, and I didn't understand what was happening until Bo started apologizing. I didn't even know Bo had a gun. He shot Dad. It was my fault, because if I hadn't come out Dad wouldn't have pointed his gun at me, and Bo wouldn't have killed him, and Mom—"

Now she's crying. It's awful, fucking awful to hear it. My baby. My Frankie.

"The gun went off, and she went right to Dad. She crawled on top of him like she could put him back together with her hands. I don't—"

"Frankie."

I can't listen anymore. I'm rocking back and forth, pressing her head into my chest, willing her to shut up with everything I've got, because there's knowing something bad happened and then there's *knowing.*

There's knowing your dad, high, pointed a gun to your sister's head and might have killed her.

There's knowing your mom didn't try to save her and didn't go to her afterward.

There's knowing that, and there's pain so huge from knowing it that the pain doesn't have anyplace to go. It just ricochets around inside you, howling.

"I did the wrong thing," she sobs.

"No."

"I should've called the police. I didn't think. I tried to think what you would say to do, but I couldn't, and you weren't there, West."

I wasn't there. I can't change it. I tried, I fucking tried to be there for her, but I couldn't.

"You did great," I say. "You did everything perfect."

It's stupid, unhelpful, but Jesus, what's helpful? I can't make it right.

I rock her, wipe her face dry, murmur nonsense until she starts to calm.

We sit in her dark room. The snow's falling outside. In the hush, the quiet, I remember all the worst times.

The time my dad hit my new kitten with his car, studied the limp body by my side, and booted it underneath the trailer next door.

The time I stood up to him and he knocked me down with a lazy fist and kicked me in the stomach so hard, I shit blood for days.

The night I got arrested out of the bakery after I found out my mom had taken him back.

The day I left Caroline at the airport in Des Moines.

The dead zone of time after the funeral when I tried to burn my life down around me so I wouldn't have to feel anything anymore, because I'd had enough. I was fucking *done*.

Frankie's worst time is worse than any of mine, and I can't fix it.

All I can do is this.

"It's not your fault." I whisper it into her hair, behind her ear. Her head is smooth and sleek under my hand, her body small, a curve against my stomach that reminds me of that kitten on my lap, soft and warm and innocent for those few hours I had it. "You didn't do anything wrong. It's them, Franks. It's them."

She presses her nose into my chest, clutching my shirt. "I don't want to live at Bo's."

"You don't have to. You can stay with me."

"Mom says you want to be alone with Caroline."

"I want you with me. You're my girl. Okay?"

She's quiet.

"I love you, Franks. I've loved you all your life, and I'm always gonna love you. And the fact that I love Caroline, too, doesn't take anything away from you. It just means I want her with me and you with me, both. It'll always be like that. You understand?"

I can feel her nod against my chest.

"I've been thinking since Christmas that you wanted to go back to Silt and I was gonna have to talk you out of it. I don't want to fight Mom for you, but if she tries to make you go back, then I'll fucking fight for you, because it's better here. It's not perfect, I know, but I think we can get it close if we work at it. If you're miserable, though, you have to *tell me* so I can try to fix it. You have to tell me everything. I can't read minds."

"Sometimes it seems like you can."

"That's because we Leavitts are fucking sharp as tacks."

She turns her head to rest her temple against my shoulder. "It's different here," she says.

"What is?"

"Everything."

"Bad different or good different?"

"Some of both."

"Yeah." Her hair smells like fruit. Cherries. "It's that way for me, too. You think you could ever get used to it?"

"Probably."

We're quiet for a minute. Her body is loose in my arms. Relaxed.

"I love you, West," she says.

And Christ, it feels good.

It feels solid. Strong enough that we can build on it. Sweeter than I expected, because she hasn't said it in months.

I hold my baby sister for a long time.

"You ever think about what I asked you? If you could do anything, be anybody, what you would want?"

"Not really."

I kiss the top of her cherry-scented head.

Say, "Start."

The package from my grandma shows up a few days into January. At first I think it was delayed by bad weather, but the postmark shows she didn't mail it until December 29.

Inside, there's a backgammon set wrapped up for Frankie, a new afghan big enough to cover the back of the couch, and a lumpy envelope with my name on it.

I slip the envelope into my pocket. Later, when Frankie's gone dancing back to her room and Caroline's talking to Paul on her headset, I put my boots on and take the letter out on the landing at the top of the stairs.

I read it holding my breath.

Dear West,

Michelle showed me the book you sent her with your pictures in it. It looks like you and your sister are doing good.

I'm sending you my 5 yr. chip from AA. I'm going to get my 10 yr. next month. I don't know what you'd want with it, but it's something I'm proud of, like you are.

I wish I could give you more. I never knew how to make things right with you.

Your uncle Jack doesn't talk about the trial anymore.

*Stephanie says they got a letter from the lawyer saying he's
given up the case so I guess that's over with.*

*Write to me when you can and tell me how you're doing.
I'll keep an eye on your mother.*

Love,

Joan

It makes me fucking cry, that letter. I don't know why.

Maybe because of the things that are so obvious, she
doesn't even have to say them.

That I'm never going home again.

I never had a home in the first place.

My mother is a child, my family is a mess, and I'm on my
own.

Joan wishes me well.

After a minute, I dry my face. Look up at the sky. Inhale.

It's one of those winter days that don't come often in Iowa,
when the temperature drops so low that it hurts to breathe,
but the sun comes out and the sky is thin blue, far away.

The snow sparkles. The world blanketed in crystal.

I pull my phone from my pocket and dial my mom. She
picks up on the second ring.

The conversation drifts for a while. The wind gusts up,
lifting powdery surface snow and sending it whirling over the
fields. I make the right noises at the right times and wait for
the moment.

Then I say it. "I want permanent custody of Frankie."

The sun ducks behind a cloud. My mom protests, argues
with me, but I just brace myself there. Let the wind blow
over me.

It's no surprise when my mom finally asks, "You'll still let
me see her?"

"Of course. I'll fly you out for the guardianship hearing, and you can stay awhile."

"I'd like that."

Then she's quiet, and I'm quiet, too. I guess we both know what it means.

"I love you, West," she says.

I say, "I love you, too." Because it's true. And because it's kind.

And because it's over.

It's a week into January when I go by the art building looking for Rikki. I want to talk to her about art therapy for Frankie.

I don't know what art therapy costs, or even if it's something that would do Franks any good, but Caroline pointed out that it's helped *her* a lot to have a therapist to talk to since the thing with Nate, and maybe I shouldn't be so close-minded about it.

I shouldn't. I'm trying not to be. Frankie's still having nightmares, so there's plenty of room for improvement, and like Caroline says, it's unlikely to hurt. Frankie will probably see it as art lessons from Rikki, which they're already more or less doing every time she goes over to Rikki's place with the sketchbook I gave her for Christmas.

I try Rikki's office, but she's not there, so I swing by the studio where she teaches her classes. I find her there with Raffe and Annie—the dude with the crazy hair from my Studio Art class and the tiny blonde he always hangs around with.

Since I quit smoking and it started snowing all the time, I haven't run into them as much as I used to, and it gives me a jolt to see them now during break.

Makes me wonder what kind of families Raffe and Annie have got, that they're here on campus in January hanging out in the art building.

They're each bent over white forms on the table that look like ceramic ice cube trays. Rikki is tapping what looks like shiny white sand into one opening with the back of a spoon. "The trick is to make sure you do not leave too much air in here," she's saying. "Because then you will have bubbles, and the frit will not melt evenly."

Raffe glances up. "Leavitt," he says.

"Hey, Raffe."

Annie acknowledges me with a dip of her eyelashes, which is all I've ever managed to get out of Annie. Raffe, I've talked to a few times, but only the kind of polite conversation that doesn't go anywhere.

You done with that?

Yeah, it's all yours.

Thanks.

"You here over break?" I ask.

"Yeah. We're doing a January-term independent thing with Rikki."

"What on?"

"Frit casting." He wiggles his fingers like a magician.

It's because of Rikki that Laurie is working in glass. He used to be satisfied making giant sculptures out of metal, but now he's got to have giant glass hammers, too, even though he wasn't kidding when he said the logistics are a fucking pain in the ass. A one-to-one casting of a glass hammer is a tough object to make, but not impossible. Multiply the scale by a thousand? Enormous fucking headache, because where are you going to get that much glass? How the fuck do you make the mold, and more to the point, where's the kiln to fire a glass hammer the size of a car?

This is the kind of stuff he pays me to try to figure out. Which, actually, I fucking love it. Best job I've ever had.

"Did you need something?" Rikki asks.

I come back to myself, realize I'm standing there staring at the molds piled with frit and daydreaming about work. "Yeah. No. I mean, it can wait. I just wanted to talk to you about something, but you're busy."

"I can make some time if it's important. Is it Frankie?"

"Nah, just class stuff," I lie.

"Are you going to be in Laurie's 3D Design in the spring?" Raffe asks.

"No, I didn't sign up."

"How come?"

I shrug. "Just didn't."

Rikki gives me a look. "What did you register for?"

"A bio class, organic chemistry, an econ seminar, and an advanced statistics thing."

"Those are all sciences."

"Econ is a social science."

"Why do you need so much science?"

"It's practical."

She sniffs. "Practical. You do not need more practical. You need more art."

This is Rikki's shtick. I need more art. I need to learn to play. I need to let myself take up more space in the world.

I've heard it enough times now that I keep thinking it'll stop digging into me, but it hasn't. Every time, I feel like she's scraping over something soft inside me. It makes me irritable. I think she knows it, too.

I think that's why she does it.

The thing is, I liked her class. It frustrated the hell out of me, but I liked it.

I like working with Laurie.

I even liked Russian history and Music in African-American Lit and Spanish, but when it came time to register for the spring semester, I went with bio, chem, econ, and math because the scholarship I'm on is worth more than fifty thousand dollars a year, and I don't know what I could *do* with art.

Nothing, probably.

I can't waste all that money on nothing.

Rikki's watching me. Her hair is in pigtails. She's got on a vest made of blue fur and underneath it a black long-sleeve top made out of leather. She should be ridiculous, but instead she makes these crazy clothes look like what everybody's supposed to be wearing.

She makes her life seem like a life anybody could have, and should, if that's what they want.

I rub my hand across my throat. Too hot. "What are you guys making?"

Raffe smiles. "We're casting tiles for color samples. Annie, where'd the book go?"

She hands it to him, and he shows me pages and pages of small glass tiles in a rainbow of colors. I ask a few questions, get some answers, ask a few more, and then we're off talking about the technique and how it works, where it can go wrong, what might be a better way.

Before I know it, I've got a spoon in my hand that I'm using to tamp down frit into the mold that was Rikki's. It's careful work, meticulous. Weighing out the components, adding the powder to the frit in tenths and hundredths of a gram. Ten grams in each opening. *Tap tap tap.*

"See, this is the kind of art I like," I say.

"How come?" Raffe asks.

"It's technique. I like the technique stuff. Or when it's a puzzle, when Laurie needs something and I have to figure out how to get some result that you want but it takes a lot of planning or science or knowledge about materials to make it happen."

"You work with Laurie?" Raffe asks.

"Yeah, I'm his assistant."

"That's tight."

"It is. It would be perfect if it was a real job, you know, like, full-time, if I could be an assistant to somebody like Laurie."

"But don't you want to make your own stuff?" Annie asks. She's got a tiny metal funnel out, and she's using it to add red pigment to a cup of frit sitting on top of a scale.

It's on the tip of my tongue to say *I'm not creative that way*, but I don't. I stop.

Because I'm trying to notice, these days, when I'm making shit harder than it has to be.

I'm trying to notice when there's something I want and I'm throwing obstacles up in front of it for no reason at all.

What I notice right now is that I was comfortable a few seconds ago, but I've started sweating, and I feel kind of . . . I don't know, furtive. Like I'm checking out porn on the Internet when Caroline's in the other room—not that I'd ever do that, but it's that kind of forbidden feeling, as if I'm going to get caught talking about something I shouldn't.

The thing I shouldn't be talking about is art.

And what I say, when I open my mouth, is, "How do you know? How is that . . . How do you convince people it's okay for you to be doing this stuff?"

Raffe exhales a laugh. "Who, like parents?"

"No, not parents." *Yourself.*

Because that's what I mean. How do I convince myself that it's okay to take art classes?

How do I make myself get out of my own fucking way?

I drop the spoon in my hand and say, "It's like— Well, take electives. You have to have so many classes for your major, whatever that is—"

"Art," Raffe says.

Annie nods. "Art."

"Okay, but pretend it's not art and you have to take bio classes, so you take those, one or two a semester, but you've got all these electives. So how do you decide what to take?"

"Whatever looks interesting," Raffe says.

"Or if I've heard it's really great," Annie says, "like Gender and Women's Studies with Professor Gates."

"Okay, well, what I do is think about work. I think what's going to be most useful to get a job that pays well. What's going to mean I'm in a position to make the most out of college."

"So how'd you end up in Studio Art?" Raffe asks.

"Fluke."

"Huh. It seems like a good fit."

"I got a B-."

"Rikki's a hard grader."

I look around, because he's talking about her like she's not here, and I realize she's not. She must have slipped out when I wasn't paying attention.

"You know that assignment with the still life, and we were supposed to paint the apple?" I ask. "My apple looked like it belonged in a children's book. This dipshit next to me, he never seemed to have the first fucking clue what was going on—swam through the whole semester in a daze—and then he paints this apple with, like, black and purple and blue and yellow and pink and white on his brush. No red at all. But when he's done, it looks exactly like an apple."

"Wait, is this Kyle?" Raffe asks.

"Is that his name?"

"Skinny kid, always made Rikki repeat the demonstrations?"

"Yeah, him."

"He's fucking gifted with colors, man."

"That's what I'm saying. So *Kyle* is creative. He should make art. But me . . . I don't want to be dicking around, wasting money on four credits when I'm not going to get anything out of it."

"Sounds like you got a job out of it," Annie points out.

"That was a fluke."

"Lot of flukes in this story," she says mildly. "You know how I got into art?"

"How?"

"I took a class in high school, started messing around with drawing and painting and sculpture. When the bell rang, I never wanted to leave."

"Same for me," Raffe says, "except it was here. First art class, and I was in the studio all the time. I'd forget to eat. Skipped meals, skipped parties, so I could be here doing this. Me and Annie—that's how we met."

"But don't you worry what you're going to do with it?"

"Rikki and Laurie seem to be surviving all right," Raffe says.

"But not everybody's as lucky or as talented as Rikki and Laurie. You could crash and burn, and then where'd you be?"

Raffe says, "I'd be a guy with a bachelor's from Putnam who knows how to work hard on something that's important to me, and who knows how to take something I'm passionate about and try to realize it, and how to communicate that passion to the rest of the world. That's not, like, wasted time. And even if it was, I'm not sure I care." He picks up a plastic tub full of frit and powder and starts shaking it to mix the color in. "Plus, dude, you're what, twenty?"

"Twenty-one."

"So, you're twenty-one. You're allowed to fuck around and experiment with stuff. I'm pretty sure it's the point of being twenty-one."

"It's not like you can only ever have one career," Annie says. "You can make art and teach school, and if you hate teaching school you can run a gas station, and if you hate running a gas station you could try your hand at embalming dead bodies, and the whole time you're making things, if that feels good."

"Embalming dead bodies?" I ask.

"Just as an example."

Raffe finishes shaking his frit and sets the container down on the table. "For what it's worth, Leavitt, you've got talent. It's just not the same as Kyle's. He's got an eye for color. You're precise, and you see things from more than one angle. You're good at solving problems, because you're fucking persistent. I could see all that just taking a class with you, and I know I'm not wrong because Laurie hired you, which he wouldn't have done if he didn't think you had something."

"He didn't hire me," Annie says. "I applied."

"He didn't hire Josh, either," Raffe says. "Or Macon. I didn't even know you were in the running for that job."

"I wasn't," I admit. "I didn't know there was a job in the first place. He just offered it to me."

"There you go."

There I go.

And actually, I feel like I'm moving. Like I've taken a step to the left and cleared a path that was blocked.

I've got a sketchbook at home full of ideas for shit that I would build or make or do if I had unlimited time and supplies. A sketchbook I've never showed anybody—not even Caroline—because it's scarier than it should be to step away from what I know is practical in favor of what might turn out to be impractical but fucking *pleasurable*.

My sister keeps drawing these grid drawings, one after another, like she can't stop. They're all she wants to do. But she keeps telling me they're not *real* art, even as she gets better and better at them.

My grandma Joan has a houseful of blankets she's knit. She makes them without patterns, and they're fucking impressive, but if you ask her anything about them she'll tell you she just does it for her arthritis.

Not because it feeds something in her to make beautiful things.

I don't know if what I want to make would come out beautiful, but fuck, I've got things I want to try just for the sake of trying it, glass I want to melt and metal I want to cut up and this idea I had for if you could take a tree and cut it into slices and suspend them, somehow, vertically, so you could see what the tree looked like when it was alive the same time you could see inside the tree and read the story of its life.

I don't know if that's art.

I guess it is if I say it is. If it makes people feel or think when they look at it.

I don't know if it would be *good* art. Could be it's just playing. But giving myself a chance to figure it out—that's what I want.

That's what I want for me, and that's what I want for Frankie, too—to be able to see me doing that, so she knows it's okay if she wants to do it herself.

I'm starting to see that if I get what I need, Frankie's going to get what she needs, too. That what's good for me and what's good for Caroline is what's good for my sister.

"Where'd Rikki go?" I ask.

"Back to her office," Annie says.

I check the clock and I'm surprised to see it's seventy-five minutes since I got here. I was supposed to be stopping for a minute. I've got to get dinner sorted out. But it's late enough now that Caroline's probably fed Frankie.

"I'd better head out," I say. "Thanks for showing me this stuff."

"You want to grab dinner?" Raffe asks. "Annie and I were going to go into town for subs."

"Thanks, but I can't."

"Oh. Okay."

I'm reminded of that day with Krishna, when he came up to me outside the art building and harassed me into coming over for dinner.

He's back in Chicago for the break.

I think tonight I'll give him a call.

"Would you guys want to come out to my place?" I ask. "Not tonight, because I don't know what Caroline's got going on, but I don't know, tomorrow? Day after? I have to warn you I've got a kid sister living with me, so if you're not into kids . . ."

I trail off.

I guess what I'm saying is, *I've got some baggage. I live off-campus with my girlfriend and my little sister. I don't really know how to have friends, and I can be a grouchy fucker if things aren't going my way, but I'd like to talk about art with you. Both of you.*

It takes a year, waiting for their reply, and I age a decade.

"Kids are good," Annie says.

"Is there anything we should bring?" Raffe asks.

It's that easy.

Just that fucking easy.

Spring comes late in Iowa, but that year was an exception. The December snow gave way to a frozen January, clear and blue, everything crystalline and sparkling.

West's eyes under that sky were all fire and ice.

His hands were cold when they moved beneath my jacket over warm skin, and I would shriek, but I loved the shock of it.

The shock of having him. Keeping him.

How that could become normal—how it could fall into a rhythm of busy days and familiar nights, but still surprise me into gratitude over and over again.

February was projects and papers, phone calls and television interviews. It was waking up early to drive to the Quad Cities for hair and makeup so I could film something for the morning news. Seeing my name in the *Des Moines Register*, sitting in a hotel conference room and answering questions for eight state senators, none of whom implied I was a slut.

All of whom shook my hand and thanked me for my service to the citizens of Iowa.

February was reading about nonprofits, political action groups, and campus organizations. Talking to activists. Thinking about guest speakers.

Planning for a future with no walls on any horizon.

February was Frankie making friends with a girl named Nadine and bringing her home to play once, then a second time, then as many nights as the two of them could get away with it.

It was Quinn back from Florence and me making time to see all her pictures and hear about her Italian escapades.

It was me making time for Bridget, too, to listen to how things were going with Krishna and give her advice she didn't need because actually, it turned out, things were going pretty well.

It was the beginning of art therapy for Frankie, her nightmares easing up, my insomnia getting a little bit less intense.

February was West at the studio or out in Laurie's shop. West talking about Raffe and Annie, West telling me what he was making, what he would try next, what he'd failed at but he had an idea, he had another idea, he had a new idea.

I gained ten pounds in February.

Then it was March, and it rained so much that the world turned brown and squelching. The snow melted away. The rug inside the front door developed a crust of mud. We had to leave our shoes on garbage bags to keep flakes of dirt from falling off us everywhere we walked.

Spring break marked a year since West left Putnam for Oregon. We gave Frankie over to the Collinses and drove to Iowa City for dinner, just the two of us. Appetizers and main courses and dessert over a flickering candle, plates passed back and forth across the table, more to talk about than we could ever say.

I laughed a lot at that dinner, because my life was so full it spilled over. West pulled me close in the truck, kissed me with the rain pounding onto the roof and the windows until I was breathless and laughing all over again.

And then there were crocuses.

April brought sunshine, the world drying out, the first questing blades of grass pushing through the earth. Rugby practices to plan. A rally to organize. Every day, some contact to be made, some reporter to talk to, some new thing to pursue.

This was how it would be. It was how we would be, always.

This full of change. This full of life.

Spilling over into words and laughter, cold hands and hot mouths, and the sound of rain drumming down.

The lawyer's office is cold.

Outdoors, the temperature is exactly perfect. Sixty-four degrees and sunny, which is unheard of for April in Iowa, so that all anyone wants to chitchat about is Gulf currents and global warming.

At Putnam, it's one of those afternoons when the entirety of the winter-pale student body emerges blinking from their dorm rooms and spreads out blankets on the lawn of the quad. Boys strip off their shirts and toss Frisbees. Girls hold their textbooks, their chem notes—whatever props they require—when really they're out there to watch the flesh parade.

I'm sitting at a conference table with the lawyer and my dad on one side of me, West and Frankie on the other. Across the gleaming cherrywood surface, Nate is flanked by his lawyer and both of his parents.

This isn't how it's normally done. My father made that abundantly clear.

It's not normal to insist on signing the papers in front of the person you've accused.

It's not normal to bring your boyfriend with you, or to invite along a girl too young to fully understand what it is she's being asked to witness.

Settlements don't usually take fifteen weeks to negotiate, either, I told my dad, *but I let you have your way. Give me this.*

The document is nothing. I don't know why I expected a sheaf of pages, binder-clipped together, covered in tape flags, when I've been part of hammering out every single one of these terms.

I guess we expect the turning points in our lives to be plastered in flags and warning signs when, in fact, most of the time our lives change when we're not paying attention. We blow past the markers without even seeing them, and then we come to the end of some path and find there's no label for it at all.

No guardrail. No dead-end sign.

Just six pages and fifteen paragraphs, with a blank line at the end where I sign my name.

"Initial here," the lawyer says, so I do that, and I watch him shove the sheets across the table to Nate.

The man holding a pen across from me isn't anyone I know. I broke up with him before the start of our sophomore year. Now we're coming up on the end of junior year, and we've slipped past estranged to the other side of it.

We're strangers.

His father slides the pages from under his hand to read them through before Nate can sign, leaving Nate with his hand wrapped around a pen and nothing to do while he waits in the cold and embarrassed silence of the conference room.

Nothing to look at but me.

We stare at each other.

He's a young man with sandy hair, blond at the tips, and a scruffy not-quite beard framing padded cheeks and bright blue eyes. He wears a dress shirt and tie. Slacks.

He wears his privilege in his clothes and his sour expression, as though he's been asked here for no reason, harassed to the limits of his tolerance, and now this.

This requirement that he look me in the eye.

This distasteful performance I've staged.

When his father puts the sheets down in front of him, Nate signs on the last page, initials where he's told to, and shoves the document across the table toward me.

"I hope you're happy," he says.

And there is this moment when any number of things could happen.

West could leap across the table and deck him.

I could ask to be left alone with Nate and take one last opportunity to give him a piece of my mind before the settlement kicks in and I'm legally obliged to avoid contact with him forever.

I thought I would do that. Fantasized about it.

I imagined what I would tell him, what words would sink right into the heart of him and make him see what he'd done, why it's wrong, why it devastated me.

I had a whole speech.

But this isn't my life here in this conference room that's cold as a tomb. Everyone is dressed for a funeral because this is the end of something—the final act of a drama that's been difficult and hurtful, complicated and rich.

A drama that's taught me more about myself than anything I went through in the years preceding it.

What Nate did to me will never go away. I will never stop

being angry, because it will never stop rearing up to hurt me. He lashed out at me, attacked me with the weapons at his disposal, and changed the contours of who I am forever.

He changed my future.

He made everything harder.

But God. Here I am with West and Frankie and my dad—these people I love more than anything. And after I walk out of this room, I'm going to get into West's car and roll down the window and stick my hand out to feel the spring air sliding through my fingers.

We're going to drive down the interstate at seventy miles an hour, and all of this will slip away.

Back in Putnam, I'll change into shorts and find a blanket, drive over to campus, plant myself on the lawn, and pretend to study while I watch the boys playing Frisbee with their shirts off.

I'm going to head home and eat dinner with West and his sister. I'm going to talk to her about why we took her out of school to be here today, what it means for my life and my future, what it means for hers.

What it is to be a woman in this world.

After she goes to sleep, I'm going to lock the bedroom door and strip down to nothing and press every inch of my body against West, my boyfriend, my guy, the love of my life. I'm going to fuck him, be fucked by him, slide against him in the glow of the bedside lamp, kiss him and pant in his ear and tell him I love him, I love him, Jesus God I love him.

All of that belongs to me.

Nate can't take it away.

I hope you're happy—that's his accusation.

It turns out that I only have one thing I want to say in response. Two words.

"I am."

———

Dude, that is fucking creepy.

It's not creepy, it's evocative.

It makes my balls shrivel up.

That's not my problem.

No, it is, though. You made it. You made this thing that shrivels my balls, so you've got to own it.

Can you stop talking about balls?

Balls are objectively relevant to the conversation.

Ball conversations are exclusionary. Pick a different metaphor.

The art building has long hallways, and at night when it's mostly deserted, they amplify every sound. I came in the door nearest the library, which means I can hear this whole conversation as I walk the span of the building.

The building is plenty long enough to figure out who's talking to who. West is the one who keeps referring to his balls. Annie's the one who doesn't want to hear it. And Raffe, I discover as I turn into the studio and get a look at what they're discussing, is the one who's created the strangest piece of mixed-media art I've ever seen.

It's a metal folding chair tipped over. On the floor, stuck beneath the seat, is a small cloth doll dressed up like an adult man. It has a miniature red wig, a little suit, and shoes.

But rather than a doll's face, it has a human face, projected onto it with a camera. Moving human features. It's talking.

"That is fucking *creepy*," I say.

They all three turn. West is already grinning. "See," he says. "I told you."

"You made that on purpose?" I ask.

Raffe smiles. If he were wearing overalls, he'd stick his thumbs under the straps and rock back and forth on his heels—he looks that proud. "Yep."

"Why?"

Annie groans. "Don't ask him why."

"But—"

Then West is beside me, dragging me across the room by the elbow. "Never mind Raffe," he says. "Look at *this*."

There's a smear of something dark on his cheekbone. His T-shirt is spattered with white spots that I would swear weren't there when he left the apartment this morning. He's wearing the jeans he wears for art stuff, the denim almost impossible to spot under a layer of paint and slip and grease and I don't even know what.

Those jeans turn my crank so hard.

So hard. Seriously, he can't ever be allowed to know. He'll hold it over me with his knowing smirks and bossy teasing.

To conceal my lust, I only allow myself quick sidelong glances at his thighs, where he's rubbed every possible art substance off his hands. The marks of all the projects that have engaged him this semester.

There are so many of them. I think if he were anyone but West, I might be worried that all the projects were a sign of some kind of manic disorder, but I know him too well to worry. I know what it means when West sits me down and says, "Close your eyes," and starts rustling around in one of the cabinets built into the room's walls.

It means he's found something he's excited about.

It means he's got something he wants to show me.

It means he's finally figuring out how to let himself try stuff, make mistakes, waste materials, *fail*.

I've never seen him so happy.

He slides his sketchbook across the table in front of me, flipped open to a page about halfway through. "Look at that," he says.

I see what looks like an exploded diagram of a tree. Trunk, roots, branches, all of them separated out with space between them, floating in the air. It isn't a picture that makes sense to me, and it makes less sense when West starts piling tree parts and metal rods on the table in front of me.

He's assembling the pieces, telling me about drill bits and cutting tools and how he tried Lucite but it was too obvious, and then he started thinking about copper pipe, the kind of fittings you use for doing plumbing, and how that would look if he fitted the pieces together that way, and Laurie suggested he look into the kind of piping that chemists use, the old-fashioned systems, because they have a kind of elegance, so he did some research on that . . .

He talks and talks, the words rushing out of him, and the whole time he's moving. Shifting from foot to foot, reaching up to fit one piece of pipe onto another, threading fittings together.

I have this thing for the way West moves.

It's worse than the jeans thing.

Especially worse because he *knows* about it.

When West is working, and happy, he gets into this physical kind of flow that unhinges the door on my libido and just lets *everything* out. I watch the muscles beneath his skin bunch and release. I watch his thighs in those jeans, his ass, his shoulders. Mostly, though, I watch his mouth, because I love to see him animated, love it when he's got this much to say about something that makes him happy.

And because it's always his mouth for me. That mouth,

and the way he moves, and the way he *is,* so . . . West. Even more West than he used to be.

More West every day.

"What do you think?" he asks.

"Hmm?"

He cocks his head. "You weren't listening to me."

"I was."

His eyes narrow, and one corner of his mouth tips up. "You weren't. You've got that look."

"I don't."

I deny it even as I'm widening my legs in the chair. Leaning into the table with both elbows and arching my back just a little bit because it tilts my hips up and tilting my hips feels good.

Tilting my hips feels positively *necessary.*

He hops up on the tabletop, putting his jeans-clad thighs directly in front of my face. Raffe and Annie aren't paying attention. West lowers his head toward me, drops his voice, and says, "What was I telling you about, Caro?"

"Copper pipes."

"That was a while ago."

"Threading tools."

"Getting warmer."

"Adhesives."

He leans down and brushes his lips over my forehead. "Lucky guess. I'm always talking about adhesives."

The way he says it, it sounds like he's telling me he wants to lick my pussy. It sends a shiver racing down my back that tightens my nipples, liquefies my low belly, and lands between my legs with a wet kiss.

West gives me a wide, dirty smile. "What brought you over here anyway? I thought you were working on that paper."

I was, but I got bored. Alone on the fourth floor of the library, my mind wandered, and it's always dangerous to let my mind wander up there, because there's too much West-and-Caroline history for my mind to get lost in.

Distracting history. The kind that makes it easy to convince myself I should take a break and come see how West's project is coming along. Just in case he's bored, too.

West never gets bored when he's working in the studio.

He is, however, usually receptive to taking a certain type of break.

"Your sister's at Nadine's for the night," I say.

His smirk widens, that wolfish gleam in his eyes intensifying. "I know."

"So I was thinking." I'm tracing a pattern on his thigh with one finger.

"What were you thinking?"

"Maybe we should do something we couldn't normally do. Instead of just spend the whole evening apart, working."

"You want to head over to the Union?" he asks. "Grab a slice of pizza?"

"I'm not sure I'm hungry for pizza."

"What are you hungry for?"

I fold my arms over his thighs, because it gives me an excuse to grope them. He's leaning in so close, our noses almost touch. "I'm not sure. Nothing sounds good."

"I bet I could change your mind."

"I should probably get back to the library."

"I'll walk you."

He jumps down, roots around in his bag, and comes up with something closed in his fist that he pushes into his pocket.

"I'm gonna walk Caro to the library," he says casually. "Back in a few."

"Sure," Raffe says. "That's completely plausible."

"If *a few* turns out to mean an hour and we bail, you want us to put your stuff away?"

"Yeah," West says. "Thanks."

He pushes me out the door with his hand on the small of my back.

We near the staircase at the end of the hall. "Where are we going?"

"Up," he says. "Ladies first."

I climb, thinking we'll go to the second floor, where there are empty music classrooms. But when we get there, West slips his hand between my thighs, cups my pussy, and says, "Keep going."

I climb some more. Throbbing.

What's on the third floor? Offices, I think. Does he have a key to an office? Or maybe we'll end up in one of the bathrooms, locked in a stall—not sanitary, but he's got his hands all over my ass and I'm breathing so fast, way too excited to care where we end up as long as it's somewhere, soon.

The landing. "Which way?"

His hand on me again, the ridge at the base of his thumb drawing a line of pressure back and forth along my slit.

Every muscle in my legs melts.

"Keep going."

"That isn't possible."

He squeezes, and I close my eyes against the hot slick pulse of it.

"Up."

I stagger upward. At the top of a short flight, I stumble into a door. West dangles a key in front of my nose.

"The roof?" I ask.

He spins me, presses me into the door, and kisses me so deeply, with so little warning, I just about black out.

Can you faint from the combination of three and a half flights of stairs and the deep and unrelenting desire to be fucked?

It seems likely.

His thigh moves between my knees. His hands grip my waist and lift me up, and I can't do anything but dissolve all over him, take his mouth and his grip and his hard heat, the beat of the pulse in his neck where my hand rests, the moan he makes when I find his cock through denim and cotton and rub my hand up and down, tracing the length and shape of him with my fingernail.

"Right here," I say. "Please."

"No."

"*Please.*"

He lowers me and backs away. "On the roof."

"Open the door, then."

He pushes me aside, unlocks it, and drags me behind him.

"Why do you have a key?" I ask.

"It's Laurie's master key."

"They give out master keys to the art building? That's not smart. That's just basically *asking* students to fuck on the roof."

"I know, right? Open season. I'm surprised there aren't twenty people up here right now." He turns and grins at me, and then we round a corner and he says, "There we go."

"What is this?"

"Grass."

"Right, but . . ."

I'm looking at a patch of lawn, about fifteen feet square. Like, just . . . Grass. On the roof of the art building. "Is this somebody's project?"

"It was some kind of prairie restoration experiment thing,

I think," he says. "But that was a long time ago, and now it's just this rooftop lawn that Rikki mows."

"Why?"

"Because she's Rikki. Strip."

"Out here?"

"I want you naked in that grass in thirty seconds. I'll make it worth your while."

"But what if there's ticks?"

"How could there possibly be ticks?"

"How should I know?"

"It's not like there's deer up here, Caro. Or foxes, or any other kind of host animal."

"We're a host animal."

"I don't think there's *that* many people fucking on this rooftop that they could be passing ticks back and forth."

"But—"

"Quit."

"But—"

He blows out an exasperated breath and whips his shirt off. The moonlight spills over his shoulders and chest, turning his skin a milky white-blue, gooseflesh and hard muscle.

Naked West chest and those jeans. Those fucking *jeans*.

When his hands go to his zipper I reach for it, because I want in on this. So much.

West pushes my hands away. "Strip."

"All *right*."

He finishes before I do, which means I push my skirt down with his gaze on me. I'm standing in my bra and panties, a little chilly, a lot turned on. "Come over here," I beg.

"Lie down."

"By myself?"

"On the grass."

"This is strange."

"Humor me."

I do as he asks, because it is a little strange, but not so strange that it's outside my comfort zone, and West doesn't make so many unusual requests that I have any reason to balk at this one.

Mostly he just loves me and supports me, bolsters my confidence when I need it, defends me, makes me laugh, makes me come, makes me happier than anyone else ever has or probably ever will.

So, sure. I'll lie down naked in this random patch of roof grass for him.

It's stiffer than I expected, prickly against my lower back, my neck. Cool on the back of my legs and my butt.

He kneels beside me.

"Is this going to turn out to be a kink of yours?" I ask. "Exposure?"

He shakes his head.

"Rooftops?"

"No." He's smiling. "I've just wanted you naked under the stars since the first time I kissed you."

He trails his hand from my neck down through the space between my breasts, almost-but-not-quite brushing my nipples, then lifting every downy hair on my stomach as he strokes his way downward.

Back and forth. Teasing me.

I close my eyes. It's too much to look at him. The intensity in his gaze. The moonlight on his skin.

He drops down to his elbow, and his face is right there, his eyes and his lips, his chin and his jaw, his mouth. So exactly like it was that night when we climbed up on the roof of my childhood home, even though almost everything is different now.

That night, I was stoned and I was scared.

I heard mean voices when I closed my eyes, hounding me, and I couldn't decide what to do about West because I wanted him, but I didn't want to get hurt.

I'd looked and looked at him that night, because I could never get enough of his face, the shapes that make him up, the beat of his heart, the heat of the life moving inside him.

"Come here," I say.

He leans down to kiss me. Shifts closer and warms me as his hand travels those last few inches and his fingers slide in. "You're wet."

"No kidding."

"Watch it," he says. "Or I might figure out you're attracted to me."

"Oh, it's not you. I was just hoping there'd be *somebody* up here who was willing to fuck me."

"Somebody who doesn't mind bossy chicks."

"Don't call me a chick."

He rubs his thumb over my clit and makes me gasp. Mumbles something that sounds a lot like, *I'll call you whatever I want.*

"Be careful," I tell him the next time I'm capable of drawing breath. "Or I'll pick someone else to be my first lady."

I guess that's all the provocation he can take, because what he says next is, "Spread your legs wider," and then he's moving inside me, hard and harder.

Fast, with his fingers sinking into the flesh at my hips.

Wow.

Breathless, I say, "You weren't kidding about wanting this."

"I was thinking about coming over to see you at the library."

"For how long?"

"Since lunch."

I laugh, and then I can't, because he's thrusting into me so hard that my whole body turns into a bow, arching up, tensing, tight. My mouth falls open.

West kisses my neck, my jawline, my throat.

The world smells green and new.

I close my eyes, and when I open them, the stars are a careless spill of diamonds decorating the night.

His thumb finds my clit and moves in slow circles in time with his thrusts.

Into me. Into me. Into me.

He eases his hand over my shoulder and down my arm, over my hip.

Pulls up my knee. Looks in my eyes.

We go deep and then deeper, falling, spinning.

When he's with me, I'm never lost.

THE FRONTIER

There are few things in life as fantastic as tackling another human being.

Like, at the top of my list of physically enjoyable things I want to be doing as much as possible, it's basically orgasms and tackling people. And sometimes I think tackling people is better, although I'll admit it also comes with a higher likelihood of getting kicked in the face.

The first time I brought down another woman on the rugby pitch, I felt like I'd cracked a code. Stolen a secret men had been keeping from me. Because the thing is, guys make it seem difficult, as though tackling requires either blind rage or shoulder pads to be even doable.

We women watch from the stands, sipping hot chocolate high in the bleachers, and there is never any suggestion that this activity might be for us. That we might have what it takes to get this job done, too.

I used to be a good girl. I sat in the stands. I followed the rules, worked hard to get straight A's, dated a nice boy, and made him wait a long time for sex.

It wasn't what I wanted, but it was in the right neighborhood, and it seemed like the thing at the time.

There is a way in which smart girls, good girls, grow up thinking that if we keep following the rules, the world will hand us what we want.

So we line up, and we wait. But no one ever shows up to deliver the goods. And the longer we wait in that line, the more likely we are to take receipt of one ration of shit after another.

Being a good girl didn't work out for me.

At the end of my junior year at Putnam, I'm not that girl anymore. I've stepped out of the line.

I've become someone else.

I am engaged, every day, in the process of becoming myself, and one of the things I understand now that I didn't used to is that every possible activity is for me. Anything and everything I might want is available to me if I'm willing to do what it takes to claim it.

Sometimes it will be fucking unpleasant.

Sometimes people will hate me for it.

That's okay.

It's okay, because on a Sunday morning in April on the Putnam College rugby pitch, I can feel the softness of the earth beneath my cleats. I can smell manure, sharp and sweet, in the wind that whips the hair out of my ponytail.

I can look to the sidelines and see Krishna and Frankie and West sitting on a blanket. The white of Krishna's smile. The light in Frankie's face when Krishna teases her and West ruffles her hair, tickles her until she's collapsed, laughing, over his legs.

I can look to my right and see my friend Quinn, big and solid, wickedly funny.

I can look to my left and see my friend Bridget, slight and freckled and redheaded, nervous because this is the first time we've managed to get her out on the pitch to give rugby a try.

I told her not to sweat it. Tackling another human being is easy. All it requires is a willingness to throw yourself at their legs and a complete refusal to let go.

That's it.

Swear to God.

I'm not big, and I'm not strong, but I could bring down a three-hundred-pound woman through the sheer force of my will. I could bring down a fucking elephant.

Facing off across the line from us is a team of strangers in red-and-black jerseys, stern mouths and ruddy cheeks and wind-whipped hair, and they're going to do this, too. We're all going to do this.

We're going to throw the ball, catch it, and run as fast as our legs will carry us.

We're going to get a bead on the carrier, sprint after her, launch ourselves through the air until she's down and we're breathless, sweating, tangled up in limbs and dirt, grass stains and grit.

I have what it takes to claim what I want. I always did.

All of us do.

That's what I tell West when he loses faith. That's what I'm always going to be here to tell him.

It's what I'll tell Frankie when she asks me, when she doubts herself, when she needs to hear it.

It doesn't take anything special to fight back against the world and all the ways it wants to box you in, hold you down, limit you, and keep you from thriving. You just have to know what it is you want to accomplish. You have to know who you want to be with and what you'll give up to get them.

You have to let yourself want what you want as hard as you can, as deep as that goes, even if it scares the fuck out of you.

Even if your want and your need are bottomless, timeless, and your fear is so big that it's hard to breathe around it.

Because in the end, fear doesn't matter. Pain doesn't matter.

You get kicked in the nose, and the disaster of the blow blooms across your face and screams through your nervous system, but then it's over.

It's over, and you're on the the other side, one blow closer to the life you want.

I've got my life locked in. I'm right in the middle of it, my friends around me, West on the sidelines, our unconventional little family together and happy.

I've got that because I went after it.

I chased it and jumped it and fucking wrestled it to the ground, and I am not ever letting go.

Ahead of me is all the work I can do in this world.

I'm not afraid.

I've got this.

"I don't know why we weren't doing this last year," Krishna says. "I don't know why I haven't been doing this every single second since I came to college."

We're sitting in the grass on the sidelines, passing Krishna's flask back and forth, sipping whiskey and watching muddy girls bruise one another. Frankie's twenty feet down the sideline, worshipping Quinn, who's taking a breather after playing the entire first half of the game.

Or first quarter.

I've got no fucking clue, actually, how this game works, but Krish has got a point. There are thirty college girls on the field flinging themselves around, and it's pretty much the best thing that's ever happened.

"I don't know how you kept this from me," he says. "You had to know I would kill to spectate this sport. I'm going to spectate the fuck out of it now. They won't know what to do with me, I'll be spectating them so hard."

"This is the first game I've made it to."

"The fuck?"

"I always had work."

He blows out an incredulous exhale. "And I always said, *Work less. You're only young once.*"

"You also said a lot of other stupid bullshit. Including *Don't tie yourself down to one chick.*"

I watch him scan the field until he locks on Bridget. She's got to be the scrappiest, tiniest, muddiest thing out there, but she's hanging in. I watch her fling her arm around Caroline's neck, attempt a chest bump, and fall down on her ass.

Then Caroline's sinking to her knees, down to her hands, her hair hanging down in the dirt, because she's laughing so goddamn hard, she can't keep herself up.

I was missing this. I can't believe I let myself miss this.

Can't believe I got here, that I get to have it now.

We're thriving.

All three of us. Not just surviving—thriving.

And seeing that, I think about Silt. How I went home thinking I would never lay eyes on Caroline again.

How I thought nothing could be harder than walking away from her, but it was.

Hard. Harder.

Too hard to take.

I went home thinking I was the sheriff, and my fight was with my dad. But the fight I got wasn't the one I expected. The gunplay all happened on someone else's watch. I ended up alone on the streets of a ghost town in full daylight, with the black borders closing in on me.

Caroline's the one who pulled me out through that pinhole, back into the light.

It's always been Caroline, because from that first day when she groped me at the library, rode my thigh, and then told me to leave her alone—as if that was a thing that could ever happen—she saw me in a way I'd never seen myself.

She knows who she is. She knows who I am. How we fit.

I've been a lot of things since I met her. Guide, villain, pioneer, exile. But I've never been the sheriff, because I didn't understand what it takes.

The sheriff isn't there to vanquish evil. He's there to keep an eye on the future. He's the guardian of the law, the protector of the rules, the fists that keep chaos at bay.

You can't be the sheriff if all you've got is someone to fight against.

You've got to have something to fight for.

Something like Frankie with Quinn on the sidelines of a rugby game. My sister in jeans and a hoodie that actually fits, her hands in her back pockets, talking and smiling and squinting into the sun.

Something like Caroline rolling over onto her back, flinging out her arms, laughing up at the sky.

A sketchbook full of ideas. A pile of copper tubing. A plan.

All of it easy.

All of it mine.

Acknowledgments

I always put a lot of myself in my stories. This time, I drew deeply on what I've learned about love, life, and what it means to survive and thrive. I'm grateful to have grown up with love and opportunity all around me, and with a life full of beauty, art, and possibility. Thanks to my parents for giving me the wide-open horizons West wants for his sister. I hope I did West and Caroline justice. I certainly tried.

As I wrote the manuscript of *Harder,* Mary Ann Rivers helped me figure out what to do when I got stuck. Serena Bell reminded me not to lose sight of the love story. My agent, Emily Sylvan Kim, held my hand, and my editor at Bantam, Shauna Summers, told me how to fix the parts I'd gotten wrong. Be glad you didn't read the book without their input.

At the research phase, I relied on a number of friends with expertise, friendly experts, and expert friends. Thanks to Erin Rathjen, Holly Jacobs, Erica Johnstone, Jeni Mokren, Marian Houseman, and Patrick Wilson for being willing to answer odd questions and talk to me about all manner of things.

Raffe's video art installation is inspired by a wonderful piece I saw at the Milwaukee Art Museum. If you're ever in Wisconsin, I can't recommend a visit too highly.

Thanks, finally, to my readers. You guys are the best.

FALL FROM INDIA PLACE

By Samantha Young

The *New York Times* bestselling author of *On Dublin Street, Down London Road* and *Before Jamaica Lane* returns with a story about letting go of the past and learning to trust in the future . . .

When Hannah Nichols last saw Marco D'Alessandro five long years ago, he broke her heart. The bad boy with a hidden sweet side was the only guy Hannah ever loved – and the only man she's ever been with. After one intense night of giving in to temptation, Marco took off, leaving Scotland and Hannah behind. Shattered by the consequences of their night together, Hannah has never truly moved on.

Leaving Hannah was the biggest mistake of Marco's life – something he has deeply regretted for years. So when fate reunites them, he refuses to let her go without a fight. Determined to make her his, Marco pursues Hannah, reminding her of all the reasons they're meant to be together . . .

But just when Marco thinks they're committed to a future together, Hannah makes a discovery that unearths the secret pain she's been hiding from him – a secret that could tear them apart before they have a real chance to start over again . . .

Fall from India Place *is available from Piatkus* now!

COME TO ME QUIETLY

By A.L. Jackson

**From the acclaimed bestselling author of *Lost to You* and *When We Collide*
comes a New Adult novel of one woman's obsession: a man who's as passionate
as he is elusive – and as tempting as he is trouble . . .**

Aleena Moore is haunted by Jared Holt. It's been six years since she's seen her brother's
best friend, the self-destructive bad boy she secretly loved in high school. As the years
pass, she knows it's time to move on. Time to decide between a practical nursing degree
and her true dream as an artist. Time to get over Jared and give another guy a chance . . .

Just when she opens her heart to her friend, Gabe, Aly returns home to find Jared
sleeping on her couch. The teenage boy she loved has grown into a man she can't resist.
Covered in tattoos and lost in rage, he's begging to be saved from his demons –
the memories of the day he destroyed his family. As the two reconnect,
their passion is hot enough to torch Aly's judgment. But can she risk
her future for a man who lives on the edge of destruction?

Come to Me Quietly *is available from Piatkus* now!